WIND WARRIOR

BOOK ONE ~ IROQUOIS SERIES

By

Cynthia Roberts

Dedication

This is my very first published book, and it would have never seen the light of day without the spiritual support of Crawford White, Chief of the Northern Arapahoe, Wind River Reservation. Your relentless guidance kept me focused through years riddled with major challenges. Because of you, I discovered the magic within myself and the strength to leave the demons in the past where they belonged.

To Janis Cohen—my soul sister, my dearest friend— —thank you from the bottom of my heart. When life kept beating me down, you were always there to help me rise above the storm.

Chapter One

Leslie detected an immediate transformation in the stranger's eyes once she reached out to stroke the tips of her fingers slowly along the strong, angular curves of his chin and jaw. She looked for a change ... a reaction that indicated perhaps she was being too bold or forward. There was none. His calm reserve showed no emotion at all.

It pleased her he did not draw away from her touch or display any signs of displeasure. She wanted to know what was going on in his mind.

Does he find me attractive? She wondered. *Would he ... maybe he might want to touch me as well.*

She could not believe such thoughts were running through her mind.

You're being scandalous! She quietly chastised and snapped her hand away. *What am I thinking! What have I done? I'm not one of those dance hall girls who stand outside the saloon down at the settlement.*

She took a step backwards and her lips quivered nervously as she attempted to smile.

She would never throw herself at a man. Leslie was shy and reserved, especially around men she did not know. She was slow to warm up to strangers and to react in such a way with a man like the one standing before her was out of character.

She could not stop staring at his lips, wondering if they would taste as sweet as honey.

She cringed and a slight whimper gave away her discomfort.

Lord, help me.

Her cheeks felt terribly flushed, and she patted at them with her palms. He made her feel brazen but knew, she could not act on it. Moments passed with words unspoken between them. Leslie was afraid she truly over-stepped her bounds.

There must be someone else in his life ... a wife or betrothed, perhaps.

She searched his eyes for a sign of disinterest reflected in their depths.

He was too difficult to read.

The silence between them became deafening and the urge to spin about on her heels and run was overwhelming. This was a mistake, a childish whim. Perhaps his stoic reserve was more out of respect, not wanting to offend her, or fear of being retaliated against?

I am such a fool ... a stupid, crazy ninny.

She lowered her head to hide her embarrassment. She had to be realistic, after all. They were from different cultures. Her kind would never approve of such a union. He was considered a savage by many of the inhabitants in her settlement.

Leslie's heart pounded rapidly when he slowly closed the gap between them and reached for her. She inhaled sharply as he tenderly clasped hold of her chin, raising it to gaze deeply into her eyes. A lump caught in her throat, and she knew she could not swallow even if she tried. Joy filled her heart as his beautiful, full lips slowly curved into a smile.

The pleasure she felt was overwhelming, and she pressed her fingers to her lips, sighing softly. She did not know his name, where he came from, or what kind of person he was. What she did know, was she felt no fear, nor apprehension in his presence. She did not hold back and allowed him to draw closer.

His beautiful, amber eyes were so captivating, and Leslie knew at that very moment she wanted to get lost in their depths for an eternity.

Am I wrong to feel this way? Will I burn in hell for having such thoughts?

He clasped hold of her tiny wrists and placed them upon his shoulder.

A warmth coursed through her veins, making her shudder and a slow rush of air escaped her lips. The shock of it surprised her. She had locked such feelings away for what seemed forever. The shock to her system was like wakening a dormant bear before Springtime. How could such a stranger make her feel so alive again? Once she buried her beloved husband, Michael, a few years back she never thought she would feel such emotion ever again.

She did not shy away from his touch. She needed, wanted, to caress more of him and slowly ran the flat of her palm down the length of his naked chest, feeling the strength of hard muscle beneath his light copper skin. It amazed her how such a masculine man could feel so soft to the touch.

Her eyes drifted again to the fullness of his lips, and she craved to have her own held captive by them.

He was the most handsome man she had ever seen, and even though he was Indian, it did not sway her from wanting to share something more with him.

The comfort and safety she felt was far from odd, even knowing it would prove disturbing to others. Leslie dismissed all doubt and worry from her mind. She never was a person to be affected by what others thought. And she was not about to start now. If he was an admirable man with a kind and compassionate heart, that was all she needed to know.

She felt an immediate connection and shivered slightly when he reached forward to tenderly move a tendril of her hair off her face. It seemed natural and right to rest her cheek against the warmth of his palm.

His thumb glided softly against her skin, and she shivered again as she tilted her head to nuzzle the side of her face against his touch. He reached his other hand to cup her face and draw her nearer.

Leslie could feel his breath caressing her skin, and she knew he was going to kiss her.

"Come. Let us ride the wind together," he whispered softly in her ear.

Slowly, his lips grazed across her cheek, barely touching skin, causing her body to tremble.

This was the moment she hoped for, and she leaned closer, raising her chin to meet the pressure of his lips. His powerful arms were tender as they softly folded about her, pressing their bodies in a heated embrace.

The loud, shrilling chatter of gray squirrels playing outside her bedroom loft window jolted Leslie from her sleep as if cold water had just been thrown at her face. She bolted upright into a sitting position.

"No!" she cried softly, as she turned to look about.

She realized it was just a dream, as she ran her palm across the spot where she could swear, she still felt the warmth of the stranger's touch.

Her eyes scanned every corner of her room, and her heart sank from the disappointing realization that she did indeed dream of the beautiful stranger once again. She turned and watched the humorous antics that continued outside her window.

"Shoo - shoo you two," she scolded. "Did you have to choose this very moment to wake me?" she continued, as she shook her head and stretched her limbs like a contented feline.

For a moment, she played back the memory of the dream that had haunted her repeatedly for the past two months.

When is this going to end? She wondered. *What does it all mean?*

For as long as she could remember, Leslie had always been taunted by such riddling dreams. Early in her childhood, she had learned not to question her special ability to envision what might take place in the very near future through her dreams. She never feared them, because they were so very much a part of her life, and she naturally assumed everyone had the same experiences in their life. That is, until she was old enough to speak and express what she dreamed with her parents.

Leslie was nearly seven when she finally began to understand what was happening to her, what she was born with. Her mother, Olivia, had sat her down and carefully told her of the special gift they both shared. It was a guarded secret that had been passed down for five generations by the feminine line on her mother's side.

Still, the dream she had just experienced was different and more personal than any she'd had before. This dream involved her emotions. She knew that this stranger was going to play a major role in her future somehow. She just did not know what, or when, or where. Each time he entered her sleep, it became more real, and her attraction for him grew stronger. She was becoming drawn to his long, dark hair and a physique that looked as though it had been chiseled from stone. He was a mystery, and she was certain it was one that would be solved sooner, rather than later.

She tried to dismiss the thought of him from her mind and hummed softly as she rose from her cot and attended to her toiletry. She filled the porcelain bowl atop her small nightstand made of pine with cold water from its matching rosebud pitcher. As she washed her face, she could not rid the stranger from her mind, or the color of his skin and the texture of his hair. Because of the way he carried himself, she knew he was a man who could be feared if the circumstance presented itself.

Who is he? Where does he live?

She had so many questions rattling around inside her head. Leslie assumed he was a member of one of the Iroquois tribes inhabiting the area. As confusing it all seemed, Leslie did not dwell on it further. For as sure as the sun was to set that very evening, she knew their paths were destined to cross, and soon. It was then, and only then, that she would be forced to deal with whatever fate had decided to deal her, and it was only then that she would find her answers.

Slowly, she descended the makeshift ladder of pine slats that began to bow slightly in the middle from her constant use.

"Are you up yet, Papa?" she called out as she looked over her shoulder.

She expected to see him sitting at the large, wood table he had constructed for them when they first arrived in the territory, from the very pine that surrounded their property.

"Yer pa ain't here, sweet thing."

Leslie halted her descent and shuddered as she recognized the voice of Red Farmer.

He moved into view with a look of hunger in his eyes as he watched her descend the final rungs of the ladder.

"Mind telling me what you're doing here?" She glared with the hatred she felt.

Red cocked an eyebrow at her boldness and licked the drool from his lower lip.

"Why don't I just shows ya?" He sneered as he took a step forward.

Leslie bolted to the cupboard at her right and, in one swift move, snatched an iron pot from its peg and flung it at Red's head.

Red was quick to twist his body in time to miss the assailing weapon and cackled devilishly as he raced from the cabin.

"Someday I'll have ya. You'll see," he threatened loudly before disappearing into the heavy brush bordering their property.

The muscles in Leslie's jaw tightened as she clenched her teeth in anger.

Why, the nerve of that no good, slithering, son of a …

She gnarled her teeth together and blew out a deep breath to calm the quivering in her belly.

She continued to sputter to herself as she gathered all the ingredients needed for the hot cakes, she would make for their morning meal. Flour splattered all over her apron when she missed her aim, and the egg she reached for broke between her fingers from squeezing too tightly.

"Dang it!" she yelled and stomped her foot in frustration as she repeated the steps.

She added a cup of cow's milk to the mixture and started to beat the batter with a vigorous fury as she contemplated whether to tell her father of Red's visit.

The cabin door swung open, and Leslie screeched loudly and jumped with a start. The bowl slipped from her hands, but luckily, she caught it before it shattered to the floor.

"I didn't mean to scare you, Les" her father, Jebidiah, apologized.

He took a deep breath as he inhaled the strong aroma of coffee coming from the pot brewing on the small iron stove in the corner of the cabin. His arms were full of chopped firewood, and with three long strides, he crossed the room to stack the logs beside the hearth.

"It's gonna be a mighty fine day." He winked and patted his belly, which was still hard with muscle despite his forty-three years. "Our traps will be full of some fine beaver pelts. I just know it!"

Leslie smiled at her father.

He was such a handsome man and still turned the heads of all the ladies in the settlement whenever he entered a room. His thick, soft brown hair favored a boyish curl that always threatened to tumble upon his forehead, and he had a contagious chuckle that afforded him many friends wherever he went.

She poured tiny round circles of the batter onto the heated frying pan and chewed at her lower lip nervously.

"Papa, I don't mean to dampen your mood, but - um ..."

"What is it, girl?" he interjected. "Let it out!"

Leslie cleared her throat and flipped the pancakes before answering. "Well, you see ... Red was here when I came down this morning."

"Here ... inside ... and you didna invite him in?"

She hesitated briefly. The last thing she wanted to do was worry her father needlessly. Especially, since he was leaving that very morning on a four-day trapping excursion. She knew if given the opportunity, he would force her to stay with one of their neighbors while he was gone. She liked her independence and was perfectly capable of taking care of herself, while he was away. She hesitated for a moment and wondered, what would be the best way to answer him and decided just to get it over with.

"Well ... no."

Her father's displeasure was obvious when his nostrils flared, and his face turned even redder as his anger rose.

She placed the bowl down upon the table and raised her palms to calm him before he exploded like a locomotive stack that needed to let loose some steam.

"Now, just cool your German temper, Papa. He might have knocked, and I did not hear him, that's all." She shrugged. "I was up in the loft and -"

Jebidiah sent her a look that quieted her immediately.

"I'm not likin' this, Leslie. I'm not likin' it at all."

He banged his fist down upon the table, and Leslie reached for the bowl as it jostled near the edge.

"What is he doing back in these parts?"

She placed a stack of golden cakes in front of him as he lowered himself onto the bench beside the table and, she leaned forward to tenderly pat his arm.

"Maybe he just wanted to apologize for all the trouble he caused last spring." She answered, even though she felt otherwise.

It bothered her to lie, but she didn't want her father to worry needlessly while he was away. She sat down across from him and poured them each a cup of coffee.

Jebidiah shook his head, and his brow furrowed with concern.

Leslie hummed softly to try and relieve some of the tension in the room. She wanted to kick herself for even mentioning the visit.

Ever since Red was banished from the settlement for stealing personal items from the graves of the local natives, her father had been on edge. Turning Red over to the authorities was necessary, she reasoned silently. What Red had done nearly caused a deadly uprising between the now friendly tribes and settlers of Hollow Pass. If her father had not intervened, she was certain everyone in the settlement would be dead right now.

"You know; I do not want you here alone. I want you staying with Tess until I return."

Leslie huffed.

The last thing she wanted to do was find herself a prisoner and locked up in a cabin with Tess Kilgallon. The woman had an Irish temper that kept most men at bay. The woman had a heart of gold, there was no denying. Still, she hovered and was more protective than a hungry grizzly sitting upstream during a salmon run. The woman would question Leslie's every move, every decision, each day while her father was gone. She just knew simple chores would elevate into major discussions and causes for concern.

"Papa, you know I can take care of myself. There is not a man in this territory who can outshoot me or fling a knife as straight and true as I. It is not the first, nor will it be the last time I have been left alone to fend for myself." She reached out to clasp hold of his hand. "Papa, I'll be just fine. Please do not fret."

Jebidiah shook his head with worry.

"Red is not a trusting man, especially where you are concerned." He pointed his fork to stress his words.

"Oh, Papa! Enough! He is not an idle-minded man. Besides, I think he's a bit scared of me." She chuckled. "You should have seen how fast he high-tailed it out of here when I flung that very pan at his head," She pointed and laughed gaily.

When her father joined in her laughter, she knew she had calmed his fear. All she had to do was convince herself.

She knew Red's intentions. He never hid the lust he felt by the way he watched and look at her. He had a terrible reputation for raping Indian women, being disrespectful and lewd around the settlement women as well. Once he learned her father was on a trapping trip, his attention would be focused on her. Leslie was sure of it. She would just have to keep her guard up. It was as plain and simple as that.

Once the morning meal was finished, Leslie and her father spent the next hour sitting by the fire and chatting about everything and anything that came to mind. She loved watching her father whittle a small cube of pine into different shapes. He was quite the craftsman, and his carvings were popular amongst the settlers. She was glad he decided not to rush right out after they ate so, they could spend a little quality time before he left.

They talked about what needed to be done before Winter turned the landscape to pure white. When Leslie mentioned the holidays, her father's eyes shrouded with sadness as he gazed her way. She knew what he was thinking; how much she resembled her mother - her hair the color of harvested wheat and eyes the color of a lime before it was ripened. It broke her heart to hear him still cry in the middle of the night, missing her dear mother so very much after all this time.

The fever, which took her mother two Christmases ago, had been completely unexpected. It had nearly taken Leslie as well. Her father was relentless in his efforts to keep them both alive. It was the longest fourteen days of their lives. Burying her mother nearly destroyed him. If she had succumbed as well, she knew it would have been the key to lock away his sanity forever.

Leslie rose from her rocker and knelt on the floor at her father's feet and placed her head upon his lap.

Jebidiah petted her hair tenderly and sighed with a contentment that warmed her deeply.

"The man who wins your heart, sweet girl, will be a man surely blessed."

She rose to her knees, placed a loving kiss upon his cheek, and squeezed him fiercely.

"He would have to be a man like you, Papa, to win my heart."

Jebidiah tilted his head to the side and ran his finger softly along her cheek.

"You have filled mine with such joy, daughter ... so much joy." He smiled and turned to look toward the window. "I best be getting my things together. Shaun will be here soon to get me."

Leslie was glad her father would be trapping with Shaun Kilgallon, their closest neighbor's son. He was an accomplished trapper, like her father, and knew how to use a gun and survive in the wilderness.

For a moment, the stranger in her dream came to mind. When she focused on what Shaun looked like, Leslie was certain there was nothing similar about the two men. Shaun's shoulders were not as wide, and he was not as tall as the stranger in her dream.

She sat back on her heels as her father rose from his chair. She looked up at his towering frame and she smiled sweetly.

Jebidiah stretched his massive arms above his head and yawned out loud. He smiled down at her, offering his hands, and lifted her up with one sweep into a warm embrace.

"Do me a favor, sweet," he kissed her forehead tenderly, "and wrap some of them hotcakes you made extra of this morning for me, will you?" He winked.

Leslie rose on her toes and kissed his nose before quickly doing his bidding as he gathered his gear and placed it by the doorway.

There was a knock, and her father opened the door to find Shaun extending a freshly baked loaf of bread in greeting.

"Me mother sent this ov'r to ye," he offered with a heavy Irish brogue, "and said ye be more and welcome to stay with her while we'r gone." He winked at Jebidiah as he crossed the threshold. "I'd feel better knowin' ye dinna stay here alone."

Leslie closed the distance between them and reached for the bread he extended. A warm sensation ran up the length of her arm when their fingers touched, and she blushed like a schoolgirl.

She stood on her toes and placed a sweet kiss on his lightly freckled nose.

"I thank you for your concern, Shaun Kilgallon but, like I told Papa, I'll be fine - like always."

Shaun reached out to caress her cheek with the palm of his hand.

His gray eyes softened tenderly. "Ye know how I feel 'bout ya, Les."

Leslie noticed the beaming smile on her father's face. It was plainly obvious he approved of Shaun's display of affection. Her eyes scanned over the contours of Shaun's face from the tuft of his wavy, auburn hair to his strong, square jaw and those thick, long lashes that curled at the edges.

She wondered what it would feel like to taste his lips in a very deep and long embrace. She smiled as she fluttered her lashes coyly his way.

"You are sweet, Shaun. I promise to be careful. I'll visit your momma often, I swear." She brought her palms together as if in prayer and smiled sweetly as she batted her eyelashes at him one more time.

Jebidiah moved to her side and encircled her waist with his arm and chuckled heartily.

"We best be going, son. Tis a lost cause trying to sway this one's mind."

Leslie laughed as well as she moved toward the table to cut the bread in half and then into slices. She wrapped the pieces in clean cloth, tucked it into her father's satchel, and then turned and embraced him warmly.

"Come home safe, Papa," she whispered into his ear. "My love goes with you."

Her father squeezed her tightly before answering, "I love you, and please, do not stray far from the cabin, and -"

Leslie interrupted, "I know, Papa. I know. Make sure I have the shotgun with me at all times. I promise, and I will," she nodded.

Jebidiah smiled as he cupped her face tenderly between his giant hands. He leaned forward and kissed each cheek softly before releasing her.

Leslie looked at Shaun and smiled.

"You be careful too. I'm depending on you to keep Papa out of trouble."

"Will ye promise ta accompany me ta the Founder's Day dance if'n I do?" he asked.

Leslie placed her hands on her hips and tried her best to look scornful.

"You bartering there with me, Shaun Kilgallon?"

Shaun chucked. "Aye," he nodded, "that I am. Just makin' sure no one else stakes their claim on ye while I'm gone." His eyes twinkled playfully.

"Well, don't stay awake nights fretting about it either. Now off with the two of you - scoot!" she replied cheerfully as she shooed them out the door.

Chapter Two

Leslie waited only a short while before leaving on a walk to her very special place, just in case the men returned for something they may have forgotten.

It was such a splendid hideaway, amid stately pines that towered nearly thirty feet tall. Rays of sunshine streamed through fissured branches to a small pond fed by a natural spring. This was her haven where she wasted away hours fantasizing about falling in love again, sharing a home with a husband, and children born of their love.

The small parcel of land they once farmed back in Ohio could not compare to the beauty that now surrounded her. She sighed deeply and breathed in the fresh open air that was peppered with the crisp scent of pine.

Her eyes scanned the area and took in the wonder and splendor of a picturesque landscape with majestic snow-capped mountains in the distance, a colorful array of wildflowers that included a mass of black-eyed Susan, yellow buttercups, and beautiful violets. She giggled with delight when she sighted a family of beavers frolicking across the pond from where she began to wash the soiled laundry, she had brought along with her to clean.

The playful critters dove to scoop mud with their wide, flat tails from the pond's bottom and then patted the wet earth upon the wide mounds they built to house their pups.

Before too long, rivulets of sweat began to flow between her breasts and saturate her chemise. The cool water against her parched skin felt refreshing, and Leslie gave in to the temptation and stripped down to her undergarments.

Like the beaver, she dove with skill and precision. Her smooth, even strokes barely caused a stir as she swam the length, and then the width, of the pond until her energy was spent. For a short while, she floated on her back and enjoyed the calming embrace of the water as it refreshed her skin. Her hair fanned out lazily behind her, glistening in the sunshine as it rippled softly upon the water's surface.

She felt at peace, renewed, and hopeful of those things yet to come in her life. Despite the stranger who continued to haunt her dreams, Leslie was certain there would be a happy future in store for her and Shaun if she ever decided it was a life, she truly wanted to share with him. They had been courting since the holidays, and she knew it would not be long before he asked her father for her hand in marriage.

The thought of marriage with him seemed almost daunting at times, the more and more she dwelt on it. Courting was nothing like it had been with her deceased husband, Michael. Whenever they could find a stolen moment, they kissed and held each other tightly, avowing not only their love but the fiery passion they could barely contain. It was not like that with Shaun. She enjoyed being in his company, but the thought of lying naked in his arms never entered her thoughts. There was a comfort between them that was warm and safe. She knew that Shaun would do anything, risk anything, and obtain whatever he could just to make her happy.

Hollow Pass was a simple settlement and having a pick of the finest in male companions to choose from was about as slim as finding a herd of pure thoroughbreds in the wild.

Leslie knew she was at a point in her life where she had to concede being alone forever or accepting a man who would do his utmost to bring happiness into her world, even if she did not love and desire him passionately. Many women in the wilderness settled for less. Many grew in love years later after children were born and after a life was created and built from sweat, hard work, and struggling together to survive.

Shaun came from a wonderful, kind-hearted family. Her father liked and respected him. Even though the light kisses they shared did not shake her to the very core of her being, she still enjoyed his touch and being held by him.

Still, Leslie could not help but wonder what it would be like to be with the stranger in her dreams. What kind of feelings would his kisses stir within her? Was he real? Did he live with one of the neighboring tribes? Would he find her attractive? Could a red man be free to love a white woman? The same questions, the same concerns, played repeatedly in her mind.

She shivered as a cool wind caressed her body, and Leslie snapped back into reality.

What am I thinking? I'm letting my dreams get carried away, she thought as she started to swim toward shore.

She could tell from the position of the sun that it was getting late, and it was time for her to return to the cabin.

She dried herself quickly, dressed, and walked to the north side of the pond to gather some fresh pine boughs so she could replace the old stuffing in her mattress later that evening. Little forest creatures scampered in every direction as she approached.

Leslie smiled as blue birds fluttered about overhead, warning each other of the human who just entered their domain. Gray squirrels chattered with bother as they skittered up the massive, gray-brown trunk of a nearby Scotch Pine to find safety amongst its branches.

She shielded her eyes from the bright sunlight and watched them briefly.

"Well, hello, you two!" she called out as their tiny heads bobbed up and down, as if in worried conversation.

"I'll be gone in just a minute," she giggled as she continued to go about her business.

It took nearly the rest of the day to work the thick, jagged branches away without destroying the soft, pine-scented needles. Meticulously, she filled the simple mattress with a blend of needles and wild game feathers that she had accumulated over the past six months and then stitched the seams tightly together.

Once the sun began its decent below the west horizon, Leslie finished tidying the cabin. She loved to watch the sky turn from azure to pink, then violet, and despite the darkness that settled in, a glorious canvas came alive with a mass of sparkling, tiny diamonds illuminating the sky. It was a ritual she practiced for as long as she could remember, earning her the pet name Stargazer.

Leslie changed into her night dress and sat in the rocker by the fireplace. As she rocked slowly back and forth, it was not long before her mind and body began to relax, becoming one with the flames that flickered and danced before her. An ominous feeling came over her, and goose bumps fluttered up and down her arms, prickling the hair at the nape of her neck. Tiny white spots danced before her eyes and clouded her vision. Her skin became flushed, and then instantly she broke into a cold sweat and felt extremely light-headed.

She knew what was happening. When her body lost control, it was nothing like having a dream. This was a real-life premonition coming over her, and it scared her to death. It was a sensation she experienced a hundred times over, and no matter how old she got, it never got any easier. It never made her feel less afraid.

Leslie forced herself to rise. She swayed and weaved as she walked toward the door. Her feet felt like she was trying to lift them out of three inches of heavy mud. The feeling grew stronger and stronger and sweat seeped from every pore of her body.

More than anything, she wanted to dart outdoors into the cool, fall night. But she tested the security of the door's bolt instead and was satisfied to find it secure. She flipped around to lean against its solid surface and support her tiny frame until the room stopped spinning.

"Relax, Leslie. Stay calm. Breathe slowly," she spoke out loud.

Is this a warning for me or someone else? She asked herself.

She ran her fingers through her hair and found it damp with sweat. She swallowed hard and rubbed her eyes with the back of her hands.

"This is *not* what I need right now!" she hollered out loud.

Leslie felt like her legs would buckle beneath her, and she slowly slid to the floor with a soft thud. She drew her knees tightly to her chest and willed the tremors that made her shake uncontrollably to subside. The pressure in her head felt like it was ready to explode. When she looked down at her hands, a loud gasp escaped her mouth.

She watched in horror as her fingers turned a soft gray, then blue, and went completely numb.

"Damnation!" she screamed and pounded the floor with her fists and shook them repeatedly to try and force some feeling back into them.

"Why, Lord? Why now? Who is it this time? Is it Papa? Is it me?" she tried to rationalize.

Now is not the time to get crazy. She thought. Her father went trapping all the time. He always returned home safe. There was nothing to fear or be afraid of. He was with Shaun. The natives were friendly. She sucked air into her lungs slowly and then expelled it to calm her racing heart.

Stop. Think. Stay calm.

It took two days to check the traps and one more to travel back to Hollow Pass and trade his pelts.

Three more days. Just three more days, she thought, *and papa will be home.*

Leslie tried to rise and used the door to steady her shaky body. Whatever bad tidings were about to befall them, she knew it was out of her control. Still, she could not quell the tears that began to cloud her vision or the sickening feeling of nausea that grew in the pit of her stomach and started to rise in her throat.

Slowly, she made her way back to the rocker and mindlessly began to rock away the seconds ... the minutes ... and focused on reminiscing about all the wonderful past events in her life. She rubbed her temples with her fingers to try and stop the insistent pounding. She knew she had to try and focus, try to get her mind on something else, even if it meant thinking about the life she shared with her deceased husband and little boy before she lost them to that fateful storm long ago. Anything would do - anything.

Just think back, she thought. *Think of anything, anything to get your mind off being afraid.*

Married at seventeen, a mother at nineteen, widowed and motherless at twenty-two, she felt as though she had lived an entire lifetime. Never in a hundred years did she think fate could be so cruel as to repeatedly plague upon one family so much pain and heartache.

Her darling three-year-old son, Jacob, and husband were taken from her together when they were caught in a winter blizzard on their way back from a visit to the local mercantile. The storm had come out of nowhere and took the town by surprise.

Leslie whispered the Lord's Prayer and begged for her father and Shaun's safety. She asked for the strength to endure what was to lie ahead and tried to fill her mind with pleasant thoughts instead.

There never was a time her father returned home empty handed, she smiled. Leslie tilted her head back and willed her body to relax, rocking slowly and trying to focus on the flames that sparked with color before her.

What surprise will you bring back for me, Papa, this time? Will it be a bottle of scented water or a bolt of fabric to sew a new dress?

She loved her father so very much. They had grown over the past two years. They relied on each other now, not just for companionship, but to create new memories and leave the painful ones behind. It was not easy. When her father first decided that they leave Ohio and settle on land that his brother Matthew deeded to them after making his fortune following the Louisiana Purchase, she was not kind to him and had reacted terribly.

Leslie remembered how upset she had been with her father back then. It was difficult for her to leave her friends, the home she grew up in, the home she started with her husband, as well as his grave and that of their son and her mother.

It took time for her to realize that Hollow Pass gave them closure and the start of a new beginning together. It took some time for her to forgive her father.

The white birch logs crackled and hissed loudly as the heat drew the moisture from its bark. Leslie rocked, oblivious to the warmth that radiated from the fire and the orange-gold flames that cast shadows on the walls around her. She continued to reflect on the past, her journey east with her father, the terrains they crossed, and the perils they survived together to settle in this cabin they now shared and had grown to love.

Soon her eyes grew heavy. The strain of worry had finally begun to take its toll. Weary and feeling drained, the effort to climb the ladder up to her loft seemed too great. Leslie moved to her father's cot instead and instantly fell into a deep sleep that, for the very first time in months, was void of recurring dreams.

Chapter Three

Leslie woke with the same dreaded fear that gnawed at her the night before. She could not shake the fact that before the day ended, tragedy could possibly rear its ugly head.

She did her best to occupy her time throughout the day with menial tasks. Around midday, she gathered wild raspberries that grew a short distance from the cabin. Soon after, she had three pies cooling on the windowsill.

Dinner time came and went without incident. Before darkness fell, she decided to go to the well for the water she needed to fill the large cauldron she would heat for the small tub they used for bathing. An unsettling feeling returned and followed her like a mountain lion stalking its prey. She could not help but wonder, if Red was still in the area, and she shivered when his face came to view in her mind's eye.

"Lord, I can't stand that man", she said aloud.

Gentle breezes blew through the pines, rustling her nightgown about her legs. She could not stop that sense of unease building inside of her and quickened her steps as she walked the beaten path that led to the well. She glanced over her shoulder repeatedly to make sure she was not being followed, and she sighed at the sight of her cozy cabin with spirals of smoke billowing upward from its chimney.

Red entered her mind again and she huffed. He was a burly man who towered over six feet tall. His shoulders were so wide that he generally had to enter most doorways sideways.

Everyone in Hollow Pass knew when Red was around. Anyone brave enough not to stand down wind of him paled when his stench wafted under their noses.

Goose bumps danced across her skin and ran up and down her spine as she scooped water into her buckets. She could envision his beady little eyes and pot-scarred face looking back at her.

A heavy fog began to roll in across the landscape, and Leslie felt extremely uncomfortable being out in the open and vulnerable to what may be lurking in the shadows. She scurried as fast as her legs and burden allowed until she reached the safe confines of her cabin.

As her water heated, she prayed again for her father and Shaun's safe return. She was so thankful there was no longer a threat from the neighboring tribes. Her father had told her when commerce with Europe began ten years ago, the League of five Iroquois Nations were establishing a firm hold on the fur trade in the territory.

Their power was once felt from Maine to as far south as the Mississippi. When they had formed their Confederacy of Tribes, they spread death and destruction throughout the entire region.

Hollow Pass had been colonized a year after the trouble began to subside. Luckily, it had been quiet since then. The settlers believed the Iroquois were not interested in them, because their small colony posed no threat to their mighty league of thousands.

Leslie lifted the heavy pot and poured its steaming contents into the copper tub they brought with them from Ohio. It was one luxury she relished immensely.

She stripped off all her clothes and tried her best to pin her heavy mass of ringlets atop her head. The soothing heat engulfed her like a warm embrace as she slipped down into the tub. Leslie cooed like a sated infant as the strain from the past two days began to melt away. Almost immediately, her eyelids felt too heavy, and she forced herself to stay awake.

She quickly washed and dried herself and left the tub to drain in the morning. Before she climbed into her father's cot, she added extra logs to the fire so, it would burn through the night and keep the cabin at a comfortable temperature.

She had just closed her eyes when a loud, persistent pounding disrupted her sleep. As the sound intensified, she turned to face the door.

Boom! Boom! Boom!

The door shook on its hinges, and Leslie bolted into a sitting position, shaking with fear.

She rose from the cot and stood frozen, unmoving. She shrieked and jumped with a start when the door rattled, and puffs of dust billowed into the cabin from the bottom.

"I'm not lifting that damn bar until I know who the hell is out there!" she bellowed.

"Damn it, ya 'lil spit fire! Tis Shaun! Open this blasted door! Yer pa is hurt!"

Leslie clutched her night dress tightly as if to help hold herself erect.

"Oh, God! Oh, my God, no!"

She shook violently as she quickly padded barefoot across the plank flooring. The fear that plagued her the last two days was now coming to life before her.

"Please, Lord," she whimpered, "don't let Papa be hurt badly. I beg of you, not to take him from me - not now."

She traced the sign of the cross on her forehead and grunted as she strained to lift the thick, heavy pine bar from its resting place. Her heart constricted painfully, and she clutched at her chest as she gazed at the near-lifeless body of her father being carried in Shaun's arms. She gasped loudly and screamed.

"No! Oh, my God! Papa!"

She moved closer to assist Shaun.

His face was drained of color as he cradled Jebidiah in his arms.

She noticed how unresponsive her father was as his limbs dangled lifelessly before her. His skin was ashen and two horrifying arrows protruded from his body. The flesh was raw and oozed blood that was almost black, which she knew was not a good sign. One arrow was embedded in her father's right upper thigh. The other, which she feared most, lay deep within his chest close to his heart. She winced as saw his clothes soaked with blood.

Shaun pushed past her and gently laid her father atop the kitchen table.

Leslie ran into the dense fog to gather fresh water from the well and then filled the iron pot hanging over the fire to boil. Again, she ventured back outdoors to gather a medicinal moss she knew grew along the pond's northern edge.

Shaun had the wound on her father's leg cleaned as much as he could by the time she returned. She could not help but worry over the unsightly yellow liquid that continued to drain from the ghastly opening. The fear that consumed her at that very moment sent shivers coursing through her body and the harsh reality of death prickled at her brain. She knew that the time it took Shaun to get her father back to safety were precious hours he could have used to attend his wounds right away.

When she looked into Shaun's worried eyes, it was almost as if he had read her mind.

"We've got ta cut the rest of these clothes away, Les." His voice quivered. "I did'na have time to stop and tend him. I had ta get clear of the savages that ambushed us."

"What do you mean savages? We're not at war with the Iroquois. They've been peaceful near three years now."

"We do'na have time to get inta this now," Shaun replied

Leslie's eyes filled with tears when she read the fear in his eyes.

Shaun reached out to tenderly caress her cheek.

"Do'na worry, lass. I'll help ya tend to yer pa." He bent forward and kissed her forehead softly. "I will'na leave ya - I promise."

She found his thick Irish brogue comforting and smiled weakly. She placed her hand over his, drew it to her lips, and kissed his open palm softly.

"I'm scared, Shaun. I don't know what I would do if you were not here. You are such a dear friend."

She noticed a flick of disappointment reflect in his eyes at her reference and looked away as she moved closer to the table. She bent and kissed her father's forehead tenderly and was shocked by the heat that warmed her lips.

"He's burning up, Shaun," she exclaimed as she moved toward the kitchen to grab a skinning knife. "We've got to move quickly!"

Immediately, she cut away her father's clothing, as Shaun tried to force whiskey into her father's mouth. Meticulously, they worked together, discarding soiled rags, washing away hardened blood, and stitching deep lacerations with her sewing thread.

Shaun directed Leslie to sit astride her father's middle and hold his shoulders down while he attempted to draw the arrow from his leg. She looked at the gruesome wound and knew it had gotten worse in the short while he had been there. She swallowed hard to fight back the nausea threatening to empty her stomach.

She forcibly blinked away the white spots dancing before her eyes and was determined not to be a swooning female at a time Shaun needed her most. She dug deep within herself to draw upon whatever reserve of strength she could muster and climbed upon the table, straddled her father, and squeezed her eyes shut.

Her father's body jerked wildly beneath her like a wild bronco. Leslie did all she could do to stay atop him and not crash to the floor.

Jebidiah moaned in agony even though he was unconscious.

Shaun quickly poured whiskey over the festering wound and flung a clean rag into the pot boiling over the open fire, swirled it around, and then used a stick to lift it out. Puffs of steam emitted from the heat it contained. Immediately, he applied some of the moss Leslie gathered earlier and laid the cloth atop it.

Leslie's father screamed and his eyes flew open, blindly searching and not focusing on anyone.

Gingerly, she moved down to his side and wiped away the tears that began to stream down his cheeks. She leaned forward and tenderly kissed each cheek and nuzzled his neck.

"I love you, Papa," she whispered close to his ear.

A wave of hysteria nearly overtook her, and she fought to control the tremors that began to shake deep within her.

"Shaun and I are going to make you well again, Papa." She forced herself to smile. "Your little Stargazer promises."

She lifted her father's head slightly and brought some whiskey to his lips.

"Take another sip, Papa. It will help you sleep and ease the pain."

Her father obeyed and drank what his strength allowed.

Leslie looked up at Shaun. She wanted to hold him as well when she saw tears streaming down his cheeks. She knew he must be feeling a terrible guilt for not keeping good his promise to keep her father safe. She reached out her hand to clasp hold of his.

"Shaun is here, Papa. He carried you all the way home and helped me tend you," She wiped the sniffles from her nose. "He' a wonderful man, Papa. Just like you've always said."

Jebidiah blinked repeatedly as if trying to focus his eyes on her.

Leslie knew he could not see Shaun even though he turned his head in that direction. She loosened her grip when her father's head went limp, and she knew he had fallen into unconsciousness once again. She turned beseeching eyes toward Shaun.

"We've got to remove that other arrow. I'm so afraid it is killing him, Shaun. He's losing too much blood."

Shaun looked from the arrow back to Leslie.

"I do'na know, lassie. Tis mighty close to ya Pa's heart. I'm afraid taken it out will kill him. If'n its near'n artery, it would be like pullin a cork from a bottle held upside down. Do ya want ta be takin' that chance?"

Chapter Four

Leslie knew Shaun's fears were valid. There was truth to what he said, but she also knew the arrow embedded in her father's chest was life threatening. The longer it remained, the less his chances of survival. She chewed her lower lip nervously and ran her fingers through her tangled waves.

"We can't leave it there, Shaun! The wound is infected. We have to do something!" she stated.

"All right, darlin'. It will'na be easy, but we will try."

He moved forward and drew her into his arms, embracing her softly, kissing her hair, her forehead, and her cheeks ever so tenderly.

Leslie's legs felt like jelly. His manly scent filled her nostrils, and she snuggled against his muscled chest. It was as though her weakness seeped into his buckskins like a sponge soaking up water, and he wrapped his powerful arms around her more tightly. She encircled her arms about his waist and burrowed her nose into the warmth of him. She missed the feel and comfort of a man's body against her own. Even though he was four years younger, she could not deny that an attraction existed between them. She just was not certain whether it was strong enough to spend a lifetime with him.

He kissed the top of her head and slowly rocked her in his arms.

"Are ya sure yer up to this?"

She leaned against his chest and sniffed back her tears.

"I don't know what I would do without you, Shaun."

He lifted her chin and kissed her lips lightly.

"I will always be here for ya, darlin' - always."

She smiled softly and caressed his unshaven cheek with her palm and read the deep love he felt for her in his eyes. It made her feel uncomfortable, because she knew that she could not return his love, not now, maybe not ever.

It made her feel guilty and selfish at that very moment because she knew she would take his strength and love and draw upon it for whatever it was worth. She prayed silently it would see them both through this terrible ordeal.

Leslie stepped out of his embrace and exhaled deeply.

"We should do this ... now."

Shaun nodded his agreement and moved to retrieve the pot from the fire. He placed it on the floor beside the table. Only a small portion of the feathered hilt of the arrow could be seen, and Shaun rolled Jebidiah to his side slowly.

Leslie noticed it had pierced straight through her father's back, and she chewed her lower lip nearly raw as she watched Shaun try to cut the sharp tip away from its shaft. His movement was swift then, as he drew the arrow swiftly from the wound.

This time, her father did not react, and Leslie poured the remainder of whiskey into both raw holes left by the invading arrow. Dark, red blood seeped from the wounds as fast as she rinsed them out. She knew they had to stop the bleeding, or her father would surely die from the extreme loss of blood, which most certainly, would be sooner rather than later.

She looked into Shaun's eyes, knowing what they needed to do next. His look was enough to confirm her worst fears, and she nodded her head in agreement.

Shaun drew the poker from its standby the hearth and thrust it into the bed of red-hot coals, while Leslie continued to apply pressure to both wounds.

She gasped, and Shaun shivered when they both noticed the hazing, red heat emanating from the poker's head as Shaun withdrew it from the coals.

Bile rose in Leslie's throat, and she swallowed hard to keep it down as she clasped a hand over her mouth. Inwardly, she agonized over the pain they were about to inflict upon her father. A whimper escaped her throat as she looked down at her father's peaceful face.

This can't be happening, she thought. She wanted to scream, *Why now?* It just was not fair they had to go through so much pain, loss, and heartache. It just was not fair.

She could feel - see - the apprehension in Shaun's eyes. The longer they waited, the less her father's chance of surviving. She reached out and touched Shaun's arm and nodded. She moved to the end of the table to take hold of her father's ankles as best she could, with all the strength she had left.

"Now, Shaun! Do it now!"

His reaction was immediate as he placed the scalding poker tip first into the wound on Jebidiah's chest and then, rolled him to his side to reach the one on his back.

Her father's ear-piercing screams ripped through her heart like a searing bolt and reverberated in her ears. Quickly, she released her hold and ran to his side, gathering him as best she could into her arms.

"Oh, Papa. Papa, I'm sorry .... so sorry we hurt you this way," she sobbed.

She wiped at the sweat on his brow with the cool cloth Shaun handed to her.

"I love you, Papa. Don't you dare leave me. Please ... please don't leave me."

Her father stirred as Shaun tended his wounds and wrapped his chest with moss and a clean, white linen cloth.

Leslie sniffed and wiped away her tears with the back of her hand.

"Can you hear me, Papa?"

A low moan escaped his pallid lips as she watched him. "Papa?"

Slowly, her father's eyes opened. His smile as proof that he knew she had spoken.

Leslie whimpered and lowered to brush her lips against his cheek, feeling the coarse stubble of whiskers against them.

"Hi there." She winked.

Her father tried desperately to speak, swallowed hard and tried again, but no words escaped.

Leslie lifted his head slightly and placed a tin cup of cool well water to his quivering lips.

"Here, Papa. Drink slowly. It will soothe your throat."

Her father gulped quickly, and he coughed uncontrollably.

"Not so fast now," she quickly spoke.

His teeth clenched tightly as he groaned much louder. His chest heaved with every painful breath he inhaled.

"Love ... you," he labored as tears cascaded from his eyes.

Leslie placed the cup down and clasped his large hand between hers, drawing it to her chest. "Me too," she replied. "No more talking now," she smiled. "You need to save your strength and try to rest."

"Don't ... be ... telling your Pa ... what to do, hear?" He smiled weakly.

Leslie returned his smile, kissed his hand softly, and nodded. His attempt at humor despite his pain did not surprise her. She knew the last thing he wanted was for her to worry. He was always calm during a crisis.

When he tugged at her, Leslie leaned in close.

"If ... if anything happens," he continued, "you must be strong."

She could not hold back the tears which threatened to escape and shook her head.

"Don't say that. Nothing will go wrong. In a few weeks, you'll be up and about and as good as new."

Her father pulled his hand from her grasp.

Leslie's heart skipped when he grimaced and suffered a painful coughing spell that nearly rocked him off the table. Blood began to trickle from the corner of his mouth, and she dabbed it away with a wet cloth.

He clasped hold of her hand once again, squeezed it, and took another deep breath before speaking.

"Promise you'll write your Uncle Matt. He will know what to do if ... if I pass." He winced and groaned once more.

"No!" She cried. "That will not happen! "

He grunted and squeezed her hand tighter.

"Promise me, child."

She raised his hand to her lips, kissed it softly and nodded.

"I promise. I love you, Papa," she whimpered. "I love you with all my heart," she cried as she lowered her head and rested it upon his chest.

He grasped the back of her neck tenderly and slowly ran his hand up and down her back.

"I love you too, precious girl."

She moved herself up upon the table, stretching out beside him. It was awkward at best as her body hung halfway off the table. She did her very best to snuggle as close as she could. She needed more than anything to be near him and feel his warmth.

It was a reassurance he was still alive - still breathing life into his lungs despite the fact it was terribly labored. He still was her father, a man whole, and the man she adored and loved.

She watched as Shaun moved quickly around the table. She felt him against her back, supporting her from behind. She could feel his emotion, as his body shook with sobs, witnessing the heart-wrenching scene of love between her and her father. She shimmied closer and could tell from her father's shallow breathing that he was sleeping. She said a silent prayer that he would survive this terrible ordeal. She needed to believe, to have faith that everything she and Shaun had done would keep him alive.

She remembered her father once telling her, "From something terrible always evolved something beautiful." She hoped the wisdom of such words held some semblance of truth, for she did not think she could survive the death of her last remaining parent. Life could not be so cruel, or could it? She turned slightly and looked up at Shaun.

He smiled as he reached forward and petted her cheek tenderly.

"Yer Pa is resting now. Come ... I need ta talk to ya."

She nodded, as he helped her off the table and took her hand, leading her to the door. She hesitated and turned to look over her shoulder.

"He will be fine. We will stay close," Shaun assured her as he handed her the shawl from the peg by the door.

The night air was brisk, and simultaneously they inhaled a deep breath and sighed.

She moved forward and perched herself atop a large tree stump just a few feet from the cabin.

Shaun squatted at the ground beside her feet. He cleared his throat nervously and gazed up at the heavens.

Leslie touched his shoulder lightly. "What is it, Shaun?"

The sadness that reflected in his eyes touched her deeply, and she dropped to her knees to face him.

"Tell me," she continued as she placed her palms alongside his face.

Shaun drew her hands to his lips and kissed her open palms.

"I do'na want ta burden ya more, Les, but for yer own sake, I must tell ya what happened out there!" He nodded toward the forest.

"Go ahead," she coaxed.

He released her hands and began to play with the fringes on his leggings as he settled onto the ground.

Leslie sat down beside him and gave him the time he needed to collect his thoughts. She knew it would be difficult for him to relive what happened out on the trail. In one respect, she did not want to know. If her safety was in jeopardy, however, it was best to know everything.

Shaun swallowed hard and ran his fingers through his hair before speaking.

"We had a full load this trip out," he smiled briefly. "I nev'r seen yer pa so pleased. We were relaxed. Our guard was down - I will'na deny. We felt safe be'n familiar territory we worked all the time, ye know?"

Leslie smiled and nodded. She could feel the tension within him begin to mount and reached out to stroke his forearm.

"You can't blame yourself, Shaun. You had no way in knowing. Papa would never blame you. You got him home."

Shaun picked up a rock and sailed it toward the wood pile with such a force, it sent some logs tumbling to the ground.

Leslie jumped, not expecting that reaction. She feared there was more. He was such a gentle soul and not the kind of man to be easily riled by anyone or any situation.

The anger did not leave his eyes when he turned to look at her.

"There were eight of them. Hurons. They were wear'n war paint to boot."

Leslie gasped and covered her mouth. "Huron! Are you sure, Shaun? They're a long way from home!" She sputtered as she turned to look in the direction of the woods.

Shaun nodded. "Aye. I'm sure, lassie. And you'll nev'r guess who was lead'n them?"

She sent him a puzzled look. *Who would she know would do such a thing*, she wondered?

Shaun spat at the ground in disgust, before speaking.

"Farmer, the bastard."

Leslie's eyes became as large as silver dollar pieces. She shook her head in disbelief over and over. She stumbled as she rose to her feet and walked mindlessly in one direction, turned, and then walked in another.

"Why? I ... don't understand."

"Revenge, I'm supposing," Shaun replied as he rose and moved to her side. "He nev'r got ov'r yer father turnin' him in."

"But he was wrong! He knew it! He even admitted to stealing from the Iroquois burial grounds," she exclaimed. "That vermin should have been hung instead of banished from the territory!"

Shaun shrugged and replied, "Well, he did'na learn, now did he?"

Her actions mirrored her exasperation as she stomped her feet and flailed her arms about.

"To purposely plot and attack another human being - a man like my father, a man who treated him with nothing but respect. Did you know Papa trapped with him when we first arrived here? He - he even tried to convince the authorities that they should give Red another chance. Arrr -," she roared as she clenched her fists and raised them skyward.

She turned toward Shaun, and tears streamed from her eyes.

"Oh, Shaun," she whimpered. "It isn't fair. Papa didn't deserve this."

Shaun held out his arms, and she moved into his embrace. She rested her forehead against his chest, and every emotion she felt let loose in a stream of sobs. Her shoulders shook with every release. She felt hopeless, beaten, defenseless, and emotionally wounded. She had no more strength to lie prey to what life continually rained down upon her. She felt as though every desire she had ever wanted, every wish she had ever dreamed, every hope she had ever prayed for was pouring from her very soul and seeping into the ground at her feet and lost forever.

Shaun tried his best to console her.

"Shh, lassie," he cooed. "Ev'rything will turn out fine," he promised as he stroked her long, golden tresses and rocked her in his arms until her sobs subsided.

Chapter Five

Leslie tossed and turned on the mattress Shaun had placed on the floor beside the kitchen table where her father was still lying. The hard surface made it nearly impossible for her to sleep straight through the night. Her mind was weary from a fitful rest, and her lower back ached from sleeping on the floor despite the thin mattress.

She propped up on her elbow and looked over by the fire, expecting to see Shaun there sound asleep in the rocker with his shotgun cradled in his arms. But he was gone. She moved to a sitting position, and despite shadows dancing across the walls of the cabin from the fire that flickered nearby, she still saw no sign of him.

It did not concern her much. He might have climbed up to her loft and fallen asleep. She draped her blanket over her shoulders, rose, placed three more logs on the fire and tip-toed to the bottom of the ladder. She climbed half-way up and called out to him.

"Shaun, are you up here?"

She looked over her shoulder to see if her father stirred. His peaceful profile made her smile and when the blanket slipped from her shoulders, she let it fall to the floor. She took two more steps and heard noises coming from outside the cabin. She started back down the ladder, stopped briefly, and listened again.

It sounded like grunting and scuffling about. She was certain of it.

Leslie hurried down the final rungs and moved to the window. Living in the wilderness made her wise to being extremely cautious, and she carefully peeked outside. She gasped loudly at the scene unfolding outdoors in the moonlight.

Shaun was desperately trying to fend off two braves, while Red Farmer stood by watching and laughing with hysterical glee. When she glanced at the door, she noticed that the large bar was still in place.

How could that be? She thought and then she realized what Shaun had done and spun around.

There under the kitchen table where her father now lay, she noticed the trap door in the floor had been raised. She was surprised that she never heard him opening the heavy door, which usually creaked loudly, especially with her lying right there beside it.

Why did he ever go outside, she wondered? *Did he hear something? Did he just wake up, and decide to use the escape route to keep a watch outside?*

When they moved to Hollow Pass, it was Shaun who convinced her father to add the cellar before building the cabin – not only to cold store the preserves she would make but to provide a hidden escape route in case of an attack that was close enough to the forest and to the rear of the cabin.

She scurried to her father's side, shook his arm lightly, and spoke loud enough to be heard.

"Papa. Papa, wake up."

When he did not stir, she reached out to touch his cheek and snapped her hand away as if it was scalded.

"No!" she cried and shaking her head in dismay. "No, this cannot be."

She leaned over his lifeless body and noticed the dark gray pallor to his skin. She placed her ear to his chest, heard no heartbeat, touched his hands, and found the skin extremely cold and rigid. She wanted to wail at the top of her lungs and lifted his stiff frame to her breast as a deluge of tears poured from her eyes.

"My God, Papa, what am I to do? What am I to do?"

Her mind drifted aimlessly. Seconds turned to minutes as she continued to slowly rock his stiff body within her arms. She could not believe what was happening. Her entire family was gone and lost to her forever. Should she stay and hope that Shaun could fend off Red? Should she take the chance and hide in the root cellar? Should she grab her father's rifle and try to help? Should she try to escape?

The ruckus outdoors got louder, and it was like an alarm clock going off inside her head, springing her into action. She knew what she had to do and tried to tap down the fear threatening to overcome her. Shaun was fighting for his life, hers was in jeopardy, and her fathers had slipped away silently in the night.

She looked quickly at the empty pegs over the fireplace where her father always hung his shotgun. It was not there. The one she had for herself was not by the door where she last left it. Shaun must have taken them both outside.

How can I help him, if I don't have the means to do so?

She thought of using her father's skinning knife, but quickly dismissed the thought. There were too many of them outside.

The minute she would open the door to take aim, two of them would surely be upon her.

No! Her mind screamed. I cannot just leave Shaun alone out there to fend for himself. He needs me. She lowered her father back down onto the table and ran to the side-board, clasping the ten-inch hunting knife in her right hand. She moved toward the window.

Instead of seeing only three assailants, there were now five, and Leslie knew that the odds were truly against her. A stream of hot tears poured from her eyes, and she sobbed openly as she came to terms with a decision, she knew wound haunt her forever.

She could not stay. As much as she did not want to leave her father behind without a proper burial, she also knew she had to escape. She had to be strong. If she owed Shaun anything as he fought for her safety, it was to escape into the forest unnoticed and quickly. There was no other choice left for her but to save herself.

Leslie moved back to her father's side, quickly said a prayer, and softly kissed his lips. She took two blankets and covered him in such a way that they hung over each side of the table, camouflaging the trap door completely from anyone's view who happened to enter the room.

She discarded her clothes and changed into a skirt she always wore when trekking through the woods and decided to wear one of her father's flannel shirts. She tucked her own knife into its protective sheath and slipped it onto the small thong she used to tie it around her upper thigh. She quickly laced up her ankle boots and looked about the cabin. She wanted to collect some food and throw it in the leather pouch lying on the floor beside the cupboard, but knew she was running out of time and decided against it.

She crawled to the table, moved aside the blanket, stepped onto the ladder, and descended into the darkness as she lowered the trap door back into place. When she reached the dirt floor she turned and tried to get her bearings. She raised her arms out in front of her and blindly felt her way about the small area.

 She knocked into one of shelves where she stacked jars of preserves, displacing one off the end. The sound of breaking glass made her jump, and she held her breath, listening intently for any noise that would indicate she had been discovered.

Moments passed in silence, and she moved forward. She found the exit door that would open to the back of the cabin. Slowly, she moved it a mere crack, peered out carefully, and listened for any signs of movement nearby. When she was certain that all was clear, Leslie crept from the cellar and pushed aside a bench kept there specifically to hide the exit door.

Once certain no one was around, she pushed the door open fully, crawled out, shut the door, and moved the bench back into place.

Silently, she hugged the ground until she reached a break in the trees and worked her way quietly parallel to the front of the cabin. She knew she was taking a chance being seen, but she had to see if Shaun was still alive. Her heart skipped a beat when she noticed one of the braves lay dead from a bullet hole in his belly.

A second had clearly taken a shot to the shoulder, and his wound was bleeding profusely. She could tell from the way he was swaying, he would not last much longer, and in a few short seconds, he fell to his knees.

Leslie looked cautiously about as she did not see Red anywhere in the clearing. She knew it would be foolish to let Shaun know she was outside. Her attention was drawn back to the cabin when she heard Shaun call out.

"Farmer yer coward – come out where I kin see ya!"

She watched as Shaun spun about, peering into the brush. His chest heaved with exhaustion, and a soft vapor escaped his breath from the crisp morning air.

A shot rang out, and Leslie jumped with fear as she watched Shaun fall backward when the bullet entered his upper thigh.

Red entered the clearing along with three more braves. In an instant, they disarmed Shaun and held him to the ground.

Shaun wrestled fiercely, but his efforts were useless when one of the warriors dug his hunting knife into his shoulder.

Leslie nearly screamed and stuffed the hem of her skirt into her mouth to muffle her sobs.

"Don't kill'm yet, ya fool!" Red bellowed as he moved forward to stand over Shaun.

Shaun kicked out with his good leg but did not make contact. The warrior on his left cuffed his chin with his fist and Shaun's head snapped sideways from the blow.

"Is the woman inside?" Red asked as he stomped his foot down onto Shaun's wounded thigh.

Shaun spat at Farmer before responding. "After what ye did, I moved her ta safety away from the settlement. You'll nev'r find her."

Red stomped him again and bellowed with rage. "Yer lying! There twasn't enough time." Red pointed to the cabin and snarled an order to the braves. "Find a way in."

Leslie was overcome with terror. She knew that Shaun was going to die, and there was nothing she could do to save him. She had to make available the opportunity he was giving to her. By the time they broke through the shuttered windows or managed to ram open the front door, she could be long gone and a far distance away.

She had to flee from the area before Red discovered she was not in the cabin and her father was dead. There was no doubt in her mind that the warriors accompanying Red could scout well. She had to leave, and it had to be now. Tears clouded her eyes as she looked one final time at Shaun.

"Thank you for loving me so much you'd give your life for me," she whispered. "I will remember you always."

Chapter Six

Leslie gathered up her skirts and quietly moved deeper into the thick forest. As soon as she was far enough away, she sprinted with the agility of a jack rabbit and the skill her father had taught her in not leaving any signs of passing.

Her direction was well chosen, as she headed deeper into the wilderness instead of toward Shaun's cabin. Not knowing how many braves were traveling with Red, Leslie did not want to chance jeopardizing his mother's safety. She prayed that they would not go there and look for her. She also knew it was out of her hands. There was nothing she could do to stop what might surely happen.

She knew also that going in the direction of the settlement was out of the question. She would have to travel too close to where the Huron and Red were right now and did not want to take that risk. So, she forged on, distraught, and scared. Her thoughts and the extreme grief she carried were her only companions.

Never would she see her home again. Never would she hear her father's laughter or know the sweetness of his embrace.

"Think, Leslie, think!" she spoke aloud. "What would Papa have you do?"

She halted and looked about. Numb, tired, frightened, she ran her fingers through her tangled tresses, and she whimpered. She looked upward as tears streamed from her eyes.

"Help me, Lord. Please, please help me. What should I do? Where should I go?"

She turned to her left, then to her right. She had no idea where she was. Whenever she ventured this far from the cabin, she was always with her father or Shaun. She looked up at the sky again and noted the position of the moon. It had to be only a few hours before dawn, and she was certain she was still heading north. She was so afraid that Red and his warriors were close behind. She shivered with fear and bolted forward, running as fast as her legs would carry her.

She stumbled along the way in the dark, tripped, and fell frequently. Branches lashed at her cheeks, pulled at her hair, slashed at her hosiery, and cut her legs. Her palms bled from the many lacerations she received when they scraped the ground to break her falls. Her pulse pounded like a locomotive in her ears, and her chest heaved with every breath she took. Her side would spasm from the toll the exertion was taking on her body.

As the faces of her loved ones passed before her eyes, she became oblivious to the direction she traveled. She tried to suck air into her lungs slowly, but her exhaustion was so great, and her body so spent, she finally gave in and fell to her knees.

Gasping heavily, she wrapped her arms about her waist and rocked back and forth in total dismay.

I cannot believe this is happening, she thought. The precious faces of her dead child and husband kept coming to mind, and she broke into hysterical tears. *How much more misery must I endure?*

She wanted to die and willed it to happen. She took a very deep breath and held it, hoping to force herself to black out, even for just a short while. She had nothing else to live for. Her family was lost to her forever. She was alone - desperately and totally alone in a wilderness foreign to her, with only the clothes on her back and nothing to eat or drink.

Her throat constricted painfully from holding her breath, and she let go with a loud wheeze. She fell to the ground utterly exhausted and sucked air back into her lungs. She cried and cried, her body craving sleep and her mind screaming to move on, for her life was in danger. As much as she wanted to lie there and sleep, she feared being a captive of Red Farmer even more.

She forced herself into a sitting position and briefly closed her eyes.

"Guide me, Lord," she spoke softly. "Give me the strength to do what I must do - to go where I am destined to be."

I need to find food, water, shelter, and a place to rest a short while, she prayed silently.

She was upset with herself for not taking the time to pack a few supplies before she left the cabin, and then, like a lightning bolt, an idea came to mind, and she squealed happily.

"Supplies!" She covered her mouth quickly with her hands when she heard her voice echo through the forest.

With renewed strength, she bolted to her feet. She turned in one direction and then spun about in the other. In all her misery, she totally forgot about the many times she hiked with her father. She shook her head to clear her thoughts and slowly massaged her temples with her fingers. There was one bluff she remembered that was her father's favorite. Immediately, a feeling, a strange sensation began to wash over her.

"Help me, Papa. I know you are here with me. Give me a sign."

Slowly, she turned and scanned the horizon that was beginning to lighten a soft pink, looking for the distinguishable landmark she sought. And there, in the distance, she saw it - a bluff that resembled the profile of a man with a hooked nose.

"Papa's peak," she whispered.

She studied it carefully to be sure and smiled. There was not a doubt in her mind it was the same formation. Leslie jumped up and down like an excited schoolgirl and clapped her hands joyously. Despite her state of distress and loss of direction, someone was looking out for her. She closed her eyes and forced herself to relax. She took in a deep breath and slowly released it, repeating the exercise three more times. She had no doubt in her mind that her father was right there at that moment by her side.

She closed her eyes and reached her arms out in front of her with her palms facing forward. Very slowly, she moved in a circle, her mind void of thought, her concentration so extreme that the sounds of nature around her ceased. She waited patiently and knew it would come - knew she would feel his energy.

"Let me know you are here, Papa. I need to know you are with me."

Completing the circle, she halted, and a slow smile graced her lips as the scent of him filled her nostrils. She breathed deeply into her lungs, recognizing the aroma of his favorite pipe tobacco, and a lump formed in her throat.

"Thank you, Papa," she murmured "Thank you for guiding my footsteps and leading me here. Stay with me, Papa - please, please stay with me and guide me to where it is I am supposed to be."

She opened her eyes and looked to the distance. Despite how close the bluff seemed, she knew better and surmised it would take another two, possibly three days to reach the base of the formation. She swallowed hard and chewed at her lower lip. It would be a long and difficult trek. To go three more days without food, even water, could prove fatal. But she knew she had to try. Hidden in a cave midway up that peak was food, clothing, and weapons - everything she needed to survive.

Concerned filled eyes embraced the direction she needed to take, and Leslie moved forward, comforted in knowing no one else knew of the cave's existence except for Shaun.

Shaun - the thought of him brought tears to her eyes. To never feel his heartbeat against her chest when he hugged her tightly or hear the sweet lilt of his Irish brogue, tore at her heart. He had given up his life for her. A sob caught in her throat as she trekked onward, missing him and her father more with every step she took. Little by little she forced the cloud of despair that hung over her to clear. She realized that being aware of everything she did from this moment forward was paramount to her survival.

She tried to tamper the tears and whimpers. She knew she needed to be alert and aware of where she stepped, not leaving any tracks, not catching her clothing, and snagging any branches. Red Farmer would be looking for her, and she could not make it easy for him.

Time passed, and the hike took its toll on her weary body and mind. Her stomach growled with hunger, and her throat ached for the tiniest drop of water. Toward late afternoon, she looked for a place to bed down for the evening. Luckily, she came upon some berries and nuts to nourish herself. It was not long before the stress of the day took its toll on her, and she fell into a deep sleep - a sleep that offered a vision more mysterious than those before.

He rides at a steady gallop upon the wind with his long, black hair whipping about him, concealing his face from view. A quiver of arrows is clutched in his hand and entwined around his muscled bicep lay a silver serpent, a symbol of the warrior's mystical power and strength. Soft, sweet whispers travel upon the wind, beckoning him to come, to find, to protect and give aid. The angelic voice he hears is alluring yet filled with such suffering and loss it beckons him onward. He prods his stallion into a hard run, pulled along by the magical force that he cannot see, yet knows is there - to help him seek her out - to help him find her.

On the third day of her venture, Leslie is only a mere mile from her climb up the bluff. It has been more than a day since she has last eaten. Her body is weak, and she can hardly place one foot in front of the other.

The muscles in her calves and thighs are burning and frequent spasms make it difficult for her to make much progress. A strong wave of hopelessness consumes her and her desire to move on is wavering. With every passing minute, her strength lessens, and doubt begins to fill her.

Leslie looked skyward and fright poked at her as ominous clouds began to filter across the sky and block out the sun. Thrashing winds ravaged about her, whipping leaves, dirt and small particles into tiny, spiraling whirlwinds about her. Her hair lashed at her face, and the cool, chilling air that moved in began to prickle her skin.

Desperately, she looked about for cover. All she could see for miles were towering, majestic pines.

"This is not good," she spoke aloud. "I've got to find shelter," her voice trembled.

She knew how menacing thunderstorms could be and turned towards the sound of rumbling in the near distance. She looked upward again, and lightning streaked across the sky as pelting rain began to fall upon her. She continued, her eyes searching for some source of cover. She saw a toppled giant pine a few feet ahead and moved quickly in that direction. As she neared, she could tell its trunk had begun to rot.

It appeared more than thirty feet long and was wedged up against a massive boulder covered with moss. The trunk of the tree had begun to lift and peel, and as she stood and stared at it, she tried to think of what she could do to work it to her advantage.

Instantly, it came to her, and she pulled her knife free and began skinning away the loose bark in one large section. When she stood the bark up against her body, it came up to her breast and wrapped around her legs.

A roaring clash echoed through the trees as another bolting streak of lightning illuminated the sky. In a matter of seconds, an extreme deluge fell upon her, followed by another deafening clash of thunder, shaking the ground beneath her feet.

Leslie fell to her knees and crawled into the narrow space where the boulder and trunk connected, dragging the bark behind her. As she lay down upon her side in a fetal position, she drew the protective bark over herself, covering her entire body. The rain pummeled heavily on top of her, and she prayed the storm would not last for long.

Each time a heavy gust of wind lifted the bark, she struggled to hold it in place. It was not long before her teeth began to chatter, and her insides shook with tremors. She spoke the

Lord's Prayer out loud, but it did not comfort her. Despite the deafening thunder that roared around her, Leslie became alert to a more familiar noise.

Her eyes grew wild with terror as the distinct, paralyzing sound of a rattler rung just inches from her head. When another flash of lightning illuminated the sky, Leslie saw the venomous serpent uncoil and raise its body to strike. She bolted into a sitting position just as it leaped forward to bite, barely missing her as she raised the bark to shield herself. She let out a piercing scream and kicked the bark away from her and bolted out into the open, slamming the side of her head as she exited.

She weaved backwards, dizzy from the blow and a deep gash that split along the side of her temple. Warm blood oozed into her left eye, and she was whirled about by the strong winds and caught up her tangling, sodden skirt as it wrapped about her legs. She rocked and swayed as nausea threatened to rise and shook uncontrollably.

Leslie began to lose her footing as she slipped in a mix of wet leaves and mud. She fell with a hard thud to the ground and screamed in excruciating pain as her shoulder popped from its socket. She could not move, even if she wanted to. Her shivering body aggravated the searing pain that traveled from her shoulder down the length of her arm.

As the pain rippled through her, another searing bolt of lightning flashed across the heavens and sliced through the fissured branches of a massive spruce that stood less than five feet from where she lay. The roaring tear of a branch pulling away from its trunk drew her attention upwards. She could see red sparks and gray smoke emanating from where the electrifying flash just hit its mark.

Before she could react and drag herself from the falling branch's path, Leslie was struck with such a force, she was knocked unconscious.

Chapter Seven

On the dawn of the second day into his vision quest, Winnokin, Chief of the Seneca Bear Clan, sat atop a sacred knoll for his spiritual renewal. Having first prepared himself by means of purifying his body in the traditional vapor bath to cast off all human influence, he came to this noble point, the most commanding of summits in all his lands. He brought with him no offerings or sacrifices other than his body paint and tobacco.

He wanted to appear before the Great Spirit in all humility, wearing no clothing except moccasins and breech clout, and rose once again to overlook the beauty of earth in all its glory.

Winnokin did not move, exposed to the elements for another full day and night. Sometimes he chanted a hymn without words or offered the ceremonial pipe. Without food or water to consume, he found his highest happiness and the motive power of his existence while in this holy place.

The League had successfully defeated the French and chased them from his people's land. They continued their steadfast control of the eastern woodlands, keeping the region void of an over-abundant settlement of English and Dutch. Except for the small colony of fur trappers and traders to their south, who pledged not to disturb their lands or break any of the League's tribal laws, it was a time of great rest for his people.

He needed this time of cleansing to redefine his pure spirit. The wars had taken their toll on him personally with the deaths of both his parents. Not that he was held accountable, but he knew his people wondered why he had not yet taken a wife.

It was uncommon for a virile warrior chief not to be joined by thirty winters. He craved loving and desiring a woman, having what his parents shared for nearly fifty winters. But to join out of duty was displeasing to him, no matter how much he yearned to have children of his own. When his needs had to be quelled, there were willing widows in camp.

Winnokin raised his arms wide to the heavens and called upon the majestic, supreme spiritual forces of nature: lightning, wind, water, and fire to guide him. He pervaded the spirits of all creation to possess his soul and mind and communicate the path his life was to lead. He had faith in all their instincts, as their combined mysterious wisdom was blessed by the Great One. He humbly accepted his voluntary sacrifice as homage to their supernatural power and continued to praise them through prayer and reverent chants.

He remained stoic as a persistent torrential storm with blustering winds threatened to carry him over the precipice. His strong resolve was soon rewarded with a mystical vision that left him bewildered yet filled him with a yearning to seek out its meaning.

From afar amid star-filled heavens, a glorious, white stallion gallops toward him, appearing almost motionless as if floating on air. Not one marking mars its coat.

Atop is a rider, her golden tresses illuminate the darkness that surrounds her. Her beautiful face mirrors fear as she gazes over her shoulder at a massive red wolf gaining upon the heels of her stead, its fangs dripping with saliva, its massive chest heaving with powerful exertion as its paws emit thunderous rumbles with each pounding romp it takes toward her.

She is not of his people but wears an embroidered skin with the markings of his Bear Clan. She turns to gaze upon him, and their eyes lock, and she briefly forgets the wolf that threatens to pounce. She smiles, and their hearts connect. Within an instant, a bolt of lightning sparks across the heavens, striking her from her mount. He reaches for her, but she plummets toward Mother Earth too far from his reach.

Her whimpers of pain reach his ears like soft whispers on the wind. "Help ... please help ... need you."

Winnokin fell to his knees, and his hands clutched his chest as if struck by a knife. He wiped the rain from his eyes, peered out into the dark void of night, and knew the woman he just saw in his vision was out there somewhere, alone and in need of his care and protection. He just knew it. He was certain he would find her running from the settlement, running to escape some perilous danger, and filled with hopeless dread.

He rose with confidence, knowing the Great Spirit had a plan for the both, and in time, they would learn together what that was.

Winnokin did not want to waste another minute and gave his thanks to his creator for sending him his vision quest.

With renewed strength, he bolted toward the cover of trees where his favorite black gelding was staked, waiting for him and quickly dressed in deerskin tunic and leggings. He swung a bag made of the same materials that held all his survival belongings and mounted his horse. In a matter of moments, he had his steed in a cantor, heading in a direction driven by some inner force that guided their way.

The rain dwindled to a soft mist after a few short hours. When he gazed up at the sky, Winnokin was pleased to see the thunderclouds dispersing as the sun began to rise above the horizon. His astute skills as a warrior made him one with the earth as he scanned the ground and surroundings for the smallest track of a female in passing. His trained hearing alerted him to every sound that echoed through the dense forest.

Fearless warrior and noble stead moved as one through the forest. They were a sight to behold and a force to be reckoned with. Winnokin's powerful, intelligent mount was accustomed to the slightest change in pressure his master applied with his thighs. Such moves were trained orders between man and beast, and the animal instinctively knew when to control his gait without blunder, so Winnokin could let go of the reins when needed to string a bow into his arrow.

It was not long when his watchful patience was rewarded as he entered a break in the forest into an open area.

Winnokin did not notice her at first, as his attention was drawn to the massive branch still smoking slightly from the lightning that had struck it earlier. As he drew closer, he could see a light-colored fabric of a garment underneath, barely covering a beautiful ivory thigh and shapely calf.

He commanded his mount to halt and jumped from its back and knelt before the small body. His loud gasp echoed as he gazed upon the face of the woman in his vision. Her hair was discolored and matted with mud and blood from a deep gash clear across the side of her forehead. Half of her body was pinned beneath the hulking limb, and he knew he had to remove the crushing weight as soon as possible.

He looked about to find a sizable rock, and the muscles in his arms bulged with exertion as he carried it a short distance, laying it opposite the woman. He then took roping he always carried with him and tied a makeshift halter around his mount's neck and connected the free end to the branch, into a secured slip knot.

He used the weight of his body to snap a thick branch free that he wedged beneath the trunk and atop the small rock he placed there earlier. With all his might, every muscle strained and exerted to lift the trunk into the air. When he was satisfied its height was far enough from the ground, Winnokin commanded this trusty stead to move backward.

The animal's powerful hind legs dug deep into the muddied earth as the strong beast reared its proud head and upper body into the air. Winnokin let go of the branch as he watched his mount's long, black mane billow in the wind and its front hoofs claw the air as it whinnied and grunted with strain, successfully plowing a few steps back and pulling the massive branch free of the white woman.

Winnokin ran forward and praised his companion as he nuzzled his head and neck with tender strokes. Quickly, he removed the halter from the animal's neck and let him graze freely as Winnokin moved forward to lift the woman away from the tree and into a small clearing.

Gently, he began to clean away the mud from her face and noticed a wound on her head that was still bleeding steadily and needed to be closed. He gathered moss from the surface of a nearby boulder to use as a poultice later and then rummaged through his bag for a medicinal plant that when crushed to a fine power and blended into a salve, would numb the area around her gash. He pulled a single hair from his horse's tail and threaded it through a bone needle used for embroidering quills onto skins, which all warriors carried to sew up battle wounds while away from camp.

He was relieved she was still unconscious so as not to feel the sharpness of his needle as it tore through her tender skin. Carefully he closed the gash with tiny, intricate stitches that would prove barely visible once the wound was entirely healed.

He thought it strange that she wore the shirt of a full-grown man and wondered if it belonged to a husband, brother or father.

Slowly he ran his hands up the arm that received the heavy blow and over her shoulder. The area where her shoulder met the collarbone did not feel right, and he moved to unbutton her shirt, lifted her carefully, and slipped the sleeve from her arm. He raised her arm to see what range of motion she had, and when he placed her arm back down by her side, he noticed how her forearm turned outward awkwardly. He was certain that her shoulder had dislocated.

Winnokin rose to his knee and placed the ball his left foot into her armpit. Carefully, he raised her arm at the precise angle and pulled upward with one quick snap and heard her shoulder pop back into place.

The woman did not move or utter a sound.

He lifted her again and slipped her arm back into the sleeve of the shirt and buttoned it back in place. The sizable knot on the side of her head concerned him greatly. If she did not awaken soon, he knew there would be great cause for concern.

He passed a small stream a few yards back and knew he needed to retrieve some fresh water. The bag he had could also be used as a water pouch, and he emptied its contents onto the ground. He brought his steed nearby and gave the animal a command to watch and protect the woman.

With lightning speed, he ran to the stream and returned with a full pouch of cool water and began to bathe away the mud from the woman's hair. Tenderly, he worked the numbing salve around the swelling, dipped the moss into the water and then covered her wound directly. Every few minutes, he continued the process until the swelling went down.

He returned for more water, built a small fire and boiled some herbal tea he would use after he cared for her and settled her comfortably. It took only moments to chop pine boughs for bedding and spread one of two saddle blankets he had with him over it. Painstakingly, he lifted her limp body into his arms and gently laid her down upon the makeshift bed and covered her with the other blanket.

Winnokin gazed upon her face and softly lifted a wavy tendril of her golden hair. It curled around his finger naturally. His heart swelled over the beauty of her.

He could not help but wonder what caused her to flee into the wilderness with not a single weapon to protect herself other than the skinning knife he found nearby, nor supplies of any kind to keep her nourished. Where were the men in her family? What kind of people were they to let someone so petite and beautiful travel in the wilderness on her own?

The whites are a very strange breed of people, he thought.

They took great pleasure in material things and not those of more importance. They destroyed the earth, killed more than they needed for food, and lusted for things that belonged to others.

He felt rage growing inside him as the thought of an abusive husband entered his mind. He did not know why such feelings of protectiveness consumed him. She was white, he was Indian, and at one time, they were great enemies. Remembering his vision quest, however, made him feel differently.

He looked at her face and hands, turned her on her side, and lifted her shirt to see if she had old bruises on her back and checked her legs. She was a mystery - a mystery he planned on solving.

No harm will further come to her, he vowed silently.

Whatever, or whoever, she is running from was now his problem and concern - for from this day forward, he would be her protector.

He took a horned cup and dipped it into the cooling tea he had set aside and brought it to her lips. Instinctively, she swallowed a few sips, and Winnokin found contentment in that.

While she slept, he took time to leave on foot and hunt for small game, his war steed again, remaining alert and watchful over her.

Chapter Eight

It was like a heavy fog was lifting from her brain as Leslie willed her eyes to open. Her right shoulder and forehead throbbed severely when she shifted her weight. Instantly, she realized the foolishness of her mistake, as pain bolted down her right arm and across her breastbone.

She cried out and willed herself to lie still and fall back to sleep, but it evaded her. The pain rippled through her body with each breath she took, and her eyes misted with tears.

She became aware of the sounds around her as dawn announced the beginning of a brand-new day. Birds chirped merrily in a tree nearby. She could hear the lone cry of an eagle as it soared somewhere overhead out of view and the drone hum of an army of black jackets as they worked nearby. She had no idea how long she had been asleep, where she was, or how she got to lie upon the bed of soft pine boughs that were beneath her.

She looked to her left and saw a neat stack of wood lying beside a small pit dug out in the ground. There was a fire burning, and it looked like something was cooking over it on a spit. She could hear the crackling of the twigs as they burned and hissing of meat juices as they dripped into the hot flames. Her stomach growled, and she could not remember when the last time was, she had something solid to eat.

She could feel the weight of a bandage wrapped around her head, and she lifted her hand to touch it.

Leslie remembered being struck by a fallen branch during a terrible thunderstorm and the weight of its impact knocking her to the ground.

Someone - but who found me? She wondered as she winced and pulled her hand away.

At first, she thought Red Farmer might have found her but, dismissed the thought immediately. Red was menacing and would not have taken such gentle care with her, for that she was certain.

Whoever it was, she felt extremely thankful but still terribly afraid. She was not sure how many days had gone by since her accident. She knew Red was still hot in pursuit of her. Still, she wanted so much to know whoever the kindhearted person might be.

Despite the throbbing pain in her head, she was comfortable. The stranger's considerate attentions were touching. She wondered where the mystery caretaker might be and called out in a raspy voice.

"Hello. Is anyone out there?"

Fear rose in her as she realized she was totally alone, helpless to whatever decided to stray into camp, attracted to what was cooking nearby. Red came to mind again, and her insides began to tremble.

She wrenched with pain as she tried to turn slightly to look behind her. Spasms coursed through her upper body.

"Oh God!" she cried out as she clutched her shoulder.

Before she spoke another word, a shadow passed over her. Leslie jerked her head to look up and shrieked with fright as the body of a tall, well-muscled, half-naked Indian stood before her, his face was void of expression.

Leslie knew from his markings that he was not Huron, because he wore his raven black hair long and free. The Huron sported a single scalp lock from their forehead midway down the middle of their head with clean-shaven sides. She wondered if he was from the tribe her father had counseled with when Red was found robbing Seneca grave sites. She could not help but gape openly at his majestic presence.

He stood tall and proud, and she could swear his light brown eyes were flecked with gold. She could not deny he was the most handsome, virile man she had ever seen.

She closed her eyes tightly for a few moments, rubbed at them with the hand of her good arm, and slowly peeked through her lashes.

She nearly jumped out of her skin and squealed like a mouse when she found him kneeling right there in front of her.

His hair gleamed in the sunlight and fell well below his shoulders. A colorful beaded headband decorated his forehead.

She could not help but gulp nervously as her eyes scanned a broad, muscular, hairless chest and flat, rippled abdomen. His powerful arms looked like they were sculpted from hard granite. Remembering the man who haunted her dreams for the longest time, she could not help but huff aloud when she recognized a thin silver bracelet on one bicep that resembled a twisting serpent.

Mindlessly, she reached out to touch it and realized what she was doing and snapped her hand away.

She saw the quizzical look on the Indian's face and found herself explaining, even though she assumed he did not understand her language.

"I'm sorry - I did not mean - it is just that my dreams - I have seen this in my dreams," she rambled.

Winnokin could not believe his ears. He did not want her to know he knew the white man's tongue quite yet and did everything he could to contain both his shock and joy.

She had visions of me as well, he thought. *It is true - the Great Spirit planned for our paths to cross after all.*

He grunted and shrugged ignorance.

"Of course, how stupid of me. You do not understand, do you?"

Leslie swallowed hard and willed her pulse to slow.

How can we communicate, if he does not understand me? She questioned herself silently.

Winnokin knew she found his looks pleasing, and he masked his amusement.

"Ni ta ya Tanye," he replied as he touched his hand to his shoulder and eye, then he touched hers tenderly.

Leslie quivered from his touch. It felt like another bolt of lightning had charged clear through her but with a more pleasing effect.

Winnokin almost broke into a smile. *She responds to my touch the way a blossom opens to the warmth of Father Sun,* he thought quietly.

Leslie knew he was questioning her wound and replied again without thinking.

"I feel like I have been kicked by a mule." She chuckled and then grimaced from the pain. She whimpered her discomfort, and when her eyes met that of the stranger's, she was moved by the compassion she read there.

"Lord, you are one beautiful man" she murmured, shaking her head absently. "I never would have thought a man such as you would come to my rescue." She shrugged. "You are certainly a sight to behold." She reached out and touched his arm lightly as she gazed softly into his eyes. "How do I, how can I thank you for all you have done?"

It was all Winnokin could do not to pull away. Her touch was magnetic and sparked a desire he had never felt with any other woman before. It would be a true test of will power not to ravage her on that very spot, and the only thing holding him back was the clear sign of her injuries and the fact that he was an honorable man and leader.

Leslie detected the immediate change in his eyes when she touched him, and for some strange reason it pleased her. She could not understand why she did not feel afraid being in the presence of this stranger kneeling before her. It was odd to feel so comfortable in his presence.

She wondered why she did not fear him as she looked into his eyes. All she read was tenderness, not ferocity in their depths. And then it dawned on her. There was no reason to fear this man. The similarities to the man in her dream were too exact to not be real. Of all the times she dreamed of him, not once was there any sign she would suffer injury by his hand.

Her stomach growled loudly again, and she made a funny face as she grasped her belly.

"I guess I am a wee bit hungry." She gestured, pointing in the direction of the fire.

Winnokin nodded slightly, and she watched him as he rose and walked toward the fire. He moved with the grace of a mountain cat, and she continued to watch him as he knelt to dish out some broth into what looked like the horn of an animal.

When he moved back beside her, he tenderly placed his hand behind her neck to help her raise her head enough to sip from the horn.

Leslie gasped with pain instantly and clutched his thigh as her eyes filled with tears.

When she looked up at him, she read the concern he felt for her in his eyes.

She patted his thigh and held up her hand.

"It is all right. Really, the pain - it will pass."

She reached for his hand and guided the horn to her lips. Beads of sweat dotted her forehead from the exertion, but the broth tasted delicious and was worth the pain. Even as tears slowly rolled down her cheeks, she took two more sips before she fell back completely exhausted.

Her pain tugged at Winnokin's heart. Instinctively, he reached out to wipe away her tears.

"Na na, Ishita. E ita shoo time (No, no, my Love. I take away the pain), he whispered softly as he dabbed a cool cloth along her forehead.

The compassion he showed warmed Leslie clear down to her toes, and she smiled up at him.

He moved from her side to retrieve a dark brown root from his belongings that she could not identify. She watched as he pounded it into a fine powder with a stone and then added water until it became a gluey salve.

When he returned to her side, he pointed to the buttons on her shirt and made the gesture for her shirt to be opened.

Leslie tried to raise the hand of her sore arm to do so and turned pale from the searing pain that shot up her arm.

Winnokin patted her hand softly and shook his head to halt her movement and lifted his hands to complete the task for her. His touch was slow and gentle as he slid her shirt past her shoulder and down her arms. He clasped the delicate strap of her chemise and slid it over her injured shoulder, exposing the swell of her right breast.

Leslie knew that any proper lady would cover herself immediately, but since he had dressed all her wounds and had already seen more than she cared to know, she gave in to the fact they were well past the stage of social propriety.

She could feel the immediate a hot flush across her cheeks the moment he began to slowly rub the salve over her entire shoulder. She raised her eyes to meet his, and there was a trace of a smile on his lips.

She was very familiar with the look of desire and passion because she had read it many times, not only in her husband's eyes, but Shaun's and Red's as well. This warrior was attracted to her. She could feel it in his touch. His body permeated that primal wanton need of a man for a woman, and her face reddened with an intensity that threatened to sear his touch. Her breath came in short, quick gasps, and she was certain her bottom lip was swollen from sucking on it nervously.

She could not believe where her thoughts were going with this man, and it both shocked and left her breathless. Just a short while ago she watched Shaun defend her life to the death. She felt as though her thoughts were a dishonor to the man he was and the selfless, genuine love and devotion he had shown her.

Still, she could not help the reaction the man before her invoked inside of her, and she wondered what it would feel like to have his lips pressed against hers.

Reading her very thoughts, Winnokin caressed her face with his right palm and then traced the length of her bottom lip with his thumb as their eyes locked in a hypnotic stare.

"My stomach is in knots," she whispered. "Our paths have never once crossed, yet I feel as though I should know who you are," she sighed.

To her surprise, he nodded.

"What is your name?" she tested.

Knowing her ploy, Winnokin did not answer, sat back on his heels, and cocked his head from side to side.

"Hmm," she responded. "Name - you name?" She pointed and touched his chest with her finger.

Winnokin played along and shrugged his shoulders, grunting his ignorance.

Frustrated, she sighed deeply and thought for a moment.

Leslie patted her chest. "Les-lee," she said and pointed to his chest. "You," she continued, shrugged as much as her sore shoulder would allow, and lifted both of her hands in question.

Winnokin continued to play along, shook his head as if not knowing, and shrugged his shoulders.

"Oh, dang!" she sputtered and slapped the ground. She gasped when the effort sent pain coursing through her shoulder.

Again, she placed an open palm on her chest and patted it lightly.

"Les-lee," she repeated and extended an open palm in his direction.

Winnokin smiled and nodded understanding while pounding his chest with his fist.

"Win-no-kin, ya!" he replied, shaking his head. "Win-no-kin," he repeated, smiling broadly.

Leslie repeated his name perfectly. "Winnokin." She smiled. "Hmm. I wonder what it means. I must learn more, so we can talk to each other."

She thought for a moment and waved her hand to catch his attention.

"Drink," she said, closing her fist and bringing it to her lips. "Drink," She repeated the action as if drinking from a cup.

Winnokin nodded his understanding, rose, and brought back what looked to her to be a rawhide water pouch.

"Kna-ga-huk," he replied, handing her the pouch.

Leslie smiled. "Knagahuk," she repeated and took a sip

Winnokin also smiled and nodded. He pointed to the fire then made the gesture as though he were shoveling food into his mouth with his fingers.

"Nuk-kna-shuk," he said.

Leslie did not know if he meant food or eating but repeated the word perfectly and was pleased with the approving smile that spread across his handsome face.

She pointed to her hair, and he responded with the Indian word. She pointed to his horse, the fire, sun, tree, and repeated each word he pronounced with clarity. The excitement tired her quickly, and she yawned with fatigue and shivered.

Winnokin knelt nearer and covered her back up with the blanket and made a sign to sleep.

"Ese nanuma, Ishita (You sleep, my love), he spoke.

Leslie smiled, not completely knowing what he said, but she figured it had something to do with falling asleep. She yawned and pretended to close her eyes. When he rose, she watched him move to the fire, throw more wood upon the flames, and settle down beside its warmth.

He took a pipe from his satchel and filled it with tobacco, lighting it with a burning twig from the fire.

A sense of contentment passed over her, and she exhaled softly. She whispered a quiet prayer to the Almighty, thanking him for her good fortune. She prayed life would be kinder and knew her destiny was in the Lord's hands. A calming filled her, and she could not help but wonder if her father knew what happened and would approve of the emotions and feelings already growing between her and Winnokin. She knew her father would respect him regardless of his heritage, for he always had a saying:

"Tis not the color of a man's skin, nor where he hangs his hat that matters, but the strength of his character, his honor, his love of the land and the Lord's creatures that marks his nobility.

"Yes, Papa," she whispered quietly. "I do believe you would like this man who has come to my rescue."

Chapter Nine

By the second day, Leslie's pain had subsided considerably. She could move about with some ease after Winnokin wrapped her arm tightly to her side with large strips torn from the bottom of her skirt.

The past couple of mornings she had feigned sleeping and quietly enjoyed watching Winnokin carry out his morning regimen. She did not know Indians were such spiritual individuals. They needed no temples or shrines to praise their Great Spirit.

Respectfully, she did not speak or do anything to distract him. It looked like he was thanking the sun and the earth with his hand gestures. Even though she could not understand his language, the tone of his voice was deeply reverent, and the words he spoke sounded beautiful to her ears. It was obvious that the outward love he showed for them was much like the love she felt for her own god and felt as though they were one and the same.

Leslie's father had a deep respect for the natives in the area and tried to learn as much about them as possible when he was alive. She knew he thought it was so very important since they shared the land and were the very first to inhabit it. Her father had told her that the Indians also praised the majestic forces of lightning, wind, water, and fire for offering their spiritual powers when needed for whatever reason. With humble acceptance, they praised their brothers, the animals of the forest, as well—who would sacrifice their bodies to preserve each of them. They also paid homage to the spirits of those they would need to hunt.

The more she witnessed, the more respect she felt for his kind and their customs. In her heart, she knew that white men could be more savage than the Iroquois, as she reflected on the atrocities Red Farmer was responsible for. Her people professed their religion but truly did not practice what they preached. Even if they sang spiritual songs or recited solemn prayers, material things held more value to so many of them.

The white man bought and sold everything, from time, labor, and the love of a woman to personal independence. Their lust for money, power, and conquest could be proven back to the beginning of time. All the Iroquois wanted out of life, was to live in harmony with nature, raise their families, and keep alive their customs and heritage.

Her impatience to learn his language increased with every passing day. She wondered if he knew Strong of Heart or was a member of his clan. When her father had traveled to his camp to plead for the safety of their settlement because of Red's wrongdoings, he was one of the elders her father had counseled with and most admired. Her father had hoped to meet with their chief, or clan Sachem as they were known, but he had gone on a pre-harvest hunt at the time.

The Seneca were the largest, most important, and fiercest warrior group of the five nations. When she looked at Winnokin, she could not imagine him as a ferocious, warring machine. His tender ministrations, since the day he found her, reflected a more sensitive, kindred spirit.

She remembered drilling her father unmercifully about what he had witnessed while amongst Winnokin's people nearly eight months ago. Even then, there was little she learned. Her father had been immediately whisked into a small dwelling with a domed roof covered in bark upon his arrival. It was large enough to hold six people. They were kept under close guard until they met for counsel after dark that same evening. While they waited, though, they were treated kindly and offered a delicious meal of cooked greens, beans, and squash.

Her father had told her animals of the forest provided the skins from which the women made their clothing. During the heat of the day, he observed most of the men wore the traditional breechclout, which was made from a strip of skin that was drawn up between their legs and held in place by looping it over a belt. Leslie's heart skipped as she watched Winnokin move about camp in the same attire. The hard muscles in his arms, legs, and back bulged and flexed with exertion as he bent, pulled, and stretched during his tasks. Very little was hidden from her view. She honestly felt guilty, even a little shameful, sitting there, enjoying seeing nearly every inch of him in his natural environment.

She admitted silently that she liked it more when he wore the breechclout than the leggings and cape shirt he changed into when the sun went down. Not that she did not admire the painstaking handiwork involved in making the particular shirt he wore each evening. She could not help but wonder, if it was a female member of his family who did his sewing and made his clothing, or if he had a wife awaiting his return.

Whoever it was, his shirt was embroidered with love and was artfully adorned with dyed porcupine quills and depicted a bright, golden thunderbolt with splatters of silver stars on a dyed black background for the night sky.

Her father had told her some of the men had tattoos on their faces. All had long, lustrous hair, some greased to add shine, some not. A number of men even plucked out their hair or cut portions to form their own distinctive style.

Winnokin, however, did not need a distinctive style. He was simply the most beautiful man she had ever seen. His high cheekbones, square jaw line, and full, sumptuous lips were intoxicating. Every muscle in his near-naked body seemed to be carved from stone as he walked about the campsite with the grace and ease of a mountain lion.

Leslie felt like a schoolgirl and had to catch herself at times for gaping at him openly. Falling for him was out of the question until she knew more about him, his family, if he was involved or promised to another, whether she was considered a friend, captive, or—or maybe even a slave.

If that was the case and he was not married, or promised to another, she would never be able to be anything more to him. She remembered the stories retold by the trappers who passed through the settlement frequently. The Seneca treated captives from warring tribes with little respect, beating them daily. Camp dogs were handled more humanely than those kept alive to act as slaves.

They did not hold whites in the highest regard, from what she understood. It was said they hated them more than their worst enemy, the Huron. It was known that all Iroquois thought themselves more superior. They scorned the whites as a soft race, absorbed in soft beds, luxurious food, drunken behavior, and who could not tell the truth even when they pledged it to paper to benefit all mankind.

She could not argue that point. The numerous treaties signed before she ever came to this region had been broken time and again. So, she could imagine how they would look upon her if he brought her back to his camp. Despite how kind he was, Leslie knew in her heart she had to depart from his company once she was strong enough to head out on her own. She still had her father's supplies safely tucked away in a cavern just a short distance up the ridge.

She knew that when the time came, she would head out on her own. The thought of being treated as a slave saddened her.

As a noble warrior, what other choice would he have? How could he defy the way of his people if it was their practice to take slaves? Was it not a human trait, despite the difference in cultures, to treat people with common decency? Could two cultures truly be so different—one a savage and the other humane?

Leslie felt confused over the fact a man like Winnokin could be so tender and caring while alone in the wilderness with her and then turn around and treat her with callous disregard; because his tradition was so inbred, he would not be able to act any differently.

Maybe he was just being kind to fatten her up enough, make her strong and healthy to trade her off to another family.

She yawned out loud, stretched, and pretended to just awaken.

Winnokin turned and smiled.

All her fears disappeared. Her heart flip-flopped in her chest as he moved toward her and knelt by her side. His manly scent filled her nostrils, and if it was not for the constriction of her bandages, she would have flung herself into his arms, even though she planned to run away.

She took a few hearty sips of the broth he offered and nodded her thanks. He went about his business, and from what she could tell, he was getting ready to go on another hunt for their next meal.

The evening before, they feasted on roasted rabbit. After he'd returned from his morning hunt, he'd spent most of the afternoon while she slept skinning the two large rabbits he had trapped. He used some kind of scraping tool she never saw before to remove the flesh from the skins until they were smooth, silken pelts that he then stretched out on pegs to dry.

After Leslie finished her broth, Winnokin untied and removed her shoes and then took the rabbit pelts and outlined each of her feet with a charred piece of wood from the fire. It was only then she realized he was making her a pair of moccasins from the rabbit skins he'd prepared the day before.

She was touched by the attention he adorned upon her. Despite her ignorance of Iroquois customs, she was certain one task a warrior did not perform was sewing of any kind. She watched him as he used his sharp hunting knife to slice a thin, narrow strip from the pelt and used it to thread through a wide-eyed needle made from some unknown piece of bone.

Using the charcoal form of her foot, he cut two separate soles, shaped a set of tongues, sides, and backs, and within two hours had custom designed a pair of moccasins that fit each of her feet like an added layer of her own skin.

Wearing the boot shoes, she had known all her life seemed natural. She knew a lot of the trappers preferred wearing skins, because they were warmer, more comfortable, and lasted longer. She just never imagined herself doing so. Now that they were covering her skin so naturally, Leslie realized what she had been missing all along.

She chuckled with delight, wiggled her toes, and clapped her hands with joy.

"Thank you, Winnokin." She smiled as she placed her palms together and bowed slightly. "Thank you, truly."

Winnokin nodded in return. He pointed to Leslie and mimicked, placing his palms together, bowing, and said, "Ni a we."

He repeated his actions and said, "Ni a we."

Her eyes lit with joy. "You are teaching me how to say thank you, I think. Ni a we," she repeated. "Thank you—Ni a we."

Winnokin's eyes shone with glee, and he pounded a closed fist to his heart as he nodded his pleasure.

"Tank you," he mimicked.

Leslie laughed and nodded.

"Yah, Niu (It is well)," he replied. "Yah, Niu."

"Are you telling me, 'You're welcome or that I did good?" She nodded happily and repeated what he said very clearly. "Yah, Niu."

She pointed to the fire and said. "Fire. Fire." She pointed again.

Winnokin nodded. "Fire. Ode ka. Fire. Ode ka."

She neared the flame and pretended to touch but pulled back quickly. "Flame," she replied. "Flame."

Aware of the game they were playing, Winnokin repeated the word as he moved near and squatted beside her.

"O do knot," he exclaimed. "O do knot."

He picked up a piece of firewood in each hand and shook them, saying, "O Yan Da. O Yan Da."

She nodded, pointed to each item, and repeated the words perfectly.

Winnokin smiled and nodded. "Ya (Yes)."

She picked up a bowl, and Winnokin stopped her, shaking his head.

"Na, Ishita (No, my love). Aga I neh (I go)."

He made the sign of shooting his bow and arrow. "Aga I neh Guk wa (I go for food)."

Leslie could not help but show her dismay. The lesson was going so well, and she enjoyed it. As much as pointing and signing was interesting, she yearned to carry on a regular conversation with him. Learning as much of his language was not only important to their personal communication. She also knew if she decided to stay with him after everything she had been through, it would prove valuable overall. She felt frustrated ... frustrated with the language barrier between them, frustrated having lost everything she valued and was comfortable to her, and frustrated dealing with her slow recuperation.

Before she could speak another word, Winnokin mounted his horse and vanished into the cover of the forest.

She stood and kicked at the ground while she absently tried to run her fingers through her hair. It was not long before she realized what a tangled mess it was. When she looked down at her dress that was terribly dirty and torn, she made a face.

"Oh, my Lord!" she exclaimed. "I must look an awful sight."

She walked over to the water pouch and exhaled noisily when she found that it was nearly empty. She turned in the direction of the forest where Winnokin had departed and wondered how far the place was where he got their water every day. She tested her shoulder, felt confident enough to walk a distance, and nodded to herself with satisfaction.

"I think a little walk will do me good," she spoke aloud. "Winnokin will not be back for a few more hours, and that will be just long enough to wash these clothes and have a good soaking myself."

With the water pouch in hand, she headed toward the trees with a light step and joyful heart.

Before her injury had occurred, Leslie knew she was close to her original destination. She could even see the rock face loom above her just a short distance away. She would have to put that adventure out of her mind for a while, until she had the strength and total use of her injured arm once again.

During her walk, she marked the path with little twigs as pointing arrows so she would not get lost. She was amazed how lush the area was with wild fruits and vegetables. When she came upon a small patch of wild onions, she folded them into her skirt to bring back with her to camp. It was not long into her walk when she heard the distinct sound of water rushing over rocks. Before even seeing the mountain stream, she anxiously unwrapped the bindings from her shoulder and disrobed.

It was quite a sight. The morning sun streamed through the fissured branches of birch, beech, pine, and oak like a stairway to heaven. Its rays reflected upon the water's surface, clear down to the stream's bed like a pane of glass. The peaceful sound lulled her like a mother's lullaby, and Leslie peeled the rest of her clothing away in a matter of minutes.

She knew time was precious and quickly found a pool steep enough so that when she sat down, the water came to her chin. She dunked beneath the surface and vigorously rubbed at her hair with her good arm until all traces of blood and mud were gone. Then she attacked her skin with a small patch of moss she pulled from along the bank.

As soon as she scrubbed herself from neck to toe, she sat along the stream's edge half emerged in the water. Since the top of her dress was torn on the whole right side and the skirt was ripped to near shreds, she still decided to wash it—it was the only thing she had besides her petticoat. She scrubbed everything as best she could, wrung out the excess water, and squeezed back into only her undergarments. She felt like she'd accomplished something worthwhile and refilled the water pouch before heading back to camp.

She used her dress like a sack to carry her newfound stash along with wild mushrooms she found growing nearby the stream. It seemed to take her longer to return to camp than to find water. She found herself terribly fatigued and could barely keep her eyes open. As soon as she entered the campsite, she curled upon her bed, which was awash in sunlight, covered herself with the blanket, and fell fast asleep in a matter of seconds.

A short while later, Winnokin entered camp and knew instantly that something was different about Leslie. Her hair shone brilliantly from where he sat atop his stead. He dismounted and approached her silently. Kneeling by her side, his breath caught in his throat. She was a sight to behold as her hair was spread out like a carpet of curly waves streaming down over her shoulders. She had kicked the blanket away in her sleep, and her shapely calf and thigh were exposed for his view. Her skin was white as a snow dove, and Winnokin craved to glide his fingers along the length of her.

Tenderly, he moved the hair from her face, and his heart skipped as he noticed the swell of her breasts and how they nearly spilled from her chemise. It took every ounce of strength not to bend low and lay sweet kisses along the soft, velvet mounds exposed before his eyes. He looked about and noticed her garment nearby filled with wild onions and mushrooms. It was obvious she ventured outside of camp and found the stream a short distance to the north of them.

He was slightly troubled that she would do so without his protection. But he also knew that she was not a woman afraid to be on her own. He wondered what she was thinking and if she was comfortable being in his company or if she still wanted to be by herself. More than anything, he wanted to know why she ran away from her people, family, and loved ones. What had driven her into the wilderness without firearms, supplies, and only the clothes on her back? What, or who, was she running from?

He could not fathom her doing anything wrong and wondered who, in fact, had wronged her. Winnokin could feel hatred welling inside of him as he looked down upon her sleeping form. He vowed that he would kill any man who had, or would do, harm to her and her family.

The Great Spirit crossed their paths for a reason. She would not have been a part of his vision quest without just cause. As head sachem to his people, he had to be careful. It was important he continue to watch, listen, and learn more about her before he confided his knowledge of the white man's tongue.

Then, and only then, would he know if she was trustworthy enough to truly open up his heart to her.

A few days passed as Leslie continued to tutor and be tutored.

Winnokin found her to be a very able student. Her eagerness to learn made it easy for her to carefully pronounce the unusual vowels and sounds of his language. It did not take long for her to gain his respect.

Winnokin felt guilty keeping the knowledge of her language a secret for so long. With each passing day, her strength grew, but he continued to lavish her with his attention to make up for his deception. It was obvious a bond was growing stronger between them, and it was becoming more difficult with the passing of each day to keep the truth from her.

Leslie took up the task of preparing their meals now that her shoulder was no longer bandaged, and her wounds were healed completely. Even though she had accompanied her father on many short hunts, and did equally well catching the smaller game, the thought of using Winnokin's weapons stirred fear within her. She was glad when Winnokin told her that in his culture, it was forbidden for a woman to touch a warrior's weapons, as they were sacred to only them. His weapons were his constant companion and never out of his reach.

She knew he would never raise them in arms against her, but still, she could not help feeling uncomfortable by their presence. His club, or Gajewa, was made of hard wood and elaborately carved, painted, and ornamented with feathers at each end. In the lower edge, a sharp-pointed deer horn about four-inches in length protruded outward. It looked as though it could inflict a fatal wound when used in close combat.

The same held true of his tomahawk, or Osquesont. He always had it strung upon his back, except during sleep when it was close by his side. It was made of some sort of iron, but the handle and blade were richly inlaid in silver. When he had shown her how he threw it, it whizzed through the air with unerring certainty as it continually revolved in the air and hit the bark of a distant beech tree with deadly accuracy. She remembered his demonstration made her shudder, knowing what the result could do to a man.

Once she became more familiar with his people's customs, she discovered that the tomahawk was the perfect symbol of war itself. To bury it, to the Iroquois, would represent peace; to raise it would declare the deadliest warfare.

It seemed his hunting absences had shortened in time. She wondered if it was because he was afraid of leaving her alone to long, or his keen sense warned him that she was anxious to leave without him. Her patience soon paid off, and he left for his usual early morning hunt. It had been two days since her last bath. Now that she was stronger and sensing Winnokin was preparing them to return to his village, she did not know when she would have another chance at privacy.

Leslie felt like a giddy child when she reached the stream. She just wanted to bathe, swim a little, and relax in the water. Despite her stiffness, she still managed to scrub her hair with both arms until it was squeaky clean.

She refused to give into the gnawing feeling that she must rush. Instead, she eased up near the bank, sitting in the shallow water, and tossed back her head. She combed her long-wet tresses with her fingers and felt the heat of the afternoon sun beating down on her naked back. The rays felt splendid, and she sighed deeply as she lost herself in its warmth and her thoughts.

A short while passed when Leslie heard movement behind her. Her eyes flew open, and she crossed her arms protectively over her full breasts, turned, and gazed over her shoulder.

Standing there tall and brazen was Winnokin, his arms crossed at his chest. He moved to lean against the ancient maple beside him with a smirk upon his face and a mischievous glint in his eye. Surprisingly, his arrogance made her temper flare.

She glided back into the water to hide her nakedness.

"What are you doing here?" she scolded. "Go! Shoo!" She waved her hand.

Winnokin stood his ground with no intention of leaving.

Leslie was infuriated. *No one can be that stupid after all the lessons in my language he has had*, she rationalized.

She slapped the water with frustration.

"How dare you just stand there? You know quite well what I just said." She fumed as her face turned scarlet with annoyance.

"So, I will do it your way. Ummm ... oh, damn! What are the words?"

Winnokin could barely contain his composure.

She hit the water with both hands and grunted loudly. "Ese ... ese ta ... um ... Ese ta I neah (You go)!" she sputtered, pointing her finger at him to leave.

Winnokin laughed loudly.

Before he could react, Leslie scooped a handful of mud from the stream's bottom and tossed it at him soundly. The force splattered mud all over his face and into his hair as it hit him dead center just below his throat.

Leslie squealed and covered her mouth. The stunned look on his face was too much to bear, and she fell back into the water, chuckling uncontrollably.

When she came up, she said, "That will teach you oh great warrior to play games with me." She laughed.

Winnokin did not reply but moved toward her, slowly wading into the water. The look on his face was a clear indication of what he was planning to do.

"Ohhh!" Leslie shrieked. "What are you doing? Get back!" She splashed as she began to move backward. "Go away, you—you big lout!" she yelped and broke into laughter again.

Winnokin ignored her threats and closed in slowly with a grin spreading from ear-to-ear.

Much to his surprise, Leslie stopped and threw her hands up in submission, unaware of the enticing sight her rounded breasts offered as they rose above the water.

"Stop! Stop! You win. You win."

Her beauty made his breath catch in his throat, and Winnokin could feel his heart pulse like thunder in his chest as she stood there in beautiful splendor just within his reach.

Droplets of water glided a path between her breasts and beaded like tear drops from the tip of each soft, brown nipple that hardened with excitement. The desire to lick the very droplets nearly drove him insane.

Leslie clearly read the passion in his eyes, and her insides tingled with the same building desire.

He closed the distance between them before she realized what he had done and gathered her into his arms. Despite the crispness in the air, the heat that radiated off his body made her shudder.

Leslie gazed upon his handsome face and saw his eyes were cloaked with the same hunger that pulsed between her thighs.

"This is not what I intended," she said breathlessly as her palms pressed against his muscular chest.

She could feel the pounding of his heart, and she smiled softly. Winnokin entwined his fingers through her silken tresses and drew her soft lips to his in an ardent kiss that sent their minds swirling.

She throbbed with desire as his tongue delved deeper into her mouth, caressing her own. She clung to him and loved the way their lips danced against each other. His hands roamed the length of her back, traveled to the soft velvet curves of her bottom, and seductively kneaded them as he crushed her harder against him.

They were mindless of the current frothing around their thighs, their passion sending tempests of desire storming to the depths of their being.

Leslie lost herself to the emotion his touch and embrace stirred within her. She forgot about wanting to leave him, being afraid of rejection, or being made a slave if she went with him. All that mattered at that very moment was the wanton hunger to lie with him for an eternity.

Winnokin lifted her from the water and moved toward shore as she wrapped her legs around his waist.

She felt the hard earth against her back as he lowered her to the ground. He warmed her cool skin with paths of fire as his hands trailed the length of her, followed by heated kisses.

They were caught up in a storm of madness as their inflamed bodies cried for a release that only their joining could subside.

Leslie never thought the touch and kiss of such a man could invoke such rapture within her. The few ardent kisses she had once shared with Shaun could not compare with the searing bliss Winnokin's offered. Even her dead husband's ardor could not ignite a fire to match the one burning within her.

She embraced his face tenderly between her palms and peered into the depths of his eyes. Their destinies had been thrown together for some reason. The many days they had spent in each other's company had bonded them. The desire they felt seared their souls. She wanted to give of herself totally, but she needed to know what she was feeling was more than just the heat of the moment. She needed to know in her heart that he loved her as much as she now knew she loved him.

She gathered whatever resolve she could muster, pulled from his embrace, and rolled to her side.

"I am sorry, Winnokin. I ... I must make you understand how I feel—what is in my heart."

The puzzled look on his face frustrated her. She touched her hand to her lips and placed her palm over her heart.

"This language barrier between us—it ... makes things so very, very difficult. If only you could understand what I must say. I cannot give my love away. I am afraid it will be tossed aside if I dissatisfy you, or find you already have a wife, or that I might become a slave if I go with you to your village."

Winnokin patted the ground beside him.

"Ese nake ho. Come here now."

Leslie's mouth flew open, and she shook her head in anger.

"No—I will not come." She scooted backward. "If you are not the most stub—"

"Come now, Ishita. Hold your tongue one moment," Winnokin interrupted sternly.

"Hold my—," she gasped loudly as the shock of his perfectly spoken English registered.

Her eyes grew wide as she realized his deception. She screeched as she picked up whatever she could find within her reach and started to throw it at him. Stones pelted him, tiny twigs caught in his hair, and dirt spattered his mouth and eyes.

Winnokin pounced forward and pinned her beneath him as he straddled her waist and held her arms above her head.

"Get off me!" she screamed as she squirmed beneath him. "You knew my language all along. You—you deceived me and pretended all this time your ignorance. What a fool I have been! You men—and to think I thought—I thought you honorable."

Her ranting got her nowhere when she realized he was attracted to something else. Her temper fumed as she watched his eyes rake over her naked body. She desperately tried her best to unseat him as she bucked like a wild stallion and panted with exhaustion. She stopped, huffed loudly, and glared at him.

"Do you intend to force me like—like a savage!"

Winnokin was shocked by the word that escaped her mouth, and he bolted backward, releasing her hands.

Leslie responded instantly and pushed him with all her might. He lost his balance. She booted his butt with her heal, and he fell face down in the muddy embankment. She lurched to her feet, grabbed a blanket to wrap around herself, and ran like lightning, squealing all the way back to camp, with Winnokin hot on her trail.

She made it to the fire pit in time to pick up a burning limb and tossed it in his direction.

Winnokin dodged it quickly, smiling as he rubbed the mud from his face. He closed the distance by jumping over the pit and held her in a powerful embrace, pinning her arms to her side.

Leslie squirmed and wiggled furiously, trying to break free from his iron grip. Tears welled in her eyes as she looked up at him.

"You are hurting my arm," she whimpered.

Winnokin loosened his grip but did not let go entirely.

"I am sorry. Will you stop the attacks on your great warrior and be still?" he teased.

"Do not make fun of me. I would never have called you that if I knew you understood. You still deceived me!" She pouted and stomped the ground with her foot.

"A warrior only deceives if he has reason. You must behave while I explain. You will listen while I speak."

Leslie glared at him, and her eyes turned a deeper shade of green. She tilted her chin proudly and snapped her head once in agreement.

Winnokin nodded his approval but continued to pin her to his chest.

"You speak of betrayal, yet I have spoken no words of promise. I have shown ignorance only until I could be sure of your loyalty and heart, little one."

He raised a hand in rebuff when she opened her mouth to speak, and she quieted.

"I am war leader to the Seneca, and the white man must not know I speak their tongue. It is a powerful weapon against them. Many speak with divided tongues. Many wish to possess the rich lands that have belonged to my people since the beginning of time. Many of your leaders have broken their promises on paper. There are only three people I trust to keep my secret—my grandfather, Strong of Heart, my closest friend, Running Elk, and his wife, Little Raven."

Leslie exhaled with surprise.

"Strong of Heart is your grandfather? Father did not tell me."

Winnokin released her and stepped back as he gazed down at her.

"What you mean, father did not tell?"

She shivered slightly and moved to sit by the fire, and Winnokin joined her.

"My father, Jebidiah, met with your grandfather and the other elders in counsel to ask forgiveness for a grave deed a man of our village did against your sacred grounds. Did your grandfather not speak of him to you?"

Winnokin nodded and reached for her hand.

"Ya, Ishita. Grandfather found your father to be an honorable man but also a foolish one to think we would punish many for the wrongful act committed by just one."

"Well, it is because of that man I ran away." She started to cry. "He attacked my father on the trail and then returned to my home to finish him off with three Huron to abduct me from my home. I only got away because the man who traveled with my father sacrificed his life so that I would have time to escape into the woods. Red Farmer is that man, and he must know by now that I escaped. He is probably looking for me right now. Oh, Winnokin! You could be in danger too! If they find us together––he is a mad man! He always wanted me, and he will track me down until he finds me and will kill anyone who stands in his way."

Winnokin reached out and drew Leslie into his arms and rocked her tenderly.

"No harm will come to you, my love. Each day and night I have tracked around our camp, and no one pursues us. I knew you ran for a reason, and I have taken heed and will continue to do so."

Leslie smiled and stroked the mud softly away from his cheek with a corner of her blanket.

"I should have known you would be so cunning."

"Know also that my people must come first." He lifted her chin to look into her eyes. "They depend on my protection, on my knowledge and strength. To speak your tongue has helped me in many conflicts. It is important no one outside my true circle know my secret. I must ask you to keep this a secret between us."

Leslie kissed his lips softly and placed his right palm over her heart.

"With every beat of my heart, I vow to honor your secret. I pledge to you this promise and whatever else you ask of me. Request anything, and I will give it freely."

Winnokin placed tender kisses all over her face and lingered at her lips while he embraced her within the strength of his arms. He wanted nothing more than to make her his wife right now at that very moment but knew he had to get her to the safety of his village.

"Come, Ishita. Let us ride the wind."

Leslie gasped. "What did you say?"

Winnokin looked bewildered. "I said come." He shrugged.

"No! After that," she pressed.

"Um ... let us ride the wind? Did I speak wrong ...?"

Leslie shook her head and patted his cheek softly. "No, my love, those words I have heard them before ... in my dreams. It all seems so clear to me now. You and I were meant to be here, to be together. I know that more than ever."

Winnokin drew her more closely to him.

"Ya. Yes. Ishita. There is nothing that can change that. Now, we must go. We have a great distance to cover before we reach my village."

When she shook her head and opened her mouth to speak, Winnokin touched his finger to her lips to stop her.

"No, Leslie. We must go before my desire for you wins over my control. I will not have you this way until you are mine. I will not anger Hawenneyu, the Great Spirit. Hear my words, so you understand and know. You will not be a slave to anyone. I am not promised to another. My heart belongs to only you."

"It does?" she interrupted.

Winnokin nodded. "Ya. Yes, it does."

She opened her mouth to reply, but he touched his finger to her lips to stop her and shook his head.

"Let me finish. When I was a boy, I ventured into the heart of the great forest with my grandfather to seek my first vision, as is the custom of my people. You were a part of my vision, Leslie, even then. I saw your face as clearly as I gaze upon it now." He tenderly caressed her face with his palm. "I knew someday our paths would cross. Before I came upon you in the forest, I sought another vision to find peace with myself after the deaths of my parents at the hands of a small band of Huron, who I believe travel with the man you have called Red Farmer."

Leslie gasped in shock and kissed his lips tenderly. She wiped away a sole tear that escaped his eye with her lips.

"I am so sorry, Winnokin. We have both suffered much and lost someone we loved dearly at the hands of this monster."

"Yes, and our love will heal each other. I knew that when I saw you in my second vision. No other has touched my heart so. You are a gift from the Great Spirit. In honor of his gift to me, I will treat you with much respect—the respect due to a sachem's wife. We will be as one for all eternity. But it must be as according to my custom, for I will not do it any other way."

He rose, pulling her up into his arms.

"Do you understand, Ishita? Do you wish it to be so? Speak now, as I will not ask this of you again."

Leslie looked into his adoring eyes.

"It is the custom of my people for a woman not to give herself to a man before they marry, but I cannot help wanting you now," she said. "The desire that burns within me is so great, Winnokin. I am afraid I will not be as strong as you," she teased and winked at him.

She reached for a lock of her hair and twirled it about her finger. Like a seasoned seductress, she let the blanket cascade to her feet and slowly stepped into her petticoat and swayed her hips as she pulled it over them.

Winnokin could not contain his amusement and chuckled.

"You are a woman to test my will. It will be a game I will enjoy, and one I will win," he replied as he slapped her bottom with a stinging smack. "So, beware who you play with."

Leslie shrieked, rubbed her backside, and stuck out her tongue.

Winnokin pulled her into his arms and kissed her sweetly.

"We must ready ourselves for travel. Come, my love, let us go home."

As they prepared for travel, Leslie smiled to herself with a happiness she had not felt in a very long time. She watched as Winnokin gathered his belongings and realized it was only a short while ago when Shaun was pledging his love to her.

Her last image of him came to mind, and it brought a great sadness to her heart. She had loved Shaun for the person he was, for the joy he brought to her life during a time when she felt empty and dead inside over the loss of her wonderful husband and son.

Fate had an unusual way of opening a window when a painful door and heartbreaking chapter was closing in her life. She knew Winnokin was to be a part of her destiny. The dreams she had for so very long had a special meaning— —their meeting. And now that she knew of his vision, there was no denying they were meant to be in each other's lives forever.

What destiny had in store for them, she did not know. The uncertainty was terrifying but knowing Winnokin would be her constant companion through it all somehow made it seem worthwhile. One day at a time, she thought. One day at a time.

Chapter Eleven

The sun was their constant mark for determining their direction of travel. They rose to its warming rays and set camp just as it began to nestle behind the majestic mountains off the western horizon.

Leslie tried to convince Winnokin to make use of the supplies her father had stored, but his stubborn side dominated her request. He made it quite clear that they could live off the land without any assistance, and it would be best to leave them untouched for use at a later date. She could not quite understand his reasoning, for she did not believe they would ever return to this region any time soon, if even ever.

Their travels took them through terrains varying in contrasts, low luxuriant river bottoms, valleys cradled among mountains, hillsides and mountain slopes closely crowded with hundreds of wide-leaved trees and wind-warped pines filled with spiky cones that clung precariously vertical to the ground. Sheer-faced, red clay cliffs reached to the sky, their sides etched with growth embedded securely, sucking life from its thin, rocky soil.

Every day was a lesson for Leslie. She learned the Seneca name for fowl, fish, animals of the forest, trees, and wildflowers.

Playfully, they frolicked like children in pools created by the felled trees of beavers building their dams or swam in mountain-fed streams that they passed during their journey.

After long days of walking, they ended each evening with an hour wrapped in each other's arms stargazing, making wishes on fallen ones, or thinking up names for constellations they did not know by way of their shape or form.

They received sustenance from what nature provided. Leslie was in awe of Winnokin's knowledge of the various herbs, nuts, and fruits that dropped from branches or grew from the earth. When she traveled on her own, she passed up many of those they ate to help satisfy their hunger, because she had feared them to be poisonous.

Wild fowl that roosted in the trees or rabbits and woodchucks that burrowed beneath their roots were hunted by Winnokin for their evening meal and prepared by Leslie.

On their sixth day of travel, Winnokin sighted a moose and decided to bring him down.

Winnokin told Leslie it was the most important component to the Seneca diet for the winter.

She watched him prepare for the hunt and did not realize the skill that was involved or how much knowledge it took to understand the prey to hunt it successfully.

He told her the moose was not only the main staple of their diet but the primary source of their clothing in the winter. Because of the long season, sleeves were needed. When the animal was skinned, it was cut at the belly and extended to include the shoulder and forelegs, providing a sleeved garment that required minimum sewing. Then a belt was used for the purpose of closing the jacket and holding up the moose skin trousers that were also made.

During the period of warm weather, both men and women wore skin loin cloths plus light deerskin shirts as protection against the sun.

"Unlike the deer, which travel in small herds and can be slaughtered in great masses," Winnokin shared, "the moose travels alone and is always hunted as such."

She watched as the muscles in his back and arms constricted as he strained to work an overhead snare, which would be triggered by the animal's weight.

Leslie loved watching him labor. Her blood heated with excitement as she wondered what it would be like to physically be made love to by such a man.

Winnokin's brow furrowed with concentration as he began to whittle an instrument from birch bark, which he would use to reproduce the mating call the moose.

"I will wait in the tree," he pointed, "with my arrow ready to strike, while you call the great moose, Ishita, with the mating flute," he relayed seriously as he handed her the finished flute.

Leslie was surprised and moved her fingers over the instrument as she examined it at every angle.

"Hmm, just what I always wanted to do—mate with a moose." She chuckled.

Winnokin scooped her into his powerful arms and renewed the passion she had tried so hard to bridle earlier with a heated, passionate kiss.

"The moose, my love, mates for life, but cannot ignite passion's flame like your great warrior can," he boasted.

"I think you may be right," she cooed against his lips as she returned his kiss with an ardor of her own.

The moose was forgotten for a short spell as Winnokin lowered Leslie to the ground that was blanketed with layers of past fallen foliage.

Slowly he lowered the strap from her petticoat as he traced her shoulder with smoldering kisses.

Leslie welcomed his probing tongue as it caressed her own then slowly trailed along the curve of her neck. Tenderly, he stopped to nibble on the lobe of her ear, whispering endearing words of love.

She ran her hands over the hard span of his broad back, relishing the feel of rippled, hard muscle working beneath her touch. She maneuvered the knot that bound together the ties of his breech clout and pulled the cloth away from his firm buttocks.

They rolled to their sides, and Winnokin moaned with desire as her warm fingers explored the mass of hair growing below his belly button. She massaged him, and he melted like butter, moaning with longing under her expert touch.

She was amazed at her own boldness but felt no shame.

Winnokin skillfully undressed her and placed sweet kisses of fire at her throat and slowly trailed downward. He teased her nipples with his tongue while his fingers delicately explored the soft flesh between her legs. Her body worked against his touch, and she moved with the same rhythm against it. He gazed into her eyes, and they were cloaked with desire.

"I will bring you to heights you have never been, my love," he vowed in a voice thick with passion.

Leslie's heart skipped a beat as she read the love in his eyes, golden like the flame of a fire. He moved lower, out of her reach. She thought she would scream from the sweet, wonderful madness he created with his tongue.

Winnokin's raven locks came loose, spraying across her belly, and she entwined her fingers into its folds. Her hips moved in unison to the splendid torture he administered. Her body shuddered as pulsing waves coursed through her, dazing her senses. Tears streamed from her eyes.

Winnokin was moved by her emotion. "Why do you cry?"

All she could do was shake her head. She held out her arms and enfolded him tightly to her breast with a kiss that was long and tender.

"Thank you for making love to me in such a way. Thank you for loving me and making me whole again."

Winnokin looked a little puzzled and leaned back slightly. "What is making love?"

"You know ... " She blushed as she pushed his chest playfully.

"I like the white man's words, 'making love.' We call it joining. But we did not make love. Do you call it, making touch?"

"Winnokin!" she squealed.

His hearty laughter was contagious, and Leslie joined him as he rolled her over playfully.

"Never feel strange with me, my love. There will be many wonderful moments such as this between us."

"But still, I have not ... you know, fulfilled you completely."

She blushed shyly.

Winnokin raised her chin to gaze into her eyes.

"Knowing I have touched your heart is all I need for now. I am glad the Great Spirit chose me to walk the path of the husband you lost. I will pray he will bless us with a child to fill that emptiness once again."

Leslie melted into his arms, content and joyously happy. It pleased her to know there would be other such moments like this between them. She was glad she had opened her heart to him when they began their journey together and told him her life's story up to when they first met along the way. The compassion he showed when she broke down in tears was so very genuine and endearing.

He vowed to fill her heart and life with happiness and promised Red would be punished for the pain he caused. He was enraged by what she had endured. The thought gnawed at him as he questioned in his mind if Red was still the one who was again pillaging their burial grounds. A tight knot grew in the pit of his stomach.

He gazed upon Leslie's face as she nuzzled peacefully against his chest. He knew Red Farmer was a man driven by evil. As sure as the sun rose and set each day, Winnokin knew they had been tracked for quite some time. The man was careless in his pursuit, but Winnokin had the advantage. He was not sure why their paths still had not crossed yet. He hoped Red was keeping his distance, because he thought Leslie was alone. He snickered to himself. Red had no idea Winnokin took care to erase his presence for quite a while. He knew men like Red Farmer.

Red had no idea Leslie was not alone. The fool expected her time in the wilderness would work to his advantage. He would be thinking her exposure to the elements, not having any supplies and in a distraught state, would make her easy prey. The last thing he would ever suspect is finding her in the company of a Seneca sachem both well fed and very much in love. Winnokin would not worry Leslie and tell her they were being tracked. His revenge for her would be sweet.

Winnokin smiled as he played softly with Leslie's curls. Red Farmer would pay dearly for the pain and anguish he inflicted on the woman Winnokin loved. He lifted a curly tendril, and he loved the way they always naturally wrapped around his finger. He would take every precaution to ensure her safety.

In a few days they would reach the outskirts of his homeland. Winnokin knew his people had expected him back from his vision quest long before now. He knew at this very moment a small contingent of his best and most fearsome warriors would have started a search pattern to find him.

Chapter Twelve

Leslie and Winnokin rested high upon a ridge to relax. The panorama took her breath away, and she gaped at the sheer splendor of it all. Her heart pounded rapidly as she gazed out over the beauty of the land.

There were five clearly outlined parallel lakes, which seemed to have been gouged from the earth by a giant hand.

Winnokin rose, turned to offer his hand to Leslie, and drew her to his side as he stood tall and proud.

"Below is the land of my people, Ishita, and the entire Iroquois Nation. By this time tomorrow, we will be home."

Her heart constricted with love as she looked upon her proud warrior, tall and handsome, with the cloudless, blue, azure sky outlining his magnificence.

She could not wait to meet the people he told her so much about: Running Elk and the woman he loved, Little Raven; his grandfather, Strong of Heart, and his grandmother, Tender Arms. Leslie wanted more than anything to love and be a part of a family once again. Silently she prayed they would look favorably upon her and accept her as one of them.

She wondered about his people. How would they view her? Would they look at her openly as an enemy? Would they approve and bless the marriage he vowed to her? She tried so hard to pay attention to his teachings. She prayed she would fit in and be accepted by everyone, from the littlest child to the wisest elder of his village.

It did not take long for them to descend to the rich, fertile valley below. Winnokin left Leslie to set up camp, while he searched for food, and scan the perimeter.

Leslie daydreamed beside the campfire as she anticipated his return. She felt content and at such peace with her life. She thought of Winnokin's strong convictions and his promise to her that his people would accept her without reservation.

His vision had been retold to them countless times, so her arrival by his side would be of no surprise, he had assured her. Many white trappers had ventured occasionally into his homeland and left as brothers with their scalps fully intact. Leslie smiled to herself when she remembered his many stories.

Winnokin had spoken reverently of his people's hospitality and how they would surrender their dinner to feed the hungry, vacate their bed to refresh the weary, and give up their apparel to clothe the naked. No test to friendship was too severe; no sacrifice to repay a favor too great; no fidelity to an agreement too inflexible.

Leslie loved the strong regard and admiration he professed for his people. How lucky they were to have such a devoted man to lead and protect them. Leslie knew in her heart that her parents would have loved and respected him in kind and taken him to their hearts for the man he was.

She was still skeptical, however, about fitting in and being a part of his extended family. More than ever, she hoped their journey together was indeed the new beginning her father had once bespoken of. She wanted desperately to fill his empty lodge with children, be his constant companion, and share in all their future life's experiences as husband and wife.

Nothing could be sweeter than love itself; she smiled absently. She reached out and etched the shape of a heart in the dirt with her finger.

When she heard movement in the trees behind her, she jumped and thought it strange, since Winnokin always took such great pleasure in catching her off guard.

She turned in the direction of the noise.

"You are getting careless, my love," she said. "Even to my untrained ears you sound like a cow breaking through the trees!" She chuckled soundly. "You might as well come out."

Leslie waited a moment, but Winnokin did not appear. Her eyes scanned the perimeter and saw nothing out of the ordinary. A deadly silence hovered over the forest, causing the hairs at the nape of her neck to prickle. Immediately her instincts told her to stand alert. Since she had no cause to doubt such warnings, she swallowed hard as she drew her father's skinning knife from Winnokin's backpack and concealed it beneath her undergarments.

 "Winnokin, this is not funny. I am hungry and grow tired of such games."

"I have a hunger greater than yours, wench, and I aim to quench it," bellowed Red Farmer as he walked into the clearing with a shotgun aimed at her chest.

Leslie froze, and the color drained from her face. She swayed from the shock of seeing him standing there in front of her.

"Don't look so shocked, darlin'. Did ya really think I'd never find ya and just let ya get away?"

When he moved in closer, her insides trembled with fear. She did not notice his fiendish accomplices anywhere in sight and wondered where they were. He took three long strides forward, and she stepped backwards, tripping over the stones of the fire pit. She lost her footing and fell and quickly crawled on her knees to further the distance between them. Her eyes searched the trees, desperately looking for Winnokin.

Red cackled as he scratched at his groin.

"Don't be look'n for that savage. I gave him one hell of a bang on the head." He laughed loudly.

"You bastard! If you hurt him, I—"

Red closed the distance between them and pulled the hammer back on his gun. The click made Leslie jump with a start.

"Don't worry. Would'n kill 'em yet," he sneered. "Wants to have some fun with 'em first, like make him watch how a real man can runt with a white woman ... especially his woman."

Leslie sat back on her legs.

"You are a disgusting hog!" she screamed. "And will rot in hell for what you have done."

Red moved forward and sat on a boulder opposite her.

"Now that's no way to be talking, darlin'. You's gonna find out what it's like to have a real man poundin' between your lilly white thighs."

"He will kill you, Red! Winnokin will take great pleasure in making you suffer. If you think for one minute I will submit to you, you pig, you are crazier than I imagined."

Red roared as he rose and fondled his manhood.

"You're right fond of the Red skin, ain't ya, Les? Did your savage tell ya it was his arrow that killed your pa?"

"You filthy liar," she screamed. "It was you and your renegade friends who ambushed my father and Shaun. I watched you bastards kill Shaun. You will pay, Red. You will pay dearly."

Red snickered and scratched the ragged growth of hair on his chin.

Leslie sat back on the ground.

"Why did you do it, Red? My father was a decent man. He treated you fairly always."

Red shrugged his shoulders and spat a wad of chewed tobacco onto the ground. "He had something I wanted. Good, rich furs they were too. Got us a good dollar." He nodded.

Leslie's voice seethed. "You no good, low down, son of a—"

"Shut your mouth, girl!" he snarled. "What I wants I takes, and you ain't in no position to bark nothing!"

He shifted his weight and scratched at his long, greasy mane and sent her an agitated look when he noticed the loathing look on her face.

"Don't be lookin' at me that way neither. Ain't never needed righteous men and families in these parts. This'n wild country. He who gets, survives. It's the law of the land and always will be."

Leslie looked away. She could not stop the tears that began to stream down her cheeks. The disregard he had for human life scared her to the core. It was not fair that a man like her father had to die, while vermin like Red Farmer still walked the earth. Life was not fair.

"Are you so ignorant and stupid to believe the good people around here will allow you to continue pillaging and murdering? Winnokin will not stand for it. You will burn in hell for the man you have become, Red. I could not think of a sweeter justice."

Red smirked as he rose.

"If that's where I ends up, I best enjoy myself now whiles I got the chance. But before I gets on with things ... gotta show ya something first." He laughed as he turned and disappeared into the trees.

He was not gone but a moment when he returned dragging Winnokin behind him like a dog on a leash. Winnokin stumbled frequently, dizzy from the blow to his head.

Leslie jumped to her feet and ran forward.

Red raised his shotgun.

"Stand fast, wench, or I'll kill em here and now!"

Leslie froze as she watched Red jerk Winnokin's bindings with a force that made him fall to the ground. Blood spurted from Winnokin's nose and smeared with dirt. She screamed and ran forward but met with the force of Red's powerful fist slamming into the side of her head. The blow knocked her backwards, unconscious.

"You will die, white dog!" Winnokin snarled as he jumped to his feet and bolted toward Red with a ferocity that shocked him.

Red slammed his shotgun into Winnokin's gut, and he fell to his knees from the blow and grunted in pain. The look of seething hatred in Winnokin's eyes made Red step backwards and Winnokin sneered.

"Hear my words, white man. I, leader of the great Seneca, will take pleasure peeling the skin from your bones while you still live and dig your heart from your chest with my bare hands. I will force it down your throat and watch you slowly die as you gasp for every breath that will not come."

The vehement tone of his voice made Red flinch nervously and swallow the bile rising in his throat. He knew the savage could put into action his very words if given the chance.

"You won't be doin' nothing of the sort caus I's the one holdin' all the cards," Red snarled in return.

He kicked Winnokin in the side of the head with his booted foot, knocking him out. Red took the end of the rope and tied it to a stake he drove into the ground, securing Winnokin's feet with a leather strip he soaked in water that would tighten as it dried. He smirked with satisfaction, knowing the pain it would cause. Red tugged at the bindings and laughed as he reached for the deerskin pouch and went to the stream to fill it.

When he returned, he threw some of the water at Winnokin's face to revive him. Winnokin shook his head and coughed as the water filled his nostrils.

"Watch and enjoy the show." Red chuckled as he licked his lips and moved toward Leslie.

Red threw the remaining water on her face, and she moaned as she slowly regained her senses. Red slapped her face viciously and the imprint of his hand left a mark on her tender cheek.

Winnokin pushed himself to his knees. He knew he had to try and stall him, keep him away from Leslie before he caused severe damage. He knew his warriors had to be within a few miles range. He tugged at his bonds and roared like a fierce mountain cat at the top of his lungs.

Red jumped with fright and turned, expecting to find the Indian had broken free from his bindings.

"It is sad that a snake like you must beat a woman half your size to prove his manhood," Winnokin sneered. "Mating must be difficult for a dog such as you. You stink worse than the dung of the animal's skin you wear."

Red glared at Winnokin. The louder and longer he laughed, the madder Red became. He rose and grabbed his shotgun, turning the butt around and clasping the barrel in his hand. He would beat his brains to a pulp to shut him up.

"Beating me will accomplish nothing, white man. You know my people will hunt you until they find you, even if you kill me. It does not matter how long it will take them, for they will find you. The death of a sachem never goes unpunished."

Red stopped in his tracks and stood there without moving, his eyes void of emotion, his breaths coming in short, heavy snorts.

Winnokin continued while he still held Red's interest.

"You know I speak the truth. You have been amongst my people more than enough to know our ways. The Huron would never allow the favor I am offering. You know they would slit your throat over less, and once they learn what you have done here, they will do that. They are smart enough to know to walk with you in friendship will make them our enemy even more. Leave now, and I will give you a three-day start."

Red looked over his shoulder at Leslie and back to Winnokin. He was, however, not a man to be talked out of anything. When he wanted something, or someone, there was not a person to stand in his way. He turned his back to Winnokin and moved toward his victim. In one quick movement he tore the right strap of her petticoat away and began to fondle the soft mound of her breast.

Leslie screamed and tried to fight him off. She rolled to her side, but he immediately forced her back and grabbed a handful of her hair. He slapped her again, making her ears ring and stars dance before her eyes. Her lip split open and began to swell and bleed. Regardless of the pain he inflicted, Red forced his mouth upon hers.

Leslie thrashed about with all her strength. Each time he forced his tongue into her mouth, she gagged and pounded his head, his shoulders and chest with clenched fists.

"You had yer chance to accept me willin'," he hissed. "Now stay still!"

Leslie let saliva and blood fill her mouth. She waited until Red lowered his face, and once he was close enough, she spit in his face, catching him off guard. As he swayed backwards to wipe at his face, she pounded her fists into his groin, and he fell sideways, clutching himself and howled out in pain.

She bent her knees into her chest then kicked out with all her might, hitting him in the head. Instantly, she leaped to her feet, pulled out the concealed knife, and tossed it in Winnokin's direction. She smiled when he tucked it underneath his thigh and turned to move. Within an instant, she caught sight of a flash escape the barrel of Red's shotgun.

The force of its discharged bullet impacted her shoulder, and her tiny frame sailed backwards into midair. She fell to the ground in a semiconscious state. She could feel the warmth of her blood running down her arm. Her head felt light, and she could hardly focus her eyes. The sounds of the forest sounded hollow and distant in her ears. When she closed and reopened her eyes, a moan escaped her lips when she saw Red standing above her, his hardened member exposed.

Red snarled. "The fight is outta ya now. I can finish what I came for."

Leslie shook her head from side to side. Tears streamed down her bruised and swollen cheeks. She did not have the strength to move or fight any more. She prayed she would pass out and mentally escape what was about to happen. Red tore away the remainder of her clothing, panting like an animal in heat.

Leslie could hear Winnokin screaming in the background. She squeezed her eyes shut tightly. Her nails dug into her palms and drew blood. The potency of his voice, the intensity of Winnokin's threats fed her, strengthened her will and reached to the very depth of her soul. His strength inspired her, fed her determination to rival what lie ahead. She knew in her heart that if he did not give up despite the state of his injuries, then neither would she.

She prayed that Winnokin cut himself loose in time. She began to squirm and buck like a possessed, deranged soul; her eyes grew wild, her face turning as red as the blood that smeared her skin, and she clawed at Red's face with her nails, marring his ugly complexion even further.

Red was taken back by the force of her rage, clenched his fist and knocked her unconscious. He became instantly furious with himself and bellowed with anger when he realized what he had done. His manhood deflated, and he pounded his fists repeatedly into the ground beside Leslie's head. He rose and adjusted his pants then lifted her from the ground and swung her over his shoulder like a sack of grain.

Winnokin stopped trying to cut himself free. He could not let Red know he had a knife and watched with disdain and helplessness. He flinched when Red poured whiskey over the hole in Leslie's shoulder to cease the flow of blood. His heart skipped when he tossed her over the back of his pack mule and covered her with a blanket and secured her with rope like she was a bundle of supplies.

"Leave her and run, white man," Winnokin screamed with a hoarse voice.

"You ain't in no position to be barkin' orders, red skin. Now shut your mouth, or I'll cut out your tongue and leave ya ta die."

Winnokin was taking a chance. He knew he could not provoke him to the point of being killed. Leslie's safety was more important.

"Your threat means nothing to this warrior. You will know what true fear is when I let my warriors torture you slowly."

Red grabbed his shotgun and aimed it at Winnokin's chest as his own heaved with fury. He stared Winnokin down as saliva drooled from the corner of his mouth. Killing the savage would be too easy. He wanted him to stay alive, to wonder where his woman was, wonder what pleasures he was having with her, if only for a little while.

Winnokin thought he pushed Red too far as he glared back at the man who resembled a rabid wolf. Going for the knife that Leslie had given him would serve no purpose right now. He had to keep it hidden. He gambled on the fact Red would get more pleasure in thinking he would be humiliated and shamed for not being able to protect Leslie.

Red closed the distance between them and rammed the butt of this shotgun into Winnokin's gut and then swept it upward, fracturing his jaw. Red snorted with glee as he kicked Winnokin in the ribs. He was satisfied he had disabled him, turned and saddled his horse and left with the satisfaction of knowing Winnokin was badly injured, and he finally had his prize possession in tow.

Chapter Thirteen

For nearly two days Red traveled north, barely taking time to rest and feed the horses.

Leslie was oblivious to her surroundings for most of the journey. When she finally awoke her screams and curses echoed throughout the dense forest. To pacify and quiet her, Red allowed her to sit astride with her hands and feet bound and wearing one of his woolen shirts to cover her nudity. He knew it would do no good to threaten her, for the spitfire had no fear of him. He threatened to gag her if she did not cease her ranting.

Leslie suspected that the bullet had passed through her shoulder. She felt weak from the loss of blood but was determined to keep her wits about her. Red made sure to cleanse her wound twice a day to ward off infection. She knew he looked upon her as his prized catch. But if she had anything to do with it, it would not be for long. She planned on parting his company the moment the opportunity availed itself.

No matter how many times she asked, Red refused to offer any information about Winnokin. For all she knew, he could be lying dead at that very moment. She kept the thought of Winnokin's strength, cunning, and fearlessness in mind and silently prayed that those virtues would see him through surviving. She was thankful Red had not attempted rape since they left the camp. She loathed his company, could barely endure his stench, and avoided any eye contact with him or light conversation. She hoped that the less appealing she appeared, the more he would leave her alone. Her luck would soon run out, for that she was certain.

Once Red was confident there was enough distance between himself and Winnokin's warriors, she knew he would break for camp and give the horses a rest. She dreaded when that day would come because she knew what he would try to do to her, and the thought of it made her stomach heave. She tried to always pay close attention to her surroundings and their direction of travel, along with any landmarks they passed.

Her father had taught her at an early age to create a poem of things you saw that stuck in your head while traveling, in case you got lost. If you kept reciting it, you would have a better chance of finding your way back. From the moment she came to, she did just that and said them over and over in her mind until they were memorized. Every time she saw something new, something unique ... she added a new verse. She was determined to find her way back to Winnokin. Nothing ... no one ... was going to stand in her way. They traveled deeper into the forest. The pines stood like sentinels, standing shoulder to shoulder thirty to sixty feet high.

When they passed beneath their massed groupings, it appeared as though all the sunlight had been distinguished. Their branches were strewn out in all directions and thickly meshed so that not a single ray could filter down through them. Often, they came upon various kinds of game feeding amongst wild berry bushes, and Red never acknowledged their presence. Trout and bass swarmed in the shallow waters of a river and various streams they crossed, but still he ignored them.

Red pushed her hard, hour upon hour, with only a mere moments rest to relieve herself, never stopping to take a break or eat a small meal, never to catch a few hours' sleep. On the third day of her abduction, around high noon, their journey finally came to a halt. Like a monument standing before her was a natural chiseled out cave in the side of a sheer mountain cliff, its entrance three feet from the ground. Leslie sat in astonishment and rubbed at her eyes.

Red turned and noticed the look of surprise on her face.

"Quite the site, hah? I came past here maybe a year back and knew it would come in right handy someday. Taint no man gonna come close without me knowin' bout it. This is one of them impregneated kind of forts you hear tell about and it's ours." He chuckled.

As she pulled up beside him, she sent him a look of disgust as he scratched his large, distended belly. He swatted the rump of her pack mule, and it reared him forward.

"Get your ass movin', woman! We's got us a home to set up."

Leslie pulled the reins in taut, and her mule hee-hawed as it reared to a dead stop. She turned slightly and gave him a dirty look as he moved near.

"Do you think I am going to share that hole with you?" she hissed. "I would rather sleep out here in the cold with the bugs and wild animals!"

Red's reaction was immediate as he swung out with his left hand and slapped her soundly across her right cheek. Since her hands were bound in front of her, she could not clasp hold of the saddle horn quick enough and tumbled to the ground with a thud and landed on her injured shoulder.

The wind was knocked out of her, and she gasped from the pain radiating down her arm and across her chest. The urge to scream was tremendous, but she refused to give him the satisfaction of knowing he hurt her.

"Get up, bitch, before I kick your royal ass up this here mountain! You sleep where I say and do my biddin'. Yer mine now and nothin's gonna change that. Now get up!"

He kicked his mare to move forward, and if Leslie had not rolled quickly to her side, its hooves would have stomped her badly.

"I heard you ... ass breath, and so did anyone else within miles of here," she retorted.

Red looked about immediately, knowing there was some truth to her words. Sound traveled fast through the forest, and he should have been more careful. He turned around slightly and glared at her as he watched her try to struggle to her feet.

"Worried, are you?" she goaded him as she chuckled loudly. "Like I said, it will be a cold day in hell before I play wife to you," she repeated and plopped her backside to the ground and gave him a look to let him know she did not plan to budge.

Red thought for a moment and noticed the circle of dark red blood seeping through the bandage wrapped around her shoulder. He knew she was hurting badly despite how hard she tried to hide it. He leaned forward and reached for the reins on her mule.

"Stay then. Yer already hungry, sore, and tired. Either the cold or wild animals will change your mind soon enough."

He kicked the mare's ribs and never looked back, confident she would come crying and looking for shelter before too long. Leslie could not believe her luck. *He thinks I will cave in like a scared little girl*, she thought. *Once I get these bindings off, I am out of here and fast.*

"Now, how did that poem go?" she asked herself as she began to work at loosening the bindings around her wrists.

Red chuckled to himself as he glanced out the entrance of the cave. The sky had already turned black, and mountain wolves were beginning their evening serenade to the moon in the distance.

"Won't be long now," he spoke out loudly. "Ain't never been a female I knows who like things that bump around at night. Jest a little more time, and she'll come crawlin' and whimperin' up a storm."

Seconds turned into minutes, and the minutes turned into an hour. What Red expected to happen never did materialize. His palms felt itchy, and beads of sweat started to dot his forehead. He knew he had been duped. He knew she ran. Red pounded his fist on his thigh. He should have thought better ... should have known Jebidiah's daughter was different than most women and be the kind to run away when given the chance.

He walked outside the cave and looked over to where his mare was staked and glad it was still there. He peered into the night and did not see any sign of her and laughed to himself.

"Looks like I gots me a runaway," he spoke against the mare's ear as he rubbed his underside. "When I gets my hands on her, she'll be pleadin' for mercy."

Red kicked out the fire with his boot and reloaded his shotgun. The provisions he carried into the cave were hidden well in a back chamber. Within a matter of minutes, his horse was saddled, and the mule secured until he returned. He was not happy when he noticed a full moon shone above.

Despite the fact it provided him ample light to track her, it also made it easier for her to escape him. His eyes began to scan over the earth, searching for the slightest sign of her passing. It did not take him long to realize he was in for quite a pursuit. She was better than he thought and did an excellent job not leaving traceable signs for him to trail. The only advantage he had was in knowing she would probably head for the Seneca village.

Leslie fell constantly over unseen rocks, strewn vines, and rotted logs. Her legs were badly skinned and bruised, and her palms and knees burned as torn flesh became exposed to the cool night air and crusts of dirt and debris gritted into her open sores. She pushed onward at an even pace, so as not to overtax herself, and kept her breathing slow and even. She did not stop or look back. Falling constantly, however, did not help her injured shoulder.

Whenever she could, she applied fresh moss to her wound that she found along the way. The loss of blood was taking its toll, and she could feel herself growing weaker and becoming dizzy from a lack of food. She tried to remember her poem, but the landscape looked different even in the bright moonlight. She tried to clear the jumbled thoughts in her mind and concentrate on each stanza.

Her breathing changed to short pants, and she stumbled more frequently. She leaned against the trunk of an elderly, crippled maple, its roots torn free and exposed upon the ground.

"Think, Leslie!" she demanded. "You have got to remember, so you can get out of here."

She took a deep sigh and thought long and hard, and the phrases slowly came to mind.

"Before me I see two white birch trees ... facing each other a lovers embrace ... branches entwined, palms bent in grace." She repeated the words repeatedly until they were branded in her mind. She pushed herself to move on and hummed the words as she moved on at a slower pace. It was almost impossible to place one foot in front of the other.

The fear of Red catching up with her forced her onward.

A few hours before dawn, she found yet another landmark. Only nine remained that she could remember. She knew if she was going to succeed, she needed to stop and give her body a chance to rest, and she looked for a means to hide herself in the process. She did not have to venture much farther when she stumbled upon a downed pine weathered and rotted with age. She checked it out and noticed that the inside was hollow enough for her to crawl inside and conceal herself.

Before she did so, she remembered the last time she crawled inside one and carefully looked to make sure there was no other occupant. Satisfied there was none, Leslie quickly looked about for something to eat and happily found some wild mushrooms and consumed them quickly to quell her rumbling stomach. In a matter of minutes, she was fast asleep.

Red's fury piqued with every foot of terrain he crossed. He had expected to find Leslie long before now, whimpering from exhaustion, hunger, and pain. How could he have misjudged her ability and willpower to escape him? His rage was his motivation. He hated being played for such a fool, and he silently vowed it would be the last time she ever did.

His horse became crippled when it stepped into a gopher hole, and he began to feel his own strength weaken being on foot for more than three hours. He knew he had to stop and rest, but he had a gut feeling Leslie was even closer than ever to being found.

He noticed that within the last hour she had become careless. It was obvious she was weak and dragging her right foot. There were continual signs of bleeding and broken branches where she passed. Red knew he finally had the advantage and decided to stop and rest for a short spell.

He emptied his canteen and finished the remainder of parched corn he carried in his side pack. His eyes burned from lack of sleep, and he dropped where he stood, giving in to the need to shut his eyes, if only for a short while.

Dawn was making its appearance when Red finally opened his eyes and sat up. He yawned loudly as he scratched at his head and heavy whiskered face. He slowly stood up and stretched his massive body, yawning loudly again and crawled over a huge, downed tree that blocked his way.

Red immediately stopped dead in place, half straddling the trunk, almost certain he heard the slightest sound of a moan. He swung his leg around and sat quietly still and listened carefully for the sound to repeat itself. A devilish smile slowly lifted the corners of his mouth when he heard it again.

Carefully he watched where he stepped as he walked around the perimeter of the huge fallen pine. He squatted down on all fours and crawled slowly as he turned the corner of its lower base and caught sight of Leslie curled up like a tiny field mouse in fetal position. Quietly he moved in position, encircled her tiny ankles, and yanked with all his might and dragged her into the clearing.

Leslie awoke with a start and began to claw at the earth as she screamed in terror.

Red's hands were all over her, ripping at his flannel shirt she wore and tore one sleeve free from the shoulder seam.

Leslie tried fiercely to fend him off, but his strength was too much for her. Even still she kicked out at him. She screamed as loud as her lungs allowed despite his repeated slaps across her face to silence her. She could feel the cool morning air on her exposed skin, and her right eye began to swell from the constant blows to her face. She could taste her blood in her mouth. She was powerless, and she knew there was nothing she could do.

My love, where are you? she thought.

She needed to know if Winnokin was dead or alive. She remembered Winnokin telling her that his warriors were expected to meet them on the trail, and she silently prayed they had found Winnokin in time.

Red pressed his knee into her abdomen, and she grunted from the pressure. She swung out with a closed fist and clipped him off the side of his head, and he barely moved. He grabbed hold of her wrists and pinned her arms to the ground above her head.

"I told ya you be mine, so stop movin', woman! Taint nothing you can do now.

The smell of his rancid breath made her stomach heave, and Leslie moved her head to the side and tried to bury her nose against the skin of her arm.

Dear God, she prayed silently, *please, please help me. Papa where are you? I need you, papa! I need you!*

Red ripped the rest of his shirt from her body, and Leslie met his eyes as her own filled with tears.

"Please, Red," she pleaded softly, "please do not do this. I beg of you."

He glared at her for a moment, and then the deep furrows between his eyes began to soften.

Leslie thought she may have succeeded convincing him and did not give up on pleading her case one last time.

"Red, I know that you are a kind man," she lied. "You were my father's friend. You hunted and trapped together when we first arrived. You ate at our table and spent special holidays celebrating in our home. My father was always, always there for you. If he did not speak in your defense, the Seneca would have tortured you slowly for what you did to them. Because of my father, you are alive today. Please Red," she began to cry softly, "please do not do this. Let me go my way, and I promise that what has happened will stay between us."

She could feel his grip lessen slightly on her wrists, and she looked deeply into his eyes. They were void of emotion. It was almost as if he did not hear her, as if the words she spoke never reached his mind. She tried to slide her wrists from his grasp but could not. The pressure of his knee did not change, and she wondered what he was thinking as he continued to look at her, not saying a word, not responding, not moving.

Leslie knew she had to move quickly and swung her right leg up fast and hard, the side of her foot striking hard against Red's temple. The blow of her foot sent him reeling backward, and Leslie moved with the speed of a jack rabbit and bolted forward. She did not care she had not a stitch of clothing covering her body except the rabbit skin moccasins Winnokin had made her and ran as fast as her strength allowed.

She heard Red's maddening growl behind her as she broke through the brush and entered the thick forest. For one brief moment she turned to look over her shoulder, and before she could catch herself, she fell down hard face forward when the tip of her foot caught underneath the exposed root of a nearby elm. The impact knocked the breath from her lungs, and Red was upon her in an instant.

He flipped her over as though she were as light as a feather, straddled her, and grabbed her throat with one large hand as he worked to unbutton his breeches with the other.

"I had me enough of you, woman," he growled.

Leslie clawed and pulled at his hand with both of hers, but his grip tightened and began to cut off the air from her lungs. She gasped and screamed as her legs flailed wildly. No matter how much she squirmed and wiggled, his thighs tightened against her, and she could not budge him off her. White spots began to dance before her eyes, and her mouth sucked hard, but the air went nowhere.

She stopped moving, and she could feel her body reacting to the lack of air it needed. Her hands dropped to the ground as her fingers became numb. Her eyes grew heavy, her temples throbbed, and her brain felt as though it would explode. This was it, she thought. She was dying. She looked one more time into Red's eyes and saw his open wide with surprise and then register horror.

A roar of agony escaped him as his hand left her throat and his body fell over her like a smothering blanket.

His scream jarred Leslie back to her senses, and the heavy weight of his body atop her told her something was wrong. She gasped air back into her lungs, but the compression against her chest was too much to bear, and she began to scream hysterically as she tried to push him off of her.

Almost immediately she heard activity about her and the sound of male voices shouting words spoken in Seneca. She tried to understand, but her mind could not register their meaning. Red's body blocked her view and she screamed again. A shadow passed overhead, and Leslie exchanged glances with a fearless, painted warrior.

The warrior kicked Red off her body and grabbed a mass of Red's hair. Without regard to her well-being, the warrior skinned away the top layer of Red's scalp with his knife. The horrifying popping, slushy sound echoed in her ears, and her mind and body granted the escape she needed as she fainted where she lay.

Chapter Fourteen

Winnokin became a man obsessed over his concern for Leslie. For nearly two days she lay in a motionless, unconscious state, her battered and bruised body a sign of the torture she had endured. His fear of losing her was as great as his obsession. She had been through so much, and he worried if her mind and the essence of her soul would heal.

No medicinal administrations aroused her from her deep slumber. He barely left her side, tenderly applying special poultices to ward off infection. With Running Elk's help, he built a special lodge to protect her from the light, misty rains that moved into the region.

Leslie's slender form was consumed with a high fever that made her hallucinate. She cried out for her parents and relived past traumatic incidents in her life. All Winnokin could do was hold and comfort her when she allowed him near her. He sponged bathed her with cool compresses and stayed by her side throughout the day and night.

Running Elk entered the lodge, concern defined on his face.

"My brother, you must take rest or you will be no good to the woman you love."

Winnokin knew his words to be true, but he could not pull himself away. Sensing his leader's apprehension, Running Elk squatted by Winnokin's side and placed a hand upon his shoulder.

"I think my words are falling upon deaf ears," he said.

Winnokin looked into his friend's eyes. The concern weighing heavily upon his heart reflected in the golden depths of his eyes.

Running Elk's heart went out to his sachem and closest friend. He knew how he would feel if it were his wife, Little Raven, lying there before him instead of the white woman known as Leslie.

"Being here will help make her strong," Winnokin replied. "I fear she will slip away from me., if I leave."

Running Elk shook his head in disagreement. "It is you, my chief, who grows weak from lack of food and sleep. You must think of your people. Who will guide and take care of them if you fall ill? What strength can the little one draw if you have none left to give?"

Running Elk took Winnokin by the shoulders and forced him to turn his way. "Listen to me as my brother and not my chief. I will stay until you nourish and replenish yourself. Go. Take in drink and food. I will send word if she awakens. I will not leave her side. You must do this."

Winnokin knew he could not argue with Running Elk. As chief, he had to keep his people's interests first always, before all else. He would be no good to anyone if he fell ill also.

He rubbed his thumb along Leslie's tiny hand. He knew his wounds were not fully healed. If he did not heed Running Elk's wise words, he was not a true chief to his people.

Winnokin looked at Running Elk and nodded.

"You are right, my brother. I will go."

Together they rose, clasped forearms, and hugged.

"I will watch her closely, my brother, as if she were my woman. Go now."

Winnokin gazed down upon Leslie's sleeping face. He squatted and caressed her fevered cheek one last time with the back of his hand then departed.

Later that evening, Leslie stirred when her fever finally broke. Her eyes felt gritty and heavy as she tried to open them. She felt like a fog settled in her brain and found it difficult to focus on her surroundings. When she did, it dawned on her that she was in a small, makeshift shelter of wood bark and poles with a hole in the ceiling to vent the smoke rising from a small fire pit that burned in the center of the room.

Her throat felt raw as she tried to swallow. She moved her head slightly to the left and noticed the frame of a huge man standing beside the fire pit with his back toward her.

She knew it was not Winnokin because he was not as tall. His broad bare back and wide muscular arms clearly distinguished him as a strong warrior. Her first thought was of panic. She did not know where she was or whose company, she was in. She wondered where Winnokin was and if the man standing before her was one of his warriors or the enemy.

She looked about for signs. There were no weapons or war shields along the walls. No provisions of any kind were about. She looked at the warrior more intently. Except for his breech clout and moccasins, he wore nothing else, and from the way he wore his hair, she knew he had to be Seneca.

She tried to speak, but only a raspy whisper escaped her lips.

Running Elk spun on his heel to look at her. A smile radiated his face when he saw that she was awake.

"My little sister has decided to join the land of the living once again," he spoke in perfect English as he moved closer.

He knelt on one knee and gently lifted her head to help her take a sip of cool water from a horn ladle. It felt refreshing as it slid down her raw throat.

She was surprised by his reference of her and wondered if she should know who he was.

"I feel I should know you," she whispered.

Running Elk placed a flat palm upon his chest.

"E Totonoman (Me Running Elk)." He nodded and smiled.

Leslie's eyes sparkled with excitement, recognizing his name and knowing it was Winnokin's best friend and second in command.

"Running Elk!" she replied happily.

He shook his head and smiled in return.

"Ya. Running Elk. My brother has spoken of me, I see."

Leslie cleared her throat and still spoke in a whisper.

"Why do you look familiar to me? Have I seen you before?"

Running Elk felt uncomfortable. He knew that scalping the red-haired man in her presence had been upsetting to her, and he did not want to remind her of the unpleasant moment.

Leslie became aware of his discomfort and looked more intensely at him. Slowly it dawned on her, and her eyes grew wide with horror. The color drained from her face when the image of Red being scalped flashed before her eyes.

"Please do not judge, or fear me, little sister," he asked in a tender voice. "What you saw was an act of combat. It is our way. Do your people not hang their enemies by the throat until dead?"

Leslie shook her head slowly in agreement.

"The Seneca take the scalp of their enemy as a trophy. It is an honor for a warrior to gain such a coup, and it is looked upon admirably by his people."

Leslie noted the concern in his eyes. She nodded her understanding. It was true the white man could be more barbaric. Red was a perfect example and deserved everything he got. She had no right to judge Running Elk or the customs of his people. She also realized there was still much to learn about the Seneca and their ways. She reached out to touch his arm.

"I ... I understand, Running Elk. I do not judge you for the customs you practice."

Running Elk smiled and nodded his thanks.

"Running Elk ... where is Winnokin? The last time I saw him he was terribly wounded. Is he ... is he ... "

Running Elk interrupted. "He rests to gain back his strength. He is well."

Leslie tried to sit up but moaned loudly as pain coursed through her body.

Running Elk tenderly touched her shoulder to stop her and shook his head.

"Do not move. My chief has not received injuries as severe as yours. He is strong and mending. You must not try to move, or your wound will not heal," he reprimanded lightly.

Leslie liked Winnokin's friend. He was a lot like her father, with the body of a bear and the heart of a kitten. She imagined he could be a worthy opponent when provoked and remembered being told he was Winnokin's equal in combat.

"Can you take me to him?"

Running Elk shook his head "Na. No. I will tell him you have awakened," he replied and exited the lodge.

Leslie's eyes felt heavy once more and she closed them. Soon she felt a cool breeze pass over her cheek and opened them to find Winnokin kneeling before her. The loving tenderness reflected in his eyes tugged at her heart. She desperately wanted him to take her in his arms, but she knew he would be reserved in the presence of Running Elk. Her eyes scanned over him, and her brows creased in a worried frown. His cheeks were badly bruised from the beating he had received, and his ribs were wrapped tightly. She looked more closely but could not see any other signs of injury and recited a silent prayer of thanks that they both survived Red's fury.

Running Elk drew near and placed a hand upon Winnokin's shoulder.

"The little one is strong, my brother."

Winnokin smiled warmly as he gazed upon Leslie. "Ya. She is strong," he answered and rose and placed his hand upon Running Elk's shoulder. "Because of you, she will walk this earth beside me, my friend."

Leslie lifted her hand toward Running Elk.

"Thank you so much for saving my life."

Running Elk took hold of her hand and placed it in Winnokin's.

"It was Hawenneyu who guided us to the campfire of our chief. But it was the driving force of his love for you that helped us find you."

Leslie smiled at them both.

"Then I will thank Hawenneyu as well and hope one day I will be given the chance to repay the honor to you, Winnokin's dearest friend." Leslie grew weary and could not stifle a loud yawn. "I am sorry. I am so tired." She sighed.

Winnokin knelt beside her and tenderly petted her forehead.

"Sleep, my Ishita," he cooed softly as he brushed her lips with a sweet kiss.

Leslie felt warm by his sign of open affection.

"Will you come sit with me later when I wake?"

"Ya. But now I must leave to prepare for our journey home, Ishita. Sleep and dream beautiful thoughts," he replied.

When Winnokin rose to leave, Leslie reached for his hand to stop him.

"Winnokin ... I ... "

She looked over at Running Elk and blushed slightly. Running Elk understood her need for privacy, bowed, and left the lodge.

Winnokin sat down by her side and took a curl in his hand and naturally wound it around his finger as he always did.

"I feared I lost you forever, Ishita."

Leslie opened her good arm, and Winnokin lowered to her chest.

Their bare skin came in contact, and the heat that radiated between them sent healing warmth to course through their veins. He was her life's blood. Softly she kissed his shoulder and neck, and Winnokin responded in kind.

He held her face between his hands and caressed her lips with a bewitching kiss, casting a welcoming spell of love over her.

"You must rest now, Ishita. It is important to gain strength before I can move you and take you home to my people and begin our life together."

Leslie sighed deeply and nodded. She did not want him to leave but knew if he stayed, she would not get her rest.

Winnokin dipped a small ladle into a bowl containing medicinal herbs to help heal her wounds and a small potion to help her sleep and raised it to her lips to drink. As she nestled comfortably upon her supple bed of robes, Winnokin stayed by her side massaging her forehead with slow, tender strokes until she drifted into a deep and contented sleep.

Chapter Fifteen

Leslie's strength grew with every passing day. She contributed her quick recovery mostly to the meticulous care of her doting benefactors.

A diversified diet consisting of fowl, fish, and hearty roasted meats helped considerably. The medicinal herbs used to dress her wounds helped immensely, to not only heal her open sores, but restored the range of movement and flexibility back to her injured arm and shoulder. Once the color returned to her cheeks and she could manage to stand without Winnokin's support, he took her on short walks each afternoon to increase her stamina and coordination.

A full week had passed, and the sun filtered through the trees and kissed the earth with its bright, white rays as they walked hand in hand across an open meadow abundant with golden sunflowers.

As their thighs brushed together, Leslie felt heady with excitement. Being alone and finally close with the man she loved was so much better than the reserve she had to practice while in the company of his warriors. She could not help feeling shy still. When she looked his way, she noticed a smile playing upon his lips and she blushed from the intense look in his eyes.

"Can we stop a while?" she asked. "Being so close to you makes me all weak in the knees."

Winnokin caressed her cheek with his thumb and led her toward a majestic blue-green spruce to be shaded from the afternoon heat.

They settled down beneath the protection of its wide branches and watched as little forest creatures scampered about and listened while the birds sang musically overhead, filling the air with their romantic sonnets.

She felt so content being with him. Spoken words weren't necessary because of the special bond they shared. Leslie rested her head upon his chest and sighed deeply. She felt safe in his embrace and lulled by the rhythmic beating of his heart. She could feel the agony and stress of the past month seep from her body as the warmth radiating from his skin and palms reached to the depth of her soul.

She prayed that the remainder of her days would finally be void of further pain and sorrow. She was confident Winnokin would protect and keep her safe, love her intensely and make her life whole again once they reached his village. She still felt a large void in her life by the loss of her family.

She looked up and gazed into his eyes. Winnokin lowered his head and tenderly kissed her mouth then lifted her upon his lap. She wrapped her arms about his powerful neck and returned his kiss, softly at first, caressing the contours of his chiseled features with her fingers. She pecked softly the tip of his nose, the cleft of his chin, each ear lobe, and then his brow.

Winnokin drew her to the ground and mimicked her moves, ending with a deeply passionate kiss, long and sedating.

Leslie moaned, and Winnokin misjudged her pleasure for pain. He drew away and took slow, deep breaths to quell the fire churning within him.

"Why do you stop?" she asked.

"Did I hurt you?" he replied.

Leslie smiled and opened her arms to him.

"No, my sweet, you did not hurt me but aroused a hunger to be one with you."

Winnokin did not move into her arms, but rather ran his fingers through his hair.

"We must return to camp before my desire for you takes control."

Leslie sat up and smiled coyly. "Would that be so wrong?"

Winnokin clasped her shoulders lightly.

"No, but it is best for now. When the sun rises tomorrow, we will break camp and begin our journey home. We must wait to join. I must keep my vow."

Leslie opened her mouth to argue the point, but the look in Winnokin's eyes told her she would not win, and she held her tongue.

He clasped hold of her hand and led her back to camp.

Everything was being prepared for their departure when they returned to camp. Their belongings had been gathered. Running Elk had a litter constructed of oak branches strung together with sinew, inter-weaved with thongs, and layered with various animal pelts to transport Leslie. The lodge she had slept in was already disassembled, and a bed was made for her beside the fire pit where the others would sleep on their final evening there.

Early the following morning, Leslie rose to find the horses were packed and all fires were extinguished. She was served a light breakfast and allowed to address her toiletry. When she was ready for departure, Winnokin swept her into his arms and settled her upon a sturdy travois.

"I can ride, Winnokin," she argued soundly. "I'm not a child or senior who needs carrying. Please let me ride beside you."

Running Elk chuckled as he moved forward and playfully ribbed Winnokin with his elbow.

"The little one is stronger than we thought. Her bite and fire has returned, has it not?"

Winnokin signed with his hands to emphasize his authority to Leslie.

"She will do as Winnokin says," he retorted.

A spark of fury shone in Leslie's eyes.

"Oh! You ... you ... "

Winnokin raised his hand to silence her.

"Neho, Ishita. Stop, my love!" he demanded. "I have spoken. Do not ask me to gamble with your safety. You have made much progress. You will do as I say and not question me again."

He turned on his heel and walked away.

Leslie glared at his retreating back and was infuriated by his superior attitude. Her father never talked to her with such a tone. She was sorely tempted to tell Winnokin exactly what was on her mind but thought best not to provoke him in front of his men. She would have her chance, and he would listen when they were alone. For now, she would relent and settled down into the travois with a huff and stubborn tilt to her chin and her arms crossed in frustration.

Winnokin mounted his stead with Running Elk by his side. They both looked in her direction, noticing her displeasure, and exchanged smiles.

Winnokin knew that fire sparked in her eyes and the matter was not over between them. The passing hours would give her temper time to cool. He chuckled to himself, knowing a life with her would not be boring. He was in love with a passionate, quick-tempered she lion, and the thought of her aroused him.

The excursion proved more tiring than Leslie had anticipated. The sun's constant beating heat drained her strength in no time. She was awed by the warriors and their tireless endurance as they effortlessly crossed countless miles of changing terrain for hours on end without a moment's rest.

She knew why Winnokin was so insistent about her traveling by travois. Hours on horseback would have been too taxing, and she found herself taking frequent short naps throughout the day. Her anger was unwarranted, and she silently promised to apologize when the opportunity arose.

The Seneca village was fixed upon the bank of one of the five Finger Lakes, its lodges protectively encamped within a tall, well-guarded stockade. The village was surrounded by a double row of wood palisades. A trench ran several feet deep around, the continuous row of stakes placed at such an angle where they inclined over the trench.

Set beyond the fortressed area was a hundred or more cultivated acres of land divided into planting lots.

Leslie sat dumbfounded as she looked down upon the glory of Winnokin's massive village and the well devised, civilized character his people exhibited.

And the white man calls them all savages, she thought. *If only we could live in harmony and learn from each other.*

Standing sentry at its entrance were two ferocious looking warriors who showed no expression other than acknowledging their leader as they drew near.

A chill ran up the length of Leslie's spine as she realized the horrid thought of meeting the two of them head on in battle. It was a great relief to know she entered their homeland under friendly terms and Winnokin's protection.

She did not expect a response from them when she passed but could not help smile. When she neared, she could not help feeling overwhelmed with respect for the strength they exuded. Her eyes were like a sponge, absorbing the sights and sounds before her as they scanned the village in its entirety.

There were no streets to be found, but rather a grouping of dwellings. She giggled to herself and turned to Winnokin as he rode up beside her.

"My people would be surprised by the greatness of your village," she said. "The white man view you as savages, but your homeland would shame many of the white villages I have seen during my travels."

She could tell her remarks pleased him, and great pride shone in his eyes as he gazed upon his village.

Children rushed forward laughing happily and jumping with glee as their entourage dismounted their horses. Winnokin helped Leslie from her travois and kept to her side as they began to walk through the heart of the village.

Winnokin's warriors passed their weapons over to the older boys following at their sides. The pride on their young faces for the honor bestowed upon them was clearly evident, and Leslie could not help but show her pleasure.

The women and elders gathered in an endless line, nodding their heads and shouting their welcome for their chief's safe return. As they gazed at her, Leslie noticed amazement, surprise, and concern on their faces.

It surprised her, however, when one beautiful maiden abruptly jumped in front of her and openly displayed her hatred. Even though Leslie's insides shook nervously, she smiled at the woman. The maiden's attitude did not change. An elder moved forward, digging her clutch into the maiden's arm, and pulled her backwards, scolding. The maiden pulled her arm from the elder's grip and made a gesture toward Leslie with her hand before disappearing into the crowd.

Leslie could not make out the heated words exchanged between them as they passed. But she was certain she was the cause and did not understand why. She looked at Winnokin and saw the fury in his eyes. It was obvious there was a connection between them, and Leslie wondered if perhaps they were lovers at one time. She made a mental note to ask him later once they were alone.

When the procession halted, they were in the center of the mighty fortress, standing beside a bark-sided lodge, tremendous in size. Standing in front of its entrance was an aged but proud-looking individual. He exuded great wisdom and authority as he eminently stood with arms crossed at his chest.

He gave the sign of welcome to all who returned and gazed briefly at Leslie and nodded slightly.

Winnokin stepped forward. The two clasped each other's forearms affectionately and exchanged words of endearment.

Winnokin interpreted Leslie's words about the village to his people, and they nodded their approval, except for the beautiful maiden, who moved to the front of the crowd. The look of hatred she sent Leslie was clear and made Leslie feel uncomfortable. She knew the woman standing just a few feet within reach would be an adversary in the days ahead.

Leslie's attention was adverted when the elder walked toward her and her heart began to beat rapidly in her chest. Her palms began to sweat, but she fought to hold her nervousness in reserve and smiled openly at him.

He needed no introduction. His resemblance to Winnokin was unmistakable, and she knew him to be Strong of Heart, Winnokin's grandfather and the man who counseled with her father. They shared the same golden eyes, square jaw, and muscular frame. Even though his hair was heavily streaked with gray, and his face was lined with age, he was still a handsome man.

"My grandson tells me the white man of your village would be shamed by our great homeland," he said proudly as he opened both his arms wide to take it all in.

Leslie held her chin high and bowed regally before him.

"Ya, Nichkotanye. Ga Wa Yete (Yes, Strong of Heart, it is so)," she responded proudly. Her eyes searched out Winnokin and her heart welled with love as she saw the pleasure her fluent words had caused.

"It is good you have learned our tongue, golden one," Strong of Heart replied. "It will make your stay among us an easy one."

He turned to his people and raised his arms wide and high. "Swah da dih go. Ese ta lichta to anda (Go, ye woman. You are welcome here this day)."

Leslie bowed. "Hineaweh, Nichkotanye (Thank you, Strong of Heart)."

Winnokin turned to speak with Running Elk and his grandfather. Together they walked toward the council lodge, leaving Leslie to stand amongst the crowd alone.

She gazed upon the various faces of his people standing before her. The elder men and women looked at her with awe and astonishment or bowed to show their respect. It was obvious they thought of her as the woman foretold to them in their chief's vision. Many nodded or signed welcome as they passed, and Leslie did so in kind. Innocent toddlers, their adorable faces bronzed from the sun, tugged at her hemline and smiled up at her with brilliant, dark eyes large as a newborn fawn.

A tall, beautiful maiden moved to the front of the crowd. Leslie guessed her to be around her age and wondered if she was another rival intent on doing battle. Her skin was flawless, and she moved with the ease and grace of a woman who held a regal title. Leslie felt uncertain how to react until the maiden knelt before her, reached for Leslie's hand, and touched her forehead to it.

"I, Little Raven, wife of Running Elk," she spoke perfectly and smiled. "My family offers our home to you."

Leslie bowed to grasp hold of her elbows and drew Little Raven to stand before her. She returned her smile.

"Hineaweh. (Thank you), Little Raven. I welcome your friendship and the gracious invitation of your family."

Little Raven extended her hand.

"Come, I will take you to a place where you can bathe away the dirt from your travels. Running Elk sent a message you would be arriving today. I had some clothes prepared for you."

Little Raven handed Leslie a one-piece doe skin shift. She smiled.

"This is for you to wear after your bath."

Leslie unfolded the dress and was amazed by the beauty of its design and its baby soft texture. The neckline was rounded, and in place of sleeves were fringed strips of a lighter hide decorated with white beads at various stages and lengths. The bottom hem was fringed to match the sleeves.

"Is this your work, Little Raven? I've never seen anything so soft and beautiful. I don't know what to say!"

Little Raven touched Leslie's arm affectionately.

"The look in your eyes, my sister, tells me what is in your heart. No words are needed."

Leslie's eyes caught sight of the hateful maiden watching them from the cover of trees off to her right and was tempted to ask Little Raven who she was. She did not want to stir bad feelings on her first day in camp. She decided it was best to watch and listen for the time and not make any quick judgments. She hoped it was something simple she could break through, get her to see what kind of person she was and slowly open her heart to want to be friends. The looks she was giving told Leslie it was going to be a difficult task.

Leslie drew her attention back to Little Raven.

"You speak my language so well, Little Raven. Did Winnokin teach you?"

Little Raven looked about to make sure no one could listen as she moved Leslie along. Leslie followed her gaze and noticed Little Raven also saw the other maiden watching them as well. She took Leslie by the elbow and led her away from the village down a small foot-worn path to a pristine lake below.

"It was Winnokin's desire that I learn the white man's tongue. But it was my husband who taught me the words."

Little Raven turned to look over her shoulder to make sure they were not being followed.

"When we are alone, we can speak your language because it will be good for me. In the company of my people, it is wise you speak the Seneca way. That is my chief's wish. I will be your teacher and help you learn the ways of my people."

Leslie nodded. "I understand, Little Raven. I will do as you and your chief wish."

While Leslie swam and washed her hair, Little Raven told Leslie about her own family who offered their home to her.

Little Raven's mother, Leluna, was married to Red Eagle, sub-chief of the Hawk Clan and leader of the False Face Society. He cured ailments, particularly those of the head, shoulders, and limbs. The masks his members wore to carry out such tasks were endowed with curative powers, enabling them to minister to the ill and injured. Little Raven told Leslie she would show her father's mask to her, but no one in the household other than Red Eagle could touch it. Her brother, Moon Stalker, was also a member of the False Face Society and did not live in their lodge but the lodge of his new bride, Metsume.

While Leslie dried herself off, she noticed they were being watched again by the same maiden as before and decided to mention it this time to Little Raven.

"Little Raven, did you not see the maiden watching us before we came down here?"

Little Raven nodded. "Ya. I know she does so now."

Leslie could not help but display her surprise as she sat down by Little Raven's side. Little Raven reached out for Leslie's hand and held it in her own.

"Do you know of the beautiful yellow flower in the forest that draws the insect with its sweet scent and then snaps itself closed to catch its prey?"

Leslie thought for a moment and then shook her head, remembering which one she spoke of.

"That is Nuchzetse, Flower that Snaps. You must be careful of her. She is not one who can be trusted with any man."

"Oh! I see. Do you think she is in love with Winnokin?"

Little Raven nodded. "She has stated openly her desire for our chief. But Nuchzetse desires all men and loves only herself."

Leslie chewed the inside of her mouth nervously.

"This could be a problem, Little Raven."

"Yes, that is so. You have been warned. Do not show your fear, or she will use it against you. You must be strong and treat her like you would an unruly child."

Chapter Sixteen

Leslie enjoyed her stay with Little Raven's family. Her only regret was not spending more time with Winnokin. The many weeks they had shared with each other were gone to her now. His duties as sachem, the countless hours he spent either in counsel over village concerns, or with sub-chiefs from neighboring clans, made it impossible for them to spend time together.

For the twelve days she had been with Little Raven, she had seen Winnokin only once. She was almost certain he was avoiding her. The mix of emotions that buzzed around in her head frustrated her and only added more dread and worry to her life. She missed the tender moments they shared out on the trail. Her lips hungered for his touch, and her body yearned for the comfort that only his arms could provide.

Little Raven did her best to keep Leslie busy, teaching her everything she needed to know, filling her hours with countless tasks, which made Leslie collapse each evening from the mental fatigue and physical exhaustion.

The bond between them became strong almost immediately, and they looked upon each other as the sister neither one had.

Leslie was pleased Running Elk had taken a liking to her as well. Even if she did not have the chance to see Winnokin, Running Elk took the time to inform her what Winnokin was doing. He told her Winnokin spoke of her frequently. When he teased Leslie and gave her a difficult time, Little Raven would scold him. Running Elk would chuckle and bend to his wife's will happily.

It was his responsibility to explain to Leslie Winnokin's duties as sachem, so she could understand that their time apart was not from lack of love, but duty to his people. He tried to make her understand what was involved, the time required to listen to the problems of all the clans: Bear, Wolf, Beaver, Turtle, Deer, Snipe, Heron, and Hawk.

Leslie promised she would try her best to be patient. She knew it would not be proper to discuss with him her dismay over Winnokin's treatment of her since her arrival. She kept those feelings to herself. It was not as if she expected him to show her any outward affection. She knew it was impossible, because right now she was not one of his people. She wondered if that was why he made no attempts to court her.

She also questioned whether being white had something to do with his avoiding her. She was too afraid to even ask that question of Little Raven, afraid of what her answer might be. Were the many council meetings he attended a discussion as to whether they could join as husband and wife?

Leslie tried to remember if Winnokin ever told her a sachem could marry beneath his social class. After all, she was not a member of any clan. She learned the Seneca had no desire to imitate the splendid achievements of the white man. The Seneca felt they were superior to her kind. They scorned the whites and thought their spirits were absorbed in wasted pleasures like soft beds, fire water, plush fabrics, and luxurious foods. The Seneca believed their happiness was independent of such weaknesses.

Leslie feared it was one thing to love her yet totally different to be able to marry. She decided the next time she was alone with Little Raven; she would ask her. She had to know the answer before she spent any more time in the village. If she could not have him as her husband, there was no point in staying. For not to be able to share her life in such a way with him, would be the greatest tragedy of all. The more she was exposed to the cultures of the Seneca, however, the more amazed she became by the importance a woman held in their society. Little Raven took her around the Bear Clan lodges and introduced her to many of the women.

She learned a wife was expected to always be dressed well, even if her husband was shabby or unclean. When a woman rose to seniority in the long house where she lived, she gradually acquired political power. The senior woman in each house could appoint a council chief and also had the power to remove him if he failed at his duties.

Little Raven's reasons were sound when Leslie asked her why the women had so much control.

"The Seneca are keepers of the western door and protect our brothers of the four other tribes. Our men must travel far to gather furs and food. Many days they can be gone on a hunt or raid. It is the women who protect the village with the younger warriors, care for the children and elderly, and tend the crops. When men are gone, women must take over."

Little Raven taught Leslie well. Her day began with lessons in drying meat on a rack, how to dry apples and squash, pound corn and wheat into grain, and prepare the ground for planting and harvest. They planted late corn and picked squash and beans in abundance, preparing much of their harvest to be stored in the underground granaries for winter use.

The most important thing, which Leslie felt true in her own society, was bearing children. When the time came for a Seneca woman to give birth, she retreated into the forest alone in the privacy of trees and shadow and washed her newborn off in water or snow before carrying the child back to a rejoicing village wrapped in either furs or deerskin.

Leslie did not know if she could follow through on that tradition and give birth alone, after experiencing the birth of one child already. She shared her fears with Little Raven.

"When it is time for one to bring forth life, a wise woman is called to assist in the birth if a doctor or medicine man is not available in my world. That way she helps the mother stay calm and if there is a problem that arises."

"It is a wise way, my sister," Little Raven interjected. "There is always one who guards from a distance in case there is need. We are not a heartless race." She smiled. "To leave a defenseless woman amid her birth cycle alone and vulnerable to harm is what you would call savage. Is it not?"

"Yes, it is." Leslie nodded. "It pleases me to know this. I fear I could not go through such a task alone. But" she sighed deeply, "I guess there will never be an easy way to bring a child into the world." She chuckled.

It was late afternoon when they began to walk the foot path that led to a private cove where all the women bathed.

They were caught up in conversation and did not notice when Nuchzetse appeared from behind a group of nimble berry bushes and tripped Leslie when she passed, causing her to reel forward and fall to the ground with a hard thud. Sharp stones lacerated her elbow, knees, and cheek.

"The clumsy white woman does not know how to walk in the moccasins of the Seneca," Nuchzetse remarked in her native tongue. "Perhaps you should include the lessons we teach our children, Little Raven." She laughed heartily.

Little Raven shot Nuchzetse a disgusted look. "It is you who needs to be taught the lesson of respect and hospitality." Little Raven spat as she bent to help Leslie rise.

"I am fine, Little Raven," Leslie replied as she brushed herself off.

She looked at Nuchzetse and lifted her head with pride. "I was not paying attention. It is my fault."

"Hmm. Just as I said," Nuchzetse rebuffed in a haughty tone. "The white woman even admits to being clumsy. Be more careful the next time, if you know what is good for you." She hissed as she bumped into Leslie when she walked past her.

Little Raven moved forward, but Leslie grabbed her elbow to stop her.

"I do not know what your problem is, Nuchzetse," Leslie called out.

Nuchzetse whirled around and moved quickly back to stand right in front of Leslie.

"You are my problem. You are white. That is enough."

"And you are Indian, and we are both women who bleed the same color. So, you need a better argument than that." Leslie countered.

Nuchzetse leaned forward and spat in Leslie's face.

"I need to do nothing more," she replied and turned on her heel and walked away.

Little Raven ran forward to take chase, but Leslie grabbed her by the arm to stop her as she wiped away the spit running down her cheek.

"She is not worth it, Little Raven. Let her go."

Little Raven stopped and turned to face Leslie. "You must watch her, my sister. She is a bad seed, and I am afraid she does not deal well with the knowledge that you and our sachem beat the same heart."

Leslie could understand the reason for Nuchzetse's hatred if she and Winnokin were courting in the open. She questioned in her mind if perhaps Nuchzetse was a scorned lover.

"Perhaps she has just cause, Little Raven. If she and Winnokin were ... "

Little Raven shook Leslie by the shoulders.

"Our chief would not lower himself to bed with such a one. She is possessed, and her lack of judgment places you in harm's way. All know his heart is full of love for you, and this displeases her greatly. You must be cautious."

Leslie shuddered. It was the last thing she thought she would have to deal with, and it still worried her terribly. There would be times when she would be alone, and her feelings were never wrong when it came to judging others. Something inside her forewarned that Nuchzetse's harassing attempts would get worse if she did not find a way to either counter them or turn her into a friend.

"I felt her hatred the moment I arrived," Leslie replied, remembering the look of contempt in Nuchzetse's eyes when they first looked at each other. "I just thought it was because I was white and being brought into your village."

Little Raven wrapped her arm around Leslie's waist and gave her a sisterly hug.

"To her you are. Do not let that worry you. Once she has come to know you, her feelings will change," Little Raven assured her as she leaned forward and placed a tender kiss on Leslie's cheek. "Come ... let us take our bath and enjoy this time together."

Leslie tried not to let the incident with Nuchzetse bother her too much while they swam, but she could not help being troubled by the vile hatred the woman openly expressed without even knowing her. She knew the maiden was up to no good by the way Nuchzetse constantly snuck around and watched her from afar all the time. Clearly, she was conniving something, and Leslie had a bad feeling gnawing at the pit of her stomach.

When they finished their swim, they sat beside each other along the water's edge and let the warm rays of the sun dry them. Leslie noticed her skin was beginning to tan a golden brown from all the time she spent in the sun hoeing in the fields, weaving corn husk baskets, or tanning hides in front of the lodge. She looked over at Little Raven and smiled softly at her. They were so distinctly different—one like a white dove and the other a black raven.

"Little Raven, can I ask you something?"

Little Raven nodded.

"Well, it has been many days since I have entered your home and have not talked to Winnokin. My heart grows heavy," she admitted sadly.

Little Raven watched Leslie draw a symbol of something in the dirt between them.

"I do not understand why Winnokin goes out of his way to avoid me," Leslie continued. She drew her knees to her chest and wrapped her arms around them. "Have I done something to offend him? Maybe Running Elk has shared this with you, or is there something I need to do ... I ... I just don't know."

Leslie noticed a sudden change in Little Raven.

"What is it, Little Raven? Why do you look at me that way?"

Little Raven softly touched Leslie's arm and ran her fingers through Leslie's hair with a worried expression on her face.

"I ... I am so sorry, my sister. I thought I told you everything, but now I realize I have not. Please, will you forgive me?"

Leslie moved to her knees and grasped a hold of Little Raven's shoulders.

"Yes, of course. What is it? Should I be concerned?"

Little Raven reached for their shifts and handed Leslie hers. As they dressed, she spoke.

"When you entered the lodge of my parents, you did so as our guest."

Leslie threw her hands up with frustration.

"What has that got to do with Winnokin and I?" she questioned, exasperated.

Little Raven reached out and grasped Leslie's forearms.

"For our chief to treat you the way you wish is not possible. Because he is chief, much is expected of him."

Leslie gasped and covered her mouth with her hands. She could not believe what she was hearing. This was her biggest fear ... not being good enough. She had to be Indian and a member of the tribe or a clan for him to even associate with her. Tears filled her eyes. This was too much to bear. A great sadness washed over her, and she felt as though she wanted to die.

Little Raven reached out and wiped a cascading tear from Leslie's cheek.

"Why do you weep, my sister?"

Leslie sent her a puzzling look.

"I do not understand," Leslie replied. She shook her head as tears continued to roll down her cheeks.

Little Raven placed a comforting arm around Leslie's shoulder, and their attention was drawn to a flock of loons that had landed nearby.

"There is no cause for sadness. It has always been our plan to make it right between you."

"But how?" Leslie asked as she turned to look at Little Raven.

Little Raven reached for her hand.

"We are to adopt you into our lodge. Not until then can Winnokin look upon you as one with the people or acknowledge his love for you openly. This is something we could not do right away. We had to observe for some time to see that you were worthy. I am sorry." Little Raven bowed her head. "He left your training to me, and I have dishonored his trust in me for lacking in my teachings." She covered her face in her hands.

Leslie reached for Little Raven's hands, drew them away from her face, and held them in her lap.

"Do not say that Little Raven. You have done a wonderful job with me. And you are also a new bride. Do not place blame on yourself. Winnokin should have told me before we arrived here. I blame him, not you."

Little Raven shook her head.

"You must not. It is I who failed. He is a great leader and cannot be bothered with such simple female concerns. All he asked of me was to teach you everything you needed to know as a woman in our village."

Leslie felt dizzy, and the color drained from her face. "Are you saying I cannot be his wife?" she asked and drew her clenched fists to her heart. "I could not bear to live in this village and know we could never be together."

Little Raven shook her head repeatedly. "No. You do not hear me. Winnokin cannot have you as his wife until you have been adopted. Once that is so, he will bring many gifts to my father to show his worth as your husband. When my father has decided the gifts may stop, an announcement will be made. I promise you, Winnokin has eyes for only you. That is all he talks to Running Elk about."

Leslie jumped to her feet and squealed with excitement.

"So what are we waiting for? Let's get me adopted!"

Little Raven chuckled at Leslie's outburst. "That we can do. But know it is our custom to wait one season before an adoption can occur. It gives the family time to learn about a person, make sure their heart is true and deserving of becoming one with a family."

"But ... that is such a long time! That means I must wait another month?" Leslie replied.

Little Raven rose and patted her hand. "Ya, that is so. But ... you have the blessing of the Great Spirit. You have been a part of his vision and know to walk the same paths of our people. This will work in your favor."

Little Raven promised to speak with her mother as soon as they returned to the lodge. The two quickly dressed and scurried back to the village as fast as their legs would carry them.

Leluna chuckled to herself as she heard the squeals of laughter and saw the excited faces of Little Raven and Leslie as they entered the village. She noticed how the villagers turned to gaze upon the happy pair as they passed by and smiled approvingly.

What beautiful young women they are, Leluna thought happily, and her lips curled into a smile as they approached. Her eyes sparkled with glee, and she rejoiced silently over their close friendship and love for each other.

The sunlight made Leslie's golden tresses glisten, and Little Raven's also shimmered when the wind caught their long mass billowing behind them as they ran hand-in-hand. They both weaved in and out of playing children and jumped over cooking fires and snoozing dogs. They came to a breathless halt before Leluna and collapsed to their knees before her, their cheeks flushed and breaths coming in short rasps as they giggled like young maidens. Leluna clucked her tongue and shook her head at them both. Little Raven and Leslie knew she was not angry with them as they noticed the twinkle in her eyes and her lips curve into a smile.

"Something tells me you are working mischief together," Leluna stated as she placed her quills and sewing down in her lap and looked from one to the other.

Little Raven and Leslie exchanged smiles. Little Raven reached for Leslie's hand and took a deep breath before speaking.

"Mother, you know our chief's heart beats with much love for Leslie."

Leluna nodded her agreement as she gazed at Leslie.

"You also know that he cannot acknowledge his love until she is one with our people," Little Raven continued.

Leluna nodded again. "That is true, my daughter," Leluna replied and looked at Leslie again. "Has my daughter told you that the lodge of Red Eagle and Leluna may adopt you should they choose?"

Leslie nodded nervously and swallowed hard as her heart pounded fiercely in her chest.

"I see this is something you hope will be?" Leluna asked as she looked more sternly at one and then the other.

Leslie was afraid Leluna was going to tell them it was an impossible task. Her look was intense, and Leslie could not read her expression. She never realized what an attractive woman Leluna truly was for her age. Her raven hair was peppered with gray. Laughter lines were etched at the corners of her luminous, brown eyes. Her teeth were perfectly shaped, and the dimple in her right cheek made her appear younger than her forty-five years.

"Red Eagle and I have spoken of this. We both would love to have you as one with our family. If Little Raven agrees, then it will be so." Leluna smiled.

Leslie's heart skipped another beat, and she looked at Little Raven, who had a mischievous glean in her eye.

"Hmmm," Little Raven replied as she touched her hand to her chin. "There is much to consider, Mother. She will be my equal, will she not?" Little Raven teased as she rubbed her chin.

Leluna nodded and could barely suppress a smile.

Leslie made a noise as her mouth dropped open.

Little Raven laughed out loud.

"I will have you as my true sister since mother and father wish it so." Little Raven chuckled again as she squeezed Leslie's hand.

Leslie ribbed her playfully in the side. "I think you will be impossible to live with."

Leluna moved forward and took hold of each of their hands and clasped one atop the other. "The Great Spirit has blessed our family and brought to us another loving heart into our home. The lodge of Red Eagle and Leluna open its door to you if you can find it in your heart to accept us as well?"

Little Raven and Leluna both had tears brimming from their eyes when Leslie gazed at them. Their love for her filled her heart with joy, and she could not stop her own tears from flowing.

"I would be most honored to call you Mother and you my true sister," Leslie replied as she opened her arms to draw them both close to her.

The three exchanged tender kisses, endearing words, and wiped away each other's tears. They did not hear Red Eagle and Running Elk approach until Red Eagle grunted loudly.

Leluna looked at her husband, smiled, and nodded. Red Eagle looked at Little Raven, and her joyous smile warmed his heart. Leluna moved to Little Raven's side and encircled her waist with her arm.

Red Eagle moved forward, and Running Elk did not move. It was difficult for Leslie to tell what was on their mind by the expressionless look on their faces, and she bowed her head respectfully in their presence.

"You must tell me, my child, what is causing such happiness in my lodge," Red Eagle stated.

Leslie clasped her hands to her breast and slowly raised her eyes to meet his gaze.

He was such a tall man with prominent, chiseled cheekbones. Penetrating dark eyes were softened by long, silken lashes that touched his broad brow. The people viewed him a lighthearted soul with dimples also that accentuated his soft, full lips. Leslie could not help but smile up at him. She looked quickly at Running Elk, and he sent her a playful wink. Immediately she relaxed.

"Leluna and Little Raven have spoken of your willingness to adopt me into your family, Red Eagle. It would please me greatly to call you father and to share in your joy, love, and happiness."

Red Eagle looked at his wife and daughter, noticing their broad smiles and nods of approval. He stepped forward and placed a tender hand upon Leslie's shoulder and caressed her cheek softly and smiled.

"It would warm my heart to call you daughter." He turned slightly and called to his son-in-law, Running Elk.

Running Elk moved forward and bowed respectfully. "Yes, my father," he spoke.

"Send a runner throughout the village this day. Tell the people of the Seneca that Red Eagle, Sub-chief of the Hawk Clan, will adopt the white woman called Leslie into his home in three days' time."

Running Elk nodded and smiled. "It is done, my father," he answered and turned immediately to do his bidding.

Red Eagle drew Leslie into his arms while Leluna and Little Raven looked on. After a moment passed, he smiled and waved them forward to join him and Leslie in a full circle of love.

Chapter Seventeen

It was predawn when Leslie awoke from a fitful sleep. No matter how hard she tried to force herself into a peaceful slumber with sweet dreams of Winnokin on her mind, it did not work. She rose from her pallet of furs as quietly as she could and wrapped a small fur rabbit cape over her shoulders. She tip-toed to the doorway and exited the home she shared with the people who would soon be legally noted as her family in the eyes of the Seneca nation. Her mind was a myriad of muddled thoughts, and the mangled mess left her confused and questioning her decision to stay with his people.

Mindlessly, she walked slowly through the massive, gated compound, reflecting on the past couple of months. She became overwhelmed with emotion and could not stay the tears which began to fall from her eyes and slowly cascade down her cheeks. Life was not fair, she thought, as the faces of her deceased husband, child, father, mother, and dearest friend passed before her eyes.

Each of them had dreams, hopes, and desires. Their lives were ended as quickly as one would snuff out a campfire. Their endings were blunt and immediate and simply not fair. She had no right to be happy, to fall in love, or start a new life. Despite her struggles through it all, regardless of the pain and extreme heartache that left scars on her heart like those left behind on ones' flesh from the lash of a whip, she felt as though she was betraying their memory and the dreams and hopes she shared and built with them.

How much must one person endure? she wondered. Many times, during sermon she would listen to various clergy proclaim that no one individual would be burdened with any more than they could humanly handle. They avowed that God would know when the weight upon their shoulders was too much. They affirmed that the more one endured, the closer they would sit at the right hand of the Lord.

Leslie could not help but snort aloud at that justification. If such was the case, she would certainly end up sitting on the Lord's lap, rather than by his side. What she had survived and suffered during her years in this god forsaken country should certainly place her in the Lord's highest honor, she rationalized.

She noticed that some of the villagers were beginning to stir as the sun rose higher in the sky. Those who started to exit from their longhouses or already standing outdoors acknowledged her as she passed. She wondered what they thought when they looked at her. Did the color of her skin matter? As soon as she asked herself that question, she knew the answer.

The Seneca were a reverent community who held much honor in the glory of what god blessed humankind with. The injustices forced upon them by "the whites" surely cast doubt in the minds of these native people, but they judged by deeds and action and not by color.

It was the white settlers who were beginning to move into the region like the waves of swallows she would watch fly south before winter cast its frozen cloak upon the land. It was the whites who judged a man by the color of his skin. Leslie could not help but wonder if her presence amongst them could make a difference. Could she possibly help them learn, take advantage of those changes brought on by the many foreigners inhabiting their lands? Was it possible if she became native to their ways, they in turn could do the same, become stronger and survive?

Was she meant to be here, she wondered? She nodded her response and knew that all the dreams she had of Winnokin had a purpose. Her visions set the stage for a future that was meant to be. As she gazed down at her moccasins, she knew that was as certain as each foot she was placing in front of the other.

 Leslie knew her destiny was to help the Seneca survive and adjust to the uncontrollable changes befalling them on a regular basis. She turned about, and her eyes scanned the bustle and activity coming alive before her. These were Winnokin's people, and they embraced her entry into their world without question. They were her destiny. Their paths were meant to cross, and she knew that the losses she suffered in life were predestined and the catalyst to making her stronger and molding her into the woman who would stand beside their leader and lead them through the challenges ahead.

When she returned to the lodge of Red Eagle, the level of excitement was both uplifting and chaotic. The women prepared a special meal of celebration for the family and the many visitors who they expected would be stopping by throughout the evening to show and express their congratulations and joy.

Winnokin and Running Elk had gone hunting as soon as Winnokin heard the news and returned with a rare white doe, which they skinned and presented the pelt to Leslie to use for her special ceremonial dress.

Winnokin was invited by Red Eagle to the celebration. Leslie could not contain her happiness when she heard the good news and was resplendent over the thought of their being together in each other's company.

A large cooking pot was prepared outside the lodge to accommodate roasting the deer, wild pig, two turkeys, and six geese that were brought by other hunters for the festivity. Twenty dozens of corn were husked and prepared for steaming. The children were given baskets to fill with all the wild berries they could find, while the older boys were sent out to hook as many trout as they could catch for smoking later.

The entire village offered Leluna their assistance because they knew that after the adoption, a wedding between Leslie and their chief would soon follow. When the sun finally set, the cooking fires were made ready and illuminated the entire area. Decorative fire poles with skins soaked in special oil were also ignited and set around the perimeter to keep the mosquitoes away.

Drums began to pound a rhythmic beat and flutes accompanied the merriment as the villagers shook their bodies in tune along with special ceremonial rattles and brightly colored pouches filled with shells.

Children and women swayed and danced to the beat as the men chided and chanted in unison in an outside circle behind them.

The men wore deerskin shirts, tailored with decorative quills and beads, strips of fur, and intertwined bark and corn husk.

The women and children had brightly colored bracelets, beads of pearls and copper adorning their necks, their own long breech cloths or deerskin dresses, skirts and tunics artfully sewn with designs representing their clan, and headbands of wampum.

Leslie received beautiful gifts from the women wrapped in fur or skins. Leluna gave her a brown leather drawstring pouch to carry her personal items, embroidered with porcupine quills, yellow and white beads, and iron bangles. Little Raven gave her a twelve-tined bone hair comb with the delicate carving of a man and woman representing her and Winnokin. Red Eagle gave her one of his prized Appaloosa mares for her own as well as a robe for the winter made from strips of beaver pelts.

When Red Eagle was done, he took Leslie by the hand and stood her in the center of the celebrants with him and raised his hands, requesting silence from the crowd.

Leslie looked around at the people before her, and her eyes rested upon the loving face of Winnokin. He looked so very handsome in his matching tunic and moccasins. The deerskin trousers he wore clung to his muscled thighs like a second skin, and the thought of him excited her.

Her heartbeat rapidly in her chest, and she wanted desperately to run into his arms.

"My friends," Red Eagle called out, drawing her attention, "the lodge of Red Eagle is pleased all you rejoice in our news to take this woman as daughter into our home."

The assemblage hooted and yelled their joy, and Leslie could not believe the depth of their excitement and acceptance of her and beamed happily.

"We also feel your joy, and our hearts have been warmed by the presence of this woman, Leslie, in our lodge," he continued. "Hear me, my brothers and sisters, as I speak for my family. It is with great happiness and pride Red Eagle accepts the woman Leslie as his daughter and has planned the adoption ceremony on the eve of the next full moon in four days' time."

Red Eagle turned Leslie to him and held her by her shoulders.

"From this day forward, let it be known that this woman will be named Leslie no more. Let my brothers and sisters now look upon the daughter of Red Eagle and Leluna, and may the Great Spirit bless this night and acknowledge the coming union of our chief and my daughter. From this day forward graciously accept her into our fold to be known as White Dove."

Leslie looked into Red Eagle's eyes, with the look of both astonishment and pride shining in her own.

Red Eagle drew her into his arms and kissed her forehead tenderly, while everyone cheered with joy around them in response to his proclamation.

They were immediately surrounded by everyone, and Leslie found herself embraced by Leluna, then Little Raven and Running Elk. Before she realized it, she was turned and held by a pair of strong arms and recognized Winnokin's masculine scent.

"The name White Dove suits you, Ishita. I am happy you have found great joy in the lodge of Red Eagle."

Leslie looked into his golden depths, and her heart skipped a beat.

"Oh, Winnokin! I have missed you so. It feels so wonderful to be in your arms."

"Yes, my love. I have missed your touch as well. I promise it will be much different between us once the ceremony is over."

Leslie laid her head upon his chest and could feel his heartbeat beneath her ear. She inhaled the smell of him and shuddered when he fondled the back of her neck with his hand.

She thought she would melt like a square of butter held over a flame from the warmth of his touch. She opened her eyes and noticed Red Eagle approaching. She smiled up at Winnokin but did not move from his embrace.

"What is this?" Red Eagle questioned with laughter gleaming in his eyes. "The minute I turn my back, a warrior tries to steal the heart of my beautiful daughter."

"I am afraid it is so, Red Eagle," Winnokin replied. He released his hold on Leslie. "My heart was pierced the very day she made her presence known to me in a vision."

Red Eagle looked at Leslie and winked. "And have you lost your heart as well to this warrior, my daughter?"

Leslie's smile was all the answer he needed.

Red Eagle grunted playfully as he rubbed his chin and surveyed the scene before him. He clasped Winnokin by the shoulder. "Then we must talk, warrior, you and I. I will decide if you are worthy of my daughter."

Winnokin looked at Leslie and winked before he turned and followed Red Eagle into her family's lodge.

Leslie's heart was full of joy as she watched them retreat.

"I would not be so sure of yourself, White Dove," Nuchzetse sneered cynically behind her. "You never know what might get in your way." She spat as she moved around to face her. "Anything can happen. Anything," she threatened with contempt and turned to walk away.

Leslie shivered and turned to search for Little Raven. She was not about to let Nuchzetse spoil her evening. She was just being a spiteful and jealous female. There was no way she would be stupid enough to make good her threats, Leslie reasoned. She did not get far when more of the villagers stopped her to express their happiness and well wishes. Leslie tried her best to remain jovial. The love being shown her was more than she could have ever dreamed of. For an entire village of hundreds, young and old, to be so accepting within such a short period of time was almost too much for her to comprehend. Why more of them did not share Nuchzetse's ideals was hard to believe. She knew the Seneca held sacred visions in the highest regard and being such a monumental part of their sachem's vision was more than enough proof to them she belonged in their lives. That is, except for Nuchzetse, who was being less virtuous and swayed by jealousy.

Leslie did not have much luck finding Little Raven. When she came upon Leluna standing beside one of the cooking fires, Leslie asked her if she knew where Little Raven had gone. Leluna informed her she had gone for a walk with her husband. Leslie told her new mother-to-be she was going to do the same since everyone was beginning to depart for the evening. She felt particularly lonely and a little despondent that Winnokin was not able to spend more time with her. She decided to head for the lake and walk along the shoreline. She knew the area was well patrolled and guarded and confident she would be safe all by herself.

It was the first time she had been totally alone since she came to the Seneca village. It felt almost awkward in a way. Every minute of her being had been worked into a lesson somehow; whatever she did, whatever she said, or wherever she went was given purpose and meaning. She almost forgot what it was like to stroll along in the still of the night, soft evening breezes whipping through her hair, carrying with it the fresh pine scent of the forest, and echoing the nightly songs of its inhabitants.

She never expected the life she was now living would turn out to be part of her destiny. When she thought of her life back in Hollow Pass, it seemed only a memory. She wondered how Shaun's parents were doing and hoped one day she could visit them and relay the truth to what happened and caused his death. His mother, Tessie, had been a great comfort to her when she first arrived. Grief for the loss of her husband and child was still so fresh in her heart like an open wound. Tessie had been a good friend and the mother she needed during a very devastating time in her life.

The old homestead flashed in her mind, and she ached to see her father but knew it would be a long time before their paths were to cross again. She questioned in her mind if he would appear to her. It had been quite some time since the last apparition. Strangely, it was almost like all the premonitions she experienced while traveling to this area had led up to the moment Winnokin came into her life. She remembered her father's last words and his expression of the happiness and joy she would find. How right he had been. She smiled to herself.

The land of the Seneca was now her home. The feeling of belonging with Winnokin's people grew stronger every day. It was something she desperately hoped to find again and needed to fill the empty void left by the many losses in her young life.

She turned and looked behind her, and the evening fires from the many lodges were still glowing brightly between the trees as they flickered in the night. When she looked to her right, their gold and orange flames reflected upon the calm, mirrored surface of the lake and Leslie felt at peace.

She tried to think what Winnokin, and Red Eagle were talking about. She expected Winnokin asked permission to court and spend time with her. If she remembered correctly, Little Raven told her a spouse had to be sought from outside one's clan and the new husband moved in with his wife's family. Having knowledge of the size of Red Eagle's lodge, she knew it could not accommodate another added family or provide the privacy a young married couple required. She made a mental note to ask Leluna when she got back.

What also puzzled her was the fact the Seneca demanded the women arrange the marriages, choosing generally a young man for an older, often widowed woman and an older man for a younger woman. It was their belief it had a great advantage of assuring the young people an experienced marriage partner, whereby a young bride was assured the security of an experienced hunter and successful warrior with status and position. A young groom had the plus of a partner wealthy in property and knowledge of parenthood and housekeeping.

Could it be respect for her own white customs, Leluna allowed Winnokin to seek permission for courting from Red Eagle instead as the dominant male figure in her life in place of her own father?

She sat down beside the water's edge and began to skip pebbles off its surface. It was hard to believe in less than four days, a formal ceremony would take place to change her life completely. She felt a little saddened about becoming a member of yet another family when the tragic loss of her natural one was so short lived. She knew Red Eagle, Leluna, and Little Raven had grown to love her. She prayed tragedy would not touch their lives once she became Seneca.

The faces of her father and mother flashed before her, and Leslie said a quiet prayer, vowing she would eternally love them and tell the children she would have with Winnokin all about the grandparents they would never see. Her life as a trapper's daughter was over. Her life as a Seneca was her new beginning. She promised herself to try her best to make it work and be happy.

 She rose and started to return to the village and stopped abruptly when she heard the soft seductive laughter of a woman coming from the edge of the trees. At first, she thought it might be Little Raven and Running Elk frolicking in the brush. She knew it was against Seneca law for a maiden to be sexually active with any man unless they planned marriage or were man and wife. She turned to move on and give them their deserved privacy but was forced to halt in her steps when the lover's conversation reached her ears.

"Do not fear me, great warrior. Let me ease your pain. Come closer to Nuchzetse."

Leslie scoffed at the maiden's words and moved closer. She was curious who the warrior was and practiced her newly taught skills as she quietly moved through the brush. The warrior's back was to her, and she could not see his face. It was clear Nuchzetse saw Leslie looking on.

The interruption did not falter her actions but rather fed her hunger. She acted more provocative, grinding her hips against the warrior's groin as she clung to him. She sent Leslie a wicked smile as the warrior bent to kiss the curve of Nuchzetse's neck.

Leslie turned and walked away in disgust. It was no concern of hers what the evil woman did as long as it was not with Winnokin or Running Elk. Leslie knew she had every right by Seneca law to disclose what she saw to the elders. Little Raven had told her such an offense could be punishable by banishment if it was a repeated offense. It could even result in losing the tip of a finger.

Leslie smiled, relishing the thought. She shook her head, knowing she could not be as cruel and did not even know who the warrior was. Still, she thought it best to confide in Little Raven. Leslie did not trust Nuchzetse since she displayed no fear at being caught at all.

When she reached her lodge, she found Little Raven was visiting with her brother's wife, Metsume, who had fallen ill earlier in the evening.

Leslie decided to walk to Moon Stalker and Metsume's lodge to wait for Little Raven. She was afraid Leluna would read her troubling thoughts and be forced to respectfully answer any questions asked of her.

Absorbed in her own thoughts, Leslie paid no attention to where she was going until she absently rammed into the solid bare chest of a warrior. The impact took her totally by surprise and sent her flying backwards. Before she fell to the ground, she was caught by the waist and looking into Winnokin's eyes and smiling face.

The electricity that passed between them was overwhelming. Winnokin scooped her into his powerful arms and trotted off with her into the trees.

Once protected behind the cover of limbs and foliage, his lips came down upon hers in a ravishing kiss that made her dizzy.

She returned his heated kisses with an urgency of her own, and Winnokin moaned with desire. The strength of his arms held her close, and when his hand slid beneath her dress and caressed the soft mound between her legs, Leslie thought madness took control of her senses.

Winnokin lowered her slightly and held her firmly against the trunk of a huge birch tree, grasping her round buttocks in his hands. She wrapped her legs about his waist and clung to his shoulders while their tongues teased each other passionately.

She could feel him harden against her, and she automatically moved her body rhythmically against him.

Winnokin followed her lead and rotated in unison. The sensation caused throbbing spasms to course through them, and their moans were softly muted by the passion of their kisses.

Their bodies shuddered collectively as the intensity of their kisses grew. He lowered himself to the ground with her tightly enfolded within his arms.

He was amazed by how pacified he felt, even though he had not penetrated her. He caressed her hair and felt exhilarated as his hands glided over her soft skin. The strong scent of pine filled his nostrils as she nuzzled even closer. He led a trail of kisses beginning at her ear and running the length of her neck, and she purred liked a contented kitten.

Leslie turned in his arms, and her eyes shown with the love she felt for him.

"How I crave you, my love. You make me feel like the most beautiful woman." She sighed as she kissed him long and tender.

Winnokin cupped her breasts and kneaded each nipple through her doeskin tunic.

"You are every bit of a woman, Ishita, a woman, who drives her warrior mad." He returned her kiss and rolled her onto her back and stretched himself atop her. "I am glad our paths have crossed. I was on my way to your lodge. Where were you headed in such a hurry?"

Leslie had to stop and think. She almost forgot about her plan to wait and talk with Little Raven. She did not want to say anything to Winnokin about Nuchzetse until she spoke with Little Raven first.

"I was going to wait for Little Raven at Moon Stalker's. I too am glad we crossed paths." She smiled, caressing his cheek, and nipping at his bottom lip with her teeth. "Did you have something to tell me?"

Winnokin smiled and kissed her nose before he rolled off her and onto his back. Leslie turned to her side and leaned on her elbow as she looked down at him, waiting for his reply.

"Ya. Red Eagle has given his blessing for us to court. I was on my way to tell you. It was Leluna who agreed to let me ask in the tradition of your custom. She knew it would please you."

Leslie sat up and clapped her hands with glee before she threw herself atop Winnokin and smothered him with kisses.

Winnokin laughed and tumbled Leslie beneath him playfully.

"It pleases me Red Eagle's decision has made you happy," he jested. "I do not have to ask then if this is your wish."

"You know you do not, you rogue." She tickled him.

Winnokin clasped her wrists and held them above her head. "Tell me anyways, Ishita. How much it pleases you to court with Winnokin?"

Leslie's eyes took on a dreamy state as they glazed with emotion.

"I do not think my heart can hold any more joy. It will surely break from the happiness I feel, my darling."

"I will make you happy, Ishita. You will never want for anything again." He released her arms and drew her even closer and sealed his vow with a kiss that told of much more to come.

Chapter Eighteen

Leslie awoke early the next morning, anxious to begin tanning the flawless white doe skin Running Elk and Winnokin had given her as a gift to use for her ceremonial dress.

Since she only had four days to finish the project, she needed to begin the process right away and did so with joyous anticipation.

The procedure was a tedious one and proved to be somewhat gruesome from the start, until she could accustom herself to the smell and feel of the texture in her hands.

The tanning was done with the brain of a dear mingled with moss and formed into a cake-like soap. With backbreaking pressure, she had to discard the hair and grain of the skin with a stone scraper. It was a very long and weary routine that made every muscle in her upper body burn and strained her previously injured shoulder.

Little Raven scolded her repeatedly throughout the morning to rest and set the task aside for a while. But Leslie refused Little Raven's attempts to persuade her.

Little Raven offered to help Leslie with as many of her chores as she could manage on top of her own. She knew the sooner Leslie finished her dress, the quicker the ceremony could be held. She could not blame her, because Little Raven remembered only two short years ago, she was rushing to complete the same task to be Running Elk's wife.

Leslie was adamant about completing the task in time and was afraid that if she dawdled, she would not accomplish what she set out to do.

After she boiled the cake of soap in water, she soaked the skin for a few hours and wrung it out then stretched it on the rack until it dried in the afternoon sun and became pliable. Each side of the skin was smoked until the skin pores closed entirely and became thoroughly toughened. When the task was executed, she cut the style to suit her frame and meticulously quilled a pattern befitting a Seneca maiden.

She thought about a pattern long and hard and collected all the necessary color beads she would need. What she did not have she bartered and begged for, but all the women were kind and generous and gave whatever supply they had to give.

When she began to work the beads and quills into the soft texture of her new shift, she did so alone to keep her outfit a surprise. Leslie took special care with her sewing because she knew her ceremonial garment would also act as her wedding dress. To give it a unique look for her special day, she managed to cut away enough material for a vest, which she would sew later with matching slippers for her feet.

Once she was finished, she sat in awe as she inspected the completed project laid out before her. She felt such tremendous pride for her beautiful workmanship accomplished in so short a time. The skin had worked into the purest white she had ever seen, with a satiny sheen and soft as the petals of a flower.

The yoke was slightly rounded and beaded with two rows of soft green quills, which would enhance the color of her eyes. There was no other color above the waistline, but the skirt stood out in splendid galore.

It was a simple masterpiece with a culmination of color and technique. Remembering Winnokin's vision, she depicted the scene with a skillful array of colors and displayed the heavens with a massive white lone star in its center. Among the heavens was sewn the image of a golden dove, with its wings open wide in flight. Beyond the dove was a multitude of tiny stars, radiating their brilliant light that led a path for the dove to follow.

Leslie's heart welled with pride when she took the garment back to her lodge to show her new family. They gasped openly in awe of her craftsmanship and were hypnotized by her interpretation and accuracy of their chief's vision.

Her two days of painstaking hard work had paid off. The many hours her fingers bled and blistered until she got use to the work was well worth the looks of admiration on their faces and their words of praise.

She left the lodge as though she were riding atop a cloud, thrilled by the exultation she received. Slowly, she walked the path that led to the bathing area, humming happily to herself and feeling so loved.

She stripped away her clothing and dove swiftly into the water with the sleekness of an otter. She knew the other women were not expected until later in the day, and she enjoyed her time alone immensely. She closed her eyes and stretched out upon her back, drifting naturally with the current, letting the cool waters relax her aching muscles. Beads of water glistened upon her silken skin, which was tanned to a soft mahogany. She felt completely at ease, somnolent and dreamy as she listened to the pacifying sounds of the forest around her.

She thought about how much her life had changed over the past few months, and it was hard to believe her future held such promise. Thinking back to the first moment she met

Winnokin, the realization he had been the stranger haunting her dreams was so obvious now. The length and style of his hair, his regal and muscular physique had been so clearly defined. It was ironic how something so dreamlike could prove so real in time. Any other woman would have been terrified waking from an injury such as the one she experienced to find an Indian standing over them, she laughed to herself. But when she first laid her eyes on his magnificence, she knew in her heart he was not a man to be feared but, one she would come to know and love. She smiled to herself, relishing the thought of how much they were already acquainted and could not wait until they could make love completely and not hold back.

A pebble instantly popped onto her belly and rolled into the crevice of her belly button. Leslie jumped with a start and quickly submerged to hide her nakedness. She spun about in all directions, looking amongst the rocks, boulders, and trees for the culprit who threw it there. Perched atop a boulder jutting out over the water above her was Winnokin with a mischievous grin upon his face.

"If the man I love finds you here gaping openly at his woman, you will smile no more warrior, I assure you," she larked and turned to swim toward shore.

Winnokin watched intently, and the blood in his veins began to boil with desire. "What brave dares to claim you as his, White Dove?" he barked. "Let him show his face, and Winnokin will show him the error of his ways!"

Leslie moved seductively as she waded from the water, teasing as her curvaceous hips swayed in front of him. Winnokin's breath caught in his chest, and his heart raced wildly. She turned around to let him take in the sight of her fully and smiled.

"You cannot have what you take for granted. I tire waiting for you, and think I may look for another," she toyed.

Winnokin jumped from the abutment in an instant and closed the distance between them and encircled her waist with his arms, drawing her snug against him.

"Do not say such things, even in jest, my love. I would kill any man who would dare to take you from me."

She ran her finger down his cheek and slowly along his full bottom lip. "I only toy with you, darling," she cooed. "My heart beats for only you." She lowered her lips and kissed his bare chest tenderly then slowly back up to his chin. "I have missed you terribly this past month."

"I know it has been hard on you, White Dove. But it has also been so for me. I tried to make it easier by not walking the same paths you did or entering a lodge you occupied. I had to be strong for both of us," he replied as he stroked her hair.

Leslie sighed and nestled her head on his chest and wrapped her arms about his lean waist.

"Still, it has been so hard. I do not think I can wait any longer."

Winnokin raised her chin and gazed into her eyes. "It will not be long. That is why I am here. To bring you good news."

Leslie's eyes lit with excitement. "What good news?"

"Tomorrow, following the rising of the new sun, the lodge of Red Eagle will adopt you as their daughter. As soon as it is so, I will abound your lodge with many gifts. They will be great, and Red Eagle will not refuse me when I ask that we be joined." He smiled.

Leslie squealed exuberantly and covered his face in kisses.

"Enough, woman!" he scolded playfully as he held her at arm's length. "You must dress and return to your lodge. There is much to prepare before the sun rises tomorrow."

Leslie curtsied regally before him. "Yes, my chief." She chuckled.

When she rose and turned, Winnokin swatted her bare behind soundly, and she jumped with a start. She turned and stuck out her tongue as she rubbed her stinging bottom.

Winnokin chuckled at her spunkiness and headed back toward the village.

Leslie hummed softly to herself as she finished drying and dressing. She could not contain her happiness and excitement that her adoption ceremony had been moved ahead of schedule. She began to waltz about in tune to a romantic melody that played in her head, and her heart sang in unison. She made a full spin with her arms open wide and her head flung back. Her golden wet waves fanned out behind her in midair and glistened in the sunlight.

And in an instant, chills riddled her body and she instantly tremored. Her arms crossed automatically, and she hugged her chest. Leslie felt as though a heavy weight lay against her chest and a rush of heat coursed through her veins, and her entire body began to perspire. It was not like when she dreamed. This was a feeling she knew all too well when she was awake. It was a warning, like an alarm was going off inside of her ... a sense of danger.

She turned slowly in a full circle and scanned the area, looking for something, someone, knowing her instincts were correct. She felt uncomfortable and was certain she was being watched and quickly moved in the direction of the village. But her warning did not come soon enough, as she stopped abruptly when Nuchzetse stepped into the open with a look of hatred that made Leslie's heart skip with fear.

The maiden's delicate features were hardened by the apparent loathing and contempt she felt toward Leslie.

"Think you have won, White Dove?" she jeered.

Leslie dropped her arms to her sides and slowly shook her head.

"Won? Oh, but I have. Winnokin loves me, and there is nothing you can do about it. And besides, you were hiding in the bushes, which is what you do very well. So, you had to hear him. Why even ask?"

Leslie moved to walk past her but, Nuchzetse blocked her way.

"I ... am ... not ... done ... with you, white dog! Our chief is blinded by your hair of gold. You are not Seneca! You will never be Seneca! I am what he needs." Nuchzetse pounded her chest. "I! Not you!"

Leslie slowly moved two steps backwards. "I am not your enemy, Nuchzetse. You are a beautiful woman who could win the heart of any warrior. You know of Winnokin's vision. We have been destined to be together. How can you question the will of your Great Spirit? It is his choice. You have no cause to question him or reason to hate me as much as you do."

Nuchzetse hesitated as she digested the truth of Leslie's words and stared at her with large, lifeless eyes.

Leslie moved slightly, but Nuchzetse side-stepped her and drew a dagger from her waist band. She gazed at the four-inch blade and swallowed hard. She raised her hand, not in defense but to try and dissuade her.

"This will accomplish nothing, Nuchzetse. It will only get you banished and bring shame to your family. Do not do this. I will forget this has happened. I want to be your friend. Nuchzetse ... please ... please put away your knife."

Nuchzetse's look was venomous. "Friends? You ask that after what you have taken from me?"

"How can I take away what was never yours to have? Think about what you are saying. Know what will happen to you if any harm comes to me," Leslie replied softly.

Nuchzetse's head snapped to the side as though she were punched by some unseen force.

Leslie took another step back as she watched a maniacal change occur before her.

Nuchzetse began to snarl with teeth clenched. Her body shook with uncontrollable tremors, and her knuckles turned white as she raised her knife to strike a deadly blow. "If I cannot have him, then neither will you," she screamed as she plunged the knife forward.

Leslie moved quickly to the side, but the blade skinned the side of her arm. Immediately she side-stepped Nuchzetse's next jab and crouched low to the ground and rolled away from the deadly swish that passed her ear. Leslie knew Nuchzetse was past the point of reasoning. She had no choice but to combat with the woman and try to defend herself until either someone happened along, she was killed, or she managed to disarm her attacker. Leslie reached for the garter under her dress, which held her own knife sheath. She drew out her blade and comfortably rolled it in her right hand, confident she could defend herself. Her father had taught her well on how to use a knife. She never ever expected it would be against another woman.

They performed a warrior's dance, circling each other, watching each other's moves, the change in expression and body language definite and intense. Leslie refused to strike out and was successful deflecting the lethal blows sent in her direction. It was not her intention to maim or kill Nuchzetse. The adrenalin pumped through her veins at an accelerated rate. It seemed as if the woodlands grew silent around them. All she could hear was her own breathing. Her sight funneled around her assailant and blocked out everything else as she focused intensely on her every movement.

Leslie's ability to react was heightened to the point of preciseness as she fought to hold onto her life. Her palms grew slick with perspiration. She was afraid she would lose her grasp and drop her knife to the ground. She could hear her own pulse thumping in her ears, and she swallowed nervously. She had to keep her control, stay focused, or her life would cease to exist. She had to be more cunning. She needed to stay alert, and her eyes became as sharp as an eagle's as she watched her attacker's every move.

Nuchzetse dove for the ground and plunged forward, slicing Leslie's right calf and then her left as she rolled over continuously out of the way.

 Leslie felt warm blood trickle down her legs. It was obvious Nuchzetse was intent on inflicting as many wounds as possible to weaken her. This is ridiculous, she thought. If I continue with the nice attitude, I will be sliced like the slaughtered meat I dry on my racks.

Leslie waited for the proper opening and kicked out swiftly at Nuchzetse's right knee with the sole of her foot and heard it snap.

Nuchzetse fell to the ground, grimacing in pain, and her dagger flew from her hand. She tried to drag herself forward and reach out for it. To no avail, Leslie managed to kick it out of her way. Nuchzetse cried openly as she clutched her dislocated knee.

It bothered Leslie to see her in such pain, and she knelt beside her. "Let me help you, Nuchzetse. We will go to the shaman and tell him you took a fall."

Nuchzetse responded with her fist and sent a hard blow to Leslie's cheek, reeling her sideways to the ground. "That is what I think of your help." She growled vehemently and dragged herself forward with a speed that surprised even Leslie.

Leslie rubbed her cheek as she rose to move forward. She halted when Strong of Heart appeared from the bushes and raised his hand for her to stop.

Nuchzetse did not see him as she continued to drag herself backward along the ground, a devilish sneer etched upon her face.

Leslie watched as she moved closer to where Strong of Heart stood behind Nuchzetse and shivered slightly knowing what the outcome would be. He stood straight and reserved, arms crossed, feet shoulder length apart. His eyes were hard and emotionless as they watched Nuchzetse move closer.

Leslie's heart skipped in her chest when Nuchzetse turned to reach out for her dagger and touched Strong of Heart's leg trouser instead.

Nuchzetse gasped loudly and jumped with fright as her head snapped around. Here hand flew to her mouth as she peered up and locked eyes with the person standing before her. Fear registered on her face as she reared backwards in shocked disbelief.

"Is this how a Seneca treats one of their own?" Strong of Heart bellowed.

Nuchzetse hung her head in shame and avoided his gaze.

"You have dishonored your family and our people with your vile words of hate and sinful actions. The council will decide your fate this night." Strong of Heart picked up the dagger at his feet and walked around Nuchzetse.

He approached Leslie and saw her many injuries. "Come, White Dove. We will see to your injuries," he said tenderly as he grasped her elbow and led her away.

She turned to look at Nuchzetse and noticed her whimpering as two warriors moved from the cover of the trees, grasped her by her forearms, and dragged her away in the opposite direction. Leslie gazed at Winnokin's grandfather and opened her mouth to speak, but he did not give her the opportunity to do so.

"Nuchzetse is no longer your concern. I watched. I heard. You gave her every chance. Now, her fate is in the hands of the elders."

Leslie stopped and turned to look at the handsome elder. "How did you know, Grandfather, what was taking place?"

"A maiden saw Nuchzetse watching you from the bushes. She knew there would be trouble and came to seek help. I was the first she saw."

Leslie bowed her head. "I know you are right, Grandfather. But still, I cannot feel great sadness for her. It is such a waste."

Chapter Nineteen

Leluna thought it would be best to delay the adoption ceremony for a few days considering what happened and to give Leslie's wounds time to heal.

Leslie argued until she was winded, trying to dissuade her stepmother's decision. Except for the bruise on her cheek and superficial lacerations on her calves, she felt fine. Her stepmother clucked at her stubbornness and commented how much she resembled Red Eagle and his own willful stubbornness and how she would fit just fine into their family.

 The ceremony was delayed until later evening to give them time to prepare. Messengers were sent to every household to notify them of the change. Her Ceremony of Adoption was going to be a simple affair in Seneca terms. Only the Hawk Clan members would be in attendance, which numbered nearly two hundred and those individuals her family wanted to personally invite.

Since Nuchzetse's family were members of the same clan, Leslie insisted they not be chastised for the deed of their daughter and wished not to show any ill-will against them.

Leluna commented how Leslie already acted with the true heart of a Seneca and the wisdom she was showing as their chief's future wife. Once they entered the counsel lodge, she searched the faces of the people who were already there. She glanced upon Nuchzetse's parents. When her mother, Willow, gazed upon Leslie, she smiled openly and bowed her head in respect. Leslie went to her and took the woman into her arms and hugged her fiercely. She was glad she extended the invitation to them.

Willow was a kind and generous woman. Her husband, Fast Arrow, was a highly respected warrior. They could not be held responsible for what their daughter had done, especially when she was a grown woman and accountable for her own actions.

Leslie asked Little Raven if she knew what became of Nuchzetse before the ceremony officially began. She was surprised to learn the decision had already been made for her to be transported to the village of their brother tribe, the Oneida, farther to the North.

Nuchzetse left shortly before dawn and guarded by a small hunting party. She would not be allowed to return home until a marriage had taken place and the birth of her first born. She also learned that the Oneida tribal chief would decide what family Nuchzetse would live with. Either one who had no daughter, an older member whose elderly spouse needed help with daily chores or placed up for a bridal auction to let his warriors bid amongst themselves.

Little Raven told Leslie she felt strongly the latter would not take place. Nuchzetse would be too resentful, even outwardly disobedient considering her present frame of mind. It had been her parents' wish, given some time that their daughter would fall in love naturally with someone and create a happy life amongst the Oneida.

When the ceremony began, it was a little hard for Leslie to understand, since she did not completely know the entire Seneca language. It still seemed to her like a longwinded address. She was given the name Ga-geh-ant Je-da-o, White Dove, and made an official member of Red Eagle's Hawk Clan.

Formally, she was introduced to her brother, mother, sister, and cousins and felt secure for the first time in a very long while. The ceremony took place in the council house located in the center of the village. The address mentioned the reason for the adoption, the name of the clan, and the persons adopting her.

Strong of Heart escorted her along with Swift of Feet, Running Elk's brother. Together they walked up and down the length of the lodge. The elders held Leslie by the arms and chanted the song of adoption as they marched, and the onlookers responded in musical accord at the end of each verse. At the end of the third lap around the lodge, the song and march ceased together.

The initiation was followed by a dance, which Leslie participated in, partnered with her new brother-in-law, Running Elk. She felt extremely awkward until she finally caught on to the beat. For the first time, her ears were regaled by Indian music. Two young men were seated on opposite sides of a drum, which looked like a nail keg, and they pounded violently with sticks as an accompaniment to the most discordant howling.

The performance had a novelty all its own, as they had no conception of musical intervals. However, the timing was exceptional and their dancing quite animated and entertaining. The atmosphere was totally different from the dinner celebration two nights before. The dancing then had been unique, and no one had sung.

 Leslie was amused and realized Winnokin's people were far from being considered songbirds. She sat down to rest and swayed to the beat of the drums. She closed her eyes, and her body relaxed to the rhythm of the music. She sensed someone standing behind her and knew that it was her beloved when she looked over at Little Raven and she winked at her. She decided to tease him a little and could not help smiling to herself. She began to sway seductively to the music, and her hair moved in soft billows as it swished and swayed about her shoulders.

Winnokin moved around to face her, and her body movements stirred his heart.

Leslie carefully peaked through the cracks of her eyelids, and she noticed the effect she had on him, as she could see the bulge beneath his loin cloth apron.

With the swiftness of a mountain cat, Winnokin scooped her into his arms and swung her over his broad shoulders in one quick sweep.

She shrieked with surprise and felt her cheeks burn with embarrassment. Everyone around them began to chuckle with amusement and applauded his actions. She kicked and hollered, but her attempts to be set free were ignored and fell upon deaf ears.

"Let me down, you big ox!" she screamed. "How dare you drag me off like a sack of potatoes. You put me down, Winnokin, or, I will ... I will ... "

It did not matter how loudly she squealed, for the villagers were out of sight. Winnokin patted her backside playfully and laughed merrily as he strolled through the compound and out the front gates.

Eventually Leslie ceased her tirade, and when they came upon the lake, she lifted herself up and momentarily wondered why they were there. Before she could question his actions, Winnokin tossed her off his shoulder and flung her out into the water. Leslie squealed in disbelief and landed with a large splash. When she broke through the surface, she sputtered water from her mouth and began to shriek obscenities at him as he stood at the water's edge with a devilish smile upon his face.

His perfect white teeth shone in the moonlight, and he chuckled loudly with his arms crossed at his chest. As he squatted on his hind legs, he sent a pebble to ripple across the surface of the lake.

"I thought White Dove needed to cool off before my warriors lost control of themselves."

She did not reply as she rose before him, looking like a drowned cat. Two can play the same game, she thought. She pretended to try and move in her water-logged attire as it weighed her down. She faked losing her balance and let out a howl as she grasped her back, pretending to be in pain.

Winnokin's smile froze on his face and faded quickly when he heard her whimper. He rose quickly and dove into the cool water, surfacing beside her. "I am sorry, White Dove. Did I hurt you?" He tenderly petted her hair. His body trembled slightly in the cool night air.

Leslie smiled to herself and slowly raised her head to meet his gaze. "It is all right, " she replied as she caressed his cheek with the palm of her hand. "I know you did not mean to hurt me."

Leslie pushed his chest with all her might, and he lost his footing, sailing backwards into the water. When his face broke the surface, she blurted out, "If anyone needs cooling off, great warrior, it is you, to quell what hardens beneath your cloth." She giggled as she ran from the water.

Before she could reach the shore, Winnokin was upon her and lifted her into his arms. He ran with her to shore where he rolled with her in the grass, and they laughed and kissed each other playfully. Winnokin pinned her beneath him and held her arms molded to her side. As she tried to squirm free, her breasts rose above the neckline of her dress and Winnokin lowered his head, using his tongue to outline a trail of fire along the white mounds exposed before him.

Leslie gasped at his touch and could feel a throbbing pulsate between her thighs.

"You take my breath away, Ishita. I must have you before I go mad," he rasped.

Winnokin kissed the scar above her eye, and slowly his lips brushed her cheek and the outline of her neck. He nipped the lobe of her ear, and she moaned with desire. Their lips found each other. What started as a tender unity soon turned to a much deeper hunger, making them want and crave even more.

Leslie met his kisses with an urgency of her own, her wanton need of him equally matched.

Winnokin's hands cupped the fullness of an exposed breast, and he rotated his thumb over its hardened nipple.

She moved beneath him, rotating her hips, and molded to the length of him. She could feel his hardness press against her, and she moved her hand beneath and stroked him slowly.

"I love the way a man feels when he hungers for his woman," she said.

Leslie's lips glided over the contours of his face, and her fingers worked at the braids of his hair and entwined in the thick, black wetness as it fanned out over his broad, muscled shoulders.

Being this close to him was nothing like the degrading encounter she experienced with Red Farmer. She knew she wanted him, needed him, and craved him completely.

"Love me ... please, my darling! Please make me yours now," she pleaded. "I do not think I can endure the fire that burns inside me much longer." Her eyes were deep pools of desire and sparkled like crystals.

Winnokin kissed her ardently and then rolled to his side and pulled her atop him. "My heart is full, White Dove. But I vowed that only when Strong of Heart joins us as husband and wife will I then take you to my bed. Only then will I quench the fire that burns between us."

As much as his words were disappointing, she knew arguing with him would do no good.

"Then you must speak with Strong of Heart and ask he perform the ceremony right away. I cannot wait, Winnokin. Please."

Winnokin rose and lifted her with him, wrapping his arms about her.

"I will do so and speak to him tonight. Before we part, there is something I must do ... "

He knelt upon one knee and took her hands in his. He kissed the tip of each finger softly and turned her palms over and placed a tender kiss there as well. When he looked up into her smiling face, his eyes glistened with tears, and he cleared his throat.

"White Dove, will you become my wife? I cannot offer those things you are used to in your world. I believe your god and mine are one and the same and decided our destiny's long before we were given life. I offer all that I am, all that I have, until our hearts no longer beat."

Leslie's eyes began to overflow with joyful tears, and she knelt in front of him. Her hand shook as she brushed her fingers over his high cheekbones and traced the outline of his jaw and the sensual fullness of his lips.

"Without you, I am nothing. With you I am everything. I want nothing more than to live forever as your woman and your wife."

Their lips embraced, sealing the commitment they vowed to each other and then they rose.

Together they walked back to the village in silence, caught up in their own blissful thoughts. Winnokin searched out Little Raven and found her sitting beside Running Elk in front of their lodge. They signed their welcome, and Winnokin held out his hand for her to rise.

She did so without question and looked at Leslie and knew what had passed between them. A gentle smile spread across her lips, and Little Raven touched Winnokin's shoulder lightly. She knew what he would ask of her, and her eyes answered before he spoke.

 "I will be glad to teach my sister, White Dove, what she needs to know," she spoke. "Hear me, my leader ... she will not be given away cheaply. If you wish to join with my sister, the bride price will be high. The women in my lodge are valued for their many talents, are they not, my husband?" she jested as she turned and winked at Running Elk.

Running Elk could barely stifle his amusement. He rose and encircled Little Raven's petite waist with his arms and happily replied.

"My wife speaks the truth, my friend. Her talents are many, and she proves them time and again." He kissed the crook of Little Raven's neck playfully. "I offer you my help in obtaining such a bride price. I'm sure you will need it." He chuckled.

Little Raven took Leslie by the hand and drew her toward the lodge and spoke loud enough to be heard.

"Do not worry, my sister. Little Raven will teach you all you need to know."

Winnokin chuckled happily. "If I truly did not need your help, your chief would take great pleasure in finding a suitable punishment for you, little one."

Chapter Twenty

Word spread quickly amongst the villagers of Winnokin and Running Elk's quest to obtain a great bride price for White Dove. The air was filled with joyous anticipation for their return, for they expected it to be nothing less than spectacular. Runners were sent out to the neighboring Iroquois tribes to announce the upcoming marriage between Winnokin, war leader and sachem of the Seneca, and Gagehant Jedao, daughter of Red Eagle, sub-chief of the Hawk Clan.

Everyone found themselves caught up in the festive activities of preparing foods for the coupling and the gifts they would award the bride and groom. Leslie's hours were filled with readying herself for marriage, and she did not think it possible to complete it all in time for the ceremony. Because Winnokin was a tribal Sachem, makeshift lodging had to be constructed outside the walls of the stockade to accommodate the visitors expected from the league: the tribal chief, sub-chief, and war leaders of the Cayuga, Oneida, Onondaga, and Mohawk nations, as well as the chiefs of their neighbors the Delaware and Algonquin.

Leslie worked on her vest to coordinate with the adoption dress she had sewn. Because she did not have time to think up a suitable pattern, she decided to cover the front panels in a rainbow pattern of green, yellow, red, and blue beads. She added a double row of yellow, red, and blue quills around the rounded neckline of her dress to coincide with her jacket and decided to quill a simple star on the top of each moccasin.

Little Raven gave Leslie beautifully designed knee-length white moccasins for when the weather turned cold.

Leslie hugged her in a fierce embrace, and her eyes misted with tears.

"You are the sister I never had and always wanted, Little Raven. I cannot believe this is finally happening. I cannot express how much you mean to me, not only for taking me into your heart but teaching me everything I needed to know about your people, your language, your customs, and so much more. Hineaweh. (Thank you), my sister."

Leluna stepped forward and offered her daughter special gifts as well. Wrapped in soft rabbit fur was a pair of silver earrings and finger rings encrusted with a star and half-moon. In a separate wrapping was a delicate string of green beads with a matching headband to set off her large eyes.

Leslie clutched the gifts to her breast and cried softly.

Leluna petted her cheek and tenderly placed a kiss upon it.

"Hineaweh, my mother. I will cherish and wear them and think of you with the greatest of love."

Leslie had a difficult time sleeping that evening. She expected Winnokin's return by bedtime, but he did not show. She started to get squeamish and wondered if he had fallen prey to their enemy the Huron. There had not been any repercussions over the two scouts massacred, who had accompanied Red Farmer during his killing spree. Maybe their tribe wanted to wait until Winnokin's guard was down, she feared. What sweeter revenge than a surprise attack upon him while he was out collecting his bride price, she thought.

She sighed deeply and moved quietly outside so as not to disturb her family. She gazed up at the sky, and her eyes scanned the heavens. What she really questioned was her own insecurity. Was happiness in her future? Her life had evolved into such a magnificent love story. Every woman dreamed from the time they were a little girl to fall madly in love with a handsome man. She had been blessed twice. She felt comforted by the serenity the night offered. She could see the silhouette of two guards in the distance, posted above a ledge that looked out over the corn fields.

The Bear Clan warriors did an excellent job taking turns every seven moons to act as sentries at various posts around the perimeter, protecting the village from raiders of opposing tribes. She could barely distinguish the stockade that encompassed the village on all three sides from where she was sitting, but she knew it was there.

One section where no stockade appeared was protected by an impenetrable wall rock, which plummeted to a sheer drop on the other side to the lake below. It made an excellent vantage point for the guards to keep watch. Just in order for them to reach their post, they had to pull themselves up hand-over-hand by a rope interwoven with sinew and secured in double lengths above.

Inasmuch as the nearest enemy tribe was over two weeks travel away, Winnokin made sure daily patrols went out each morning before sunrise to scan the entire area, an area that spanned a three-hour trek. It was an added precaution, and his warriors were always alert, ready to strike, ready to protect their homeland and their people.

Leslie heard someone stir within the lodge and smiled when Little Raven appeared with a light robe draped around her shoulders.

"Are you ill, my sister?" she asked. She reached out and touched Leslie's forehead with the back of her hand.

"No. I am fine, my sister. I cannot sleep, that is all." Leslie shrugged.

Little Raven smiled as she sat down beside her and cuddled her shoulder to Leslie's as she drew the robe around them both.

"I too could not sleep the eve before I was to join with Running Elk. They will be home soon, White Dove. I say after the sun is high in the sky. You will see." She bumped against her playfully.

Their heads touched tenderly as they listened to the peaceful sounds of the night. An owl hooted in the distance, and frogs croaked their evening serenade as they floated upon the lily pads in the nearby lake.

"Do you worry every time Running Elk must leave the village?"

"Ya, I do." Little Raven nodded. "I swear my heart stops beating until my eyes gaze upon him once more when he returns. It is our way and has always been so."

"Is married life as wonderful in your custom as it is in ours?" Little Raven asked.

"Um. More, I think. As a people we cherish every breath, every sound and touch. We take nothing for granted. The best part," Little Raven chuckled, "is falling asleep and waking up in the arms of the man you love."

"Oh, I think you lie, my sister," Leslie teased. "I have a feeling there is something you are not sharing with me."

The two of them tried to stifle their giggles so as not to awaken Leluna and Red Eagle. They wrapped their arms around each other and looked up at the twinkling stars overhead.

"We are lucky, you and I, White Dove. We have both been blessed with the love of a great warrior."

"Ya, Little Raven. We are blessed, and I cannot wait until they return to us."

The following day, moments after sunrise, a commotion was building outside Red Eagle's lodge. When Leslie arose to peer out the doorway, she was motioned away by her father and told to remain in the dwelling until someone told her otherwise. She obeyed respectfully with giddy excitement and felt as though a thousand butterflies danced inside her stomach. It was apparent that Winnokin and Running Elk had returned and were displaying at that very moment the gifts he brought to offer for her hand in marriage.

Little Raven helped her to dress into something appropriate, and Leluna began to brush her long, golden tresses and work them into a braid. They waited patiently by her side as Red Eagle wagered with Winnokin.

Leslie could hear the excited exclamations and sighs of the villagers, and she could not sustain her intense impatience as each moment passed. She paced back and forth, and her animations proved entertaining for her sister and mother, who chuckled and remarked gaily.

"Oh, shush you two!" Leslie turned and scolded. "One would think they were bargaining for a side of beef! I will go mad if father does not decide soon!"

She wrung her hands nervously over and over as she continued to pace about the lodge. Little Raven interpreted for Leluna the words Leslie ranted in English, bringing more giggles from them both.

"You two are quite a pair, you know. This is not fair, Mother." She stomped her foot. "Is it to be yes, or no? Why do they barter so long?"

Leluna spoke calmly as she sat down beside the fire pit.

"You are held in the highest regard, my daughter. Your father will not go easy on Winnokin. But do not fear. With Running Elk's help these past two days, your father will not be able to deny the gifts they have brought for you and the family. This much I know." Leluna smiled and nodded.

With that spoken, Red Eagle called out.

"Gagehand Jedao. Ese anke ho! (White Dove, you come now.)"

Leslie leaped for the door, and Little Raven stepped in front to block her exit. "Do not appear so willing, my sister. Let Winnokin wait and think you are still deciding."

"Are you crazy?" Leslie squealed. "I have waited too long and do not intend to torture either one of us for another moment!"

Little Raven held her ground and Leluna joined her.

"If you run in haste, my daughter, Winnokin will think you will jump at his every word." She interjected.

Leslie considered Leluna's words and found them to be wise and nodded.

"You are both right. I am sorry. My heart is most anxious. I will let him stew for a few more minutes."

"Stew?" Leluna questioned. "What has food got to do with it?"

Leslie burst out laughing, shaking her head. "No ... not stew as in food, Mother. It is a white saying meaning to wait ... make him wait."

The puzzled look on Leluna's face made Leslie chuckle more, and she moved forward to hug her.

"I know, Mother. We whites are a strange breed. Do not trouble over trying to understand us."

Leslie stood with them as they all held hands and Leluna spoke a short prayer, asking for the Great Spirit's blessing. Her heart pounded frantically in her chest and threatened to burst wide open. The time had finally come, she thought. Winnokin waits just outside my door to openly proclaim his love for me.

They waited for her name to be called out one more time, and Leslie followed behind as Leluna and Little Raven exited the lodge. As she walked into the bright morning sunlight, Leslie noticed the entire village had turned out to witness the exchange between Winnokin and Red Eagle. She blushed with anticipation and excitement. Her embarrassment did not go unnoticed and brought about playful remarks and laughter from many of the braves.

Winnokin moved to her right, flanked by her father and Running Elk. She turned to meet his gaze, and the golden flecks of his eyes sparkled with excitement. He spoke in his native tongue with clarity for all to hear.

"Hear me now, people of the hill. I have come forward this day to ask if I may join with White Dove. Her father has agreed to my wishes and has accepted my bride price on her behalf."

Leslie lowered her eyes demurely and blushed when a great uproar arose from all who gathered before them. When she looked up and spanned the mass of young and old, warrior and maiden, before her, she was absolutely astounded. If she were to guess, every single person within the compound were in attendance ... each with the look of splendid joy on their faces.

Winnokin watched her reaction, and his heart filled with love. His loins stirred with desire, knowing soon their bodies would join in a lover's dance, lasting until both of their hunger was sated. He moved forward and took both of her hands in his.

"I ask you, White Dove, to open your heart and look favorably upon those gifts I have brought for you. I stand here a humble man waiting to hear that you wish nothing more than to share with me this life I offer to you." He moved closer and drew her to his chest, holding her about the waist. He spoke above a hush in English for only her to hear. "I love you, Leslie, and wish not to live the rest of my days without you by my side as my wife."

She returned his heated gaze and wanted to ravish his lips with her own but knew she could not. Winnokin knew what was on her mind by the way she gazed at his mouth and the desire that radiated in her eyes.

A slow, radiant smile curved his lips, and he reverted to his own language as he took both of her hands in his and placed them over his heart.

"Come, White Dove ... see what I have gathered in homage of my love for you."

He took her by the hand, and she fought to control an overwhelming desire to kick up her heels with joyous glee. She could not see in front of her since his large frame blocked her view.

The villagers were ecstatic, clucking their tongues, clapping their hands, the children jumping and hopping about excitedly. When Winnokin stopped and turned to face her, the crowd parted behind him to reveal his accomplishments over the past two days with Running Elk's assistance. He moved to the side, encircled her waist, and watched for her reaction.

Leslie gasped loudly as her eyes scanned the area before them.

She looked at Winnokin, and he smiled as he coaxed her forward to get a closer look. Piled high before her were spectacular mounds of beautiful furs and pelts in every size, color, and texture that anyone could ever imagine. Slowly she stepped closer and tried to make a mental note of every detail, every item her eyes took in.

"Oh, my lord!" she spoke repeatedly.

Whatever she needed to run a Seneca household had been attended to. There were baskets in various sizes and weights, fish net holders, ladles, pottery, and clay bowls. She saw two stunning pairs of intricately designed moccasins, turquoise bracelets in aqua and red. A lavish full-length red fox robe to keep her warm during the winter was held out before her. An excess of fur covers they would use to soften their sleeping pallet were scattered before her feet by four of the village children. To her right she noted a mass amount of additional wares and clothing items, which were gifts to her family, along with dried fish, venison, fowl, and fruits that hung from strands on racks that stood nearly three feet tall.

Tears of happiness streamed from her eyes, and she sniffled as she gazed at the multitude of individuals who would soon be her people to lead beside their sachem. They loved and accepted her without question. It did not matter the color of her skin. It did not matter that she was not a true Seneca by blood. They adored her for her kindness and compassion. They respected her for the person she was. They honored her as the woman destined by their Great Spirit to join with their leader.

She turned to express her amazement and gasped even louder as she stepped backwards in disbelief. Her hands flew to her mouth, and she cried openly.

Winnokin stood before her, holding two bridles in each hand attached to four of the most magnificent white stallions she had ever laid her eyes upon. This was the most revered of gifts and the highest bride price ever bestowed upon a Seneca maiden.

Leslie could not move. She felt as though her legs had turned to stone. Her hands did not leave her face and were still pressed tightly against her lips. Tears streamed from her eyes, and her head shook slowly from side-to-side in disbelief. Winnokin took three steps forward.

"This is all I have to offer, along with my heart, my love, my life," he vowed. "Will you take me as your husband for the rest of all eternity?" he asked, opening his arms wide.

"Oh, Winnokin!" she cried, running forward into his arms. She did not care if it was against custom and kissed him ardently.

Winnokin dropped the bridles and gathered her into his arms and returned her kiss.

"Ya, my love. I will take you for my husband." She cried as she hugged him fiercely. And for only his ears to hear, she whispered, "You are my heart, my love, my life."

Chapter Twenty-One

A wedding amongst the Seneca was a very romantic affair. Leslie and Winnokin's company assembled at the council lodge where they sang a melodious hymn in honor of the couple.

As Leslie prepared herself for her wedding day, she could not believe her ears and turned to listen. More than she cared to admit, her ears had been pained many times by the uncomplimentary gale of voices coming from her own village songsters. She was certain they could not be the same ones signing now.

"They are not our people?" she questioned, making a corny face at her mother.

Little Raven could not contain herself and broke into hilarious laughter.

"Shame, daughter," Leluna said as she waved her finger and tried her best to look stern. "Our people try their best to make merry any occasion. But no, they are not our people."

"Mother, is that the best you can do ... making merry?" Leslie chuckled as she shook her head and raised her eyes to the ceiling.

Leluna clucked her tongue and swatted Leslie's backside, which only made her shriek with laughter even harder.

The three women moved forward and joined in a hug and shared kisses and stood quietly to listen to the beautiful voices and fluted sounds that floated throughout the village.

Your smile brings light into the darkness ~ You fill my heart with joy, you give me hope and peace of mind ~ You are my life, you are my world, you are my love ~ Your smile brings light into the darkness ~ My world has no meaning, without you by my side ~ You are my partner, my heart dances, my soul rejoices ~ Your smile brings light into the darkness ~ From this day forward life has meaning ~ Together we walk as one, love as one, live as one ~ Our love will be the light to take away the darkness

Leslie's eyes filled with tears as the beauty of the love song touched her heart.

Leluna tenderly wiped the droplets from her cheeks and placed a soft kiss in their place.

"It is time, my daughter. Winnokin waits for you."

Leslie breathed in deeply and let it out slowly as she nodded her head.

"Ya, Mother. I feel as though a thousand butterflies dance inside of me. Today is a new day, a new beginning, and I am ready to take that journey."

Leluna wrapped her arm about Leslie's waist and touched her daughter's forehead with her own.

"Come, my daughter, we will start that journey together."

Leluna turned slightly and reached for Little Raven, also encircling her waist. Together the three stepped into the morning sunshine and slowly made their way through the crowds to the ceremonial lodge.

The gathering of people greeting them was beyond any Leslie ever could have expected, and she felt tremendously overwhelmed. It was difficult to comprehend that so many would hold her in such a regard, in such extreme importance.

When they stood at the far end of the council lodge, all in attendance turned to look at her. She heard many words of praise for the outfit she wore, and her heart was full of pride and joy. She looked upon the smiling faces of all those before her, and she returned their nods and smiles in kind.

An aisle was left open for her to pass down, and she slowly walked to the front of the room, greeting her guests along the way as they patted her arms.

Before entering, Leluna handed her a few cakes of unleavened corn bread, which she would present to Winnokin's grandmother, She Who Speaks Softly, who was waiting at the far end of the lodge beside Winnokin. The bread was a symbol, representing her usefulness and skill in the domestic art.

Leluna and Little Raven followed behind as tradition required. When Leslie reached the halfway point, they moved to her side to escort Leslie the rest of the way.

Leslie could pick out Winnokin, even from a distance. For their wedding day he wore his raven black hair loose upon his shoulders, except for a small section that was tied with a leather strap and adorned with an eagle feather.

He was clothed in the purest white doe-skin leggings, moccasins, loin cloth, and tunic adorned with leather fringes, which ran along the sides of his arms, beginning at his shoulder down to his cuffs. Entwined in the fringes were multi-color beads of yellow, green, and white. A pattern was quilled in the center of his tunic which represented the wings of a white dove touching the points of a gleaming five-point star.

As she moved near, her eyes never left his, and she trusted Leluna and Little Raven to guide her the rest of the way and lead her to his side.

It was hard to believe a fierce warrior and tribal sachem could show so much emotion, and her chest ached to hold him as she witnessed tears glistening in his eyes.

Leslie moved in front of She Who Speaks Softly and handed her the corn bread. She in turn offered a gift of venison to Leluna, proving Winnokin's ability to provide for his new wife.

The exchange of gifts concluded the contract, which bound Winnokin and Leslie in marriage. Together, Leluna and Little Raven escorted her to Winnokin's side.

Winnokin was taken aback by her beauty and in awe of the workmanship and intricate bead work she added to her wedding attire.

Her eyes continued to hold his in a loving embrace as she proceeded toward him.

The eldest male of the clan, Strong of Heart, rose to speak before them as he tied their wrists together with a leather thong, representative of their unity.

"You have taken this woman, Winnokin, for your wife. She leaves her mother, her father, her sister, her brother to be your woman. Do not forget to love her. As she has left everything for you, be kind to her and always remember these words. The Great Spirit looks down and hears what you have promised. Remember, Hawenneyu can see all, and if you are not true, he will know it. Love this woman you have claimed for your wife."

Strong of Heart lifted his eyes to the heavens and extended his arms wide and sang a chant in resonant accord. When he finished, his stance did not change, and he offered up his final prayer.

"Great Spirit, hear the words of Strong of Heart, medicine man of the mighty Seneca and grandfather to Winnokin, sachem of the Seneca. My heart rejoices my grandson's vision has been fulfilled, and we praise your kindness and blessing. Look upon the young of heart standing now before you, who proclaim their love for each other. Guide them through their many years as man and woman. Give them the wisdom to make the right choices, the insight to raise their children in the way of the Seneca, and the strength to endure the hardships which may come to pass. Bless them, Great Spirit with a love, strong and binding, which will stand the test of time. Hear this grandfather's wishes, Great Spirit. It is the last wish I will ask, as their love and happiness will bring me much joy and many great-grandchildren to teach the customs of my people. Neho."

Winnokin drew his skinning knife from his sheath and sliced the leather bond that held them in ceremony. They turned to face each other, and their lips met in a kiss filled with promise and love.

Their guests quickly ascended upon them with words of congratulations for their continued joy and happiness. Half a score of men and women took Winnokin by the hand and, in turn, gave as much advice as they thought fit, expecting him to benefit from their experience.

No words were offered to Leslie. It was expected that Winnokin would guide her and teach her all she needed to know. She found herself laughing at the seriousness with which the counsel was given, for she knew her husband was most experienced in the ways utmost important in her mind.

The feast immediately followed as six long tables were inundated with overflowing spreads of food. There were smoked bass and trout, roasted venison, and wild turkey and geese to feed the entire assemblage of well-wishers. Cooked squashes, steamed corn, and other various vegetables added to the colorful setting. There also were ladles of honey and maple syrup to blanket freshly baked corn cakes and muffins; and ever-flowing punches and fresh fruits to devour.

It was a celebration expected to continue straight through the night. The songs sung in their honor were beautifully serenaded. Again, Leslie could not believe her ears when three of the braves softly sang a melody of love accompanied by two warriors who played the flute.

Winnokin held Leslie close in front of him, with his arms about her. The feel of his heart beating against her back sent a thrilling sensation to course through her, and Leslie could not believe her happiness.

As the warriors sang, Winnokin interpreted the words for her and whispered them in her ear. When his breath caressed her ear, her stomach shivered with excitement.

The words he told her were one's that bespoke of a love everlasting and infinite, of a man and woman who would die without the love of the other. Should the man fall from sickness or combat, the lips of his loved one would inspire new life or strength to fill his being, and the man would be as he was before.

When the love song was over, the other village drummers took over the celebration, and the evening took on an upbeat air.

The depth and emotion of the words touched Leslie deeply, and she could not help but cry.

Winnokin turned her to face him.

"Why do you weep, my love? Are you not happy to be the wife of Winnokin?"

He wiped the tears from her cheeks, and she shook her head.

"Oh no, darling! Nothing has made me happier."

"Then why the tears?" he asked, kissing her cheek tenderly.

"The words are so full of love ... they have touched my heart and made me realize how happy I am and how deep my love is for you."

"Come, Ishita. Let us get something to fill our stomachs and then we will say goodbye to our families."

He led her to the tables where the food was spread for all to take and enjoy. They ate until their hunger was satisfied. They searched for Little Raven and Running Elk and expressed their farewells and also did the same with Leluna and Red Eagle and Winnokin's grandmother.

Strong of Heart waited for them in front of the massive gates that stood open at the entrance to the stockade.

Winnokin smiled at his grandfather and clasped his forearm as they drew near.

"May your journey be a safe one, my son. I know it will be a joyous one for both of you."

"Thank you, Grandfather. We will do our best to see that a great-grandchild sits upon your knee soon." Winnokin grinned as he drew Leslie to his side.

Leslie blushed at his reference and both men chuckled.

Strong of Heart raised her chin and smiled at her. "It pleases this old man's heart to see my grandson so loved by you, White Dove. I welcome you into our family. May your days be blessed and filled with much joy."

"Thank you, grandfather. I vow to you that my love for your grandson shall never die."

She bowed her head respectfully then threw her arms about his neck and hugged him fiercely. She took his handsome, aged face between her hands and placed a tender kiss upon each of Strong of Heart's cheeks.

Strong of Heart wrapped his arms about her and squeezed her in return. He then moved toward Winnokin and hugged him as well and patted his back. He stepped away and pointed out to the distance.

"Go now, both of you, and begin your new journey in life together."

Together they walked through the clearing and moved outside the stockade.

"Where are we going, Winnokin?" Leslie asked.

"It is my wish that we are totally alone, my wife, and away from the playful antics of my warriors."

"Is it far? Should I change first?"

Before she had time to ask another question, they came upon one of her white stallions, which was staked to the ground, packed with extra clothing. Winnokin swiftly mounted and bent to lift Leslie up behind him. She snuggled closely and encircled her arms about his middle and—at the moment—left her future in his capable hands.

Chapter Twenty-Two

For nearly an hour they rode in a direction that took them east. In the moonlit glow of the night, she could make out the image of a makeshift tepee and could tell a fire burned within, as inviting spirals of smoke released into the night from the vented hole in its ceiling.

The heat from the fire greeted them like a welcoming host upon entering. As her eyes adjusted to the soft hue of the firelight, she noticed the painstaking care that was taken to make their temporary home comfortable and cozy.

Her cookware was to one side of the tepee and their personal belongings to the other. Opposite the entrance was a pallet slightly raised off the earth abounded with soft furs of fox, beaver, and rabbit pelts sewn together to form a spread.

"This will be the home we will share for a time while a new lodge is constructed by my warriors. Until then, you are mine to share with no one. Come, Ishita. I desire to taste the wine your fruit has to offer."

Leslie folded into his open arms willingly. Skillfully, he disrobed her slowly, devouring her beauty as she stood naked before him.

The silkiness of her skin was defined from the glow of the fire. Shadows danced romantically upon the walls of their quarters as the two moved together seductively.

Leslie undressed Winnokin in kind and returned his passionate kisses with an intensity that took their breaths away.

When their naked bodies touched, Winnokin could not restrain himself further, lifted her into his arms, and carried her to their luxurious pallet. The soft furs made her purr with delight as she stretched like a contented feline upon them.

Winnokin's ardent gaze consumed every inch of her, and his fingers traced the length of her shapely legs and firm thighs, over her silky buttocks, and cupped a round breast in each of his hands. He lowered his lips and felt her shudder under his touch.

His lips trailed lower, and he tenderly kneaded the inside of her thighs.

Leslie found herself caught somewhere between oblivion and heaven as she rode a cloud of ecstasy. A soft moan escaped her, and Leslie's insides throbbed from the fire his touch ignited. She lifted her hips and rotated in response to the rhythm he created, and he lowered his mouth. She whimpered as his seduction played havoc with her body, and she exploded with pulsating tremors.

"Winnokin! Please, take me now! I cannot bear it any longer!"

He lifted his weight upon her and guided himself inside her slowly.

Leslie gasped. It was as if she were a virgin again ... it had been so long since she had made love. But the slight discomfort was instantly forgotten as their bodies began to move in harmony. She wrapped her legs about him tightly, and he cupped her round bottom with his hands to help her meet his every thrust.

Their hunger for each other was strong, their kisses consuming, their tongues caressing, teasing, and arousing them to the point of explosion. They rode the pinnacle of passion, sating each other's hunger until their bodies climaxed together as one. Time stood still as they held each other tenderly, until their heated bodies cooled, and their heartbeats slowed to a pace of contentment.

"At last, you are mine, Ishita." Winnokin sighed and he kissed her tenderly ... deeply. "Many, many days my body threatened to explode from wanting you so."

"Promise me, my husband, that every day we will love each other like this. Promise me it will always be like this between us," she replied.

"I promise. Until our bodies are too old to perform what our heart and our soul desires, I will forever want and love you." He kissed her again, ever so slowly.

Leslie outlined his full, sensuous lips with the tip of her finger as she gazed into his beautiful eyes.

"Winnokin. Was ... was I ... ummm ... I mean ... did I—"

"Do not be afraid to say what is in your heart, White Dove," he interjected.

She blushed. "Did ... did I please you, my love?"

Winnokin chuckled, and he squeezed her to him. "Did you not feel the rapid beat of my heart or the tremors that passed between our bodies? No other woman has ever given completely what you have this night. Only you can sedate this warrior's hunger, my woman, my wife."

His words were all she needed to hear, and Leslie beamed with a radiance that accentuated her beauty even more.

"I am so happy, my love. All I want is to please and love you for the rest of my days."

"As do I, Ishita. There is so much more I will teach you. You have only begun to learn what Indian magic can be created between lovers. Together we will climb heights never reached. Come," he rolled to his side and stood, drawing her up with him, "we will take a swim together in the moonlight to clean our bodies of sweat. When we return, we will delight in each other again."

They walked hand-in-hand to the river's edge and slowly waded out until it reached their chests. The surface glistened as the full moon above reflected its radiance. They swam and floated upon their backs, hands entwined, not wanting to break contact or the magic of the moment.

Crickets and frogs inhabiting the shoreline harmonized in accord. Words spoken would only break the spell cast between them, so none were needed. They were separated from the outside world, safely in a cocoon their love had created, a wonderful, blissful fantasy they both silently prayed would last forever. When their skin began to prickle from the cool, night air, and retreated back to shore.

Winnokin lifted Leslie into his arms as they neared the shallow water and held her lips to his in a kiss she did not want to end. Their wet skin glistened as their mouths remained bonded while he carried her back to the tepee. He settled her upon their nuptial bed and left her side briefly to add more wood to the dying flames. When he turned, he read the look of hunger in her eyes, and his manhood came to life as wanton desire flowed through his veins once again. He went to her, and their bodies united.

Their lovemaking this time was slow, tender, exploring as they caressed, and did not leave an inch of flesh untouched. He showed her what aroused him, and she did the same. The lessons between them carried on into the night, and time held no meaning for the young lovers. Winnokin ran his palm over her curvaceous backside. His slow, tender strokes were sedating, and Leslie's eyelids became heavy as the heat from his body warmed her.

Soon their breathing slowed, and together they gave in to the exhaustion of the day, their bodies pacified, their hunger sated, and their unity consummated.

Chapter Twenty-Three

Just before dawn, Leslie awoke and quietly pulled herself free from Winnokin's. It had turned chilly in the tepee, and the flames from their campfire had burned down to coals. She rose slowly and moved to the small stack of logs Winnokin had brought inside, added a few of them to the red coals, and waited for them to ignite into flames. She wrapped herself in a robe and moved outside the entrance.

It would be a while before the sun would rise. A low fog cradled the earth as she slowly walked to the river and sat near its edge. She hugged her knees to her chest and cradled her chin on her knees. The sounds of the night were comforting as she heard the distant hoot of an owl coming from the forest to the right of her.

Her eyes scanned the heavens, and she felt a strong calming sense of belonging and peace wash over her. She watched as a star in the distance sparkled more brilliantly than the mass of others around it, and then its light flickered incessantly as though it were going to burn out. She was mesmerized by its show, and she watched it intently as it fought to maintain its brightness amongst the bed of millions surrounding it.

Her brows knitted tightly together as she became oblivious to her own surroundings. The air about her permeated with the sweet scent of roses, yet when she looked about, there were none in sight. It was then she sensed a presence and drew her eyes from the star she had been watching and looked over her shoulder, to her right, to her left, and saw no one. Patiently, she waited. Silently, she watched.

She did not sense fear, only a calming warmth wash over her again ... a warmth she had felt many times before. The sky began to take on a light of its own, yet it was not dawn. A pink haze began to take shape, and the night creatures about her abruptly stopped all sound. Leslie's heart began to pound in her chest, and her breath quickened as the haze became an apparition and moved to hover above the water's surface only a few feet from where she sat.

It was like a misty fog and then a billowy cloud that had no definite form, but yet there was a feeling, a sense of masculinity about it. Leslie swallowed hard, and a soft sob escaped from her throat. There was something familiar about it, but how could it be, she wondered. And then, it dawned on her.

"Papa!" She gasped. "Papa, is that you?" she whispered softly as she crawled forward on her knees and teetered slightly as her palm slipped over the edge and hit the water.

Her robe slipped from her shoulders, and she drew herself up on her knees and reached her hand forward, hoping to touch, to feel something she once knew to be familiar. The image flickered and dimmed, and she cried out, fearful it would disappear completely, and drew her hand away.

"No! Please ... do not leave!"

She had no knowledge that Winnokin watched only a few feet behind her, mystified and in awe of the scene taking place before him.

A hushed voice, distant yet audible, broke the silence.

"I and happy am I."

Leslie gasped as she clutched her hands to her heart.

"Oh, Papa. It is you, and you know. You know I have found love?"

"I know. You are now with husband and child."

"Child?" she questioned. "There is no child, papa."

She waited for a reply and shook her head, bewildered, unsure of his meaning, and then the thought struck her like lightning. Leslie stood, and her robe slipped to the ground at her feet.

"Are you saying I am with child? You know this ... I am with child, papa?"

She cried joyously as her eyes overflowed with tears and ran down her cheeks as she placed her palms over her belly.

"The seed grows within you. Go with love. Share your joy. Be happy. We will never speak again, until your time comes to pass."

Leslie shook her head and stepped into the water, wading out, her arms stretched before her, reaching out, trying to touch, hoping to feel something ... anything.

"No! No! You cannot go, Papa ... "

"Life moves on, daughter. Now that you have found love, I can do so with a happy heart. My time here is done."

"Oh, Papa! I miss you so. I ... I love you, Papa. You will be with me all—"

Before she could finish her words, the star she had watched earlier became ablaze with a brilliant, radiant light and streaked across the sky, plummeting to earth. The mist above the water dissipated into thin air slowly before her.

"Goodbye, Papa," she whimpered, blowing a kiss in the direction of the mist.

She took a few steps backward and dropped to her knees. She felt terribly weak, and when she tried to stand, she slumped into the water and her body shook uncontrollably as she sobbed into her hands.

Winnokin came up from behind her, his voice quivering heavily with emotion as he knelt in the water behind her and wrapped his arms protectively about her.

"White Dove, what have I seen?"

Leslie turned in his arms and noticed the look of total astonishment on his face as he glanced at the sky, out at the water, and back to her again, his mouth agape and his brow knitted tightly with worry.

"You saw and heard?" she whispered.

Winnokin nodded slightly and reached out to softly wipe the tears from her cheeks with his thumbs.

"Ya. I do not doubt the gift you spoke to me of, but to witness such a vision without ... without fasting and praying to the Great Spirit is a power like none I have ever seen."

Leslie laid her cheek against his and sobbed softly. "Oh, Winnokin. A part of me is gone forever."

Winnokin lifted her into his arms and carried her to shore. He covered her with her robe and rocked her in his arms as he stroked her hair.

"Do not cry, Ishita. Your father will always be with you. He is gone of body, but his spirit lives on in the land of the Great Spirit. He will always watch over you, always love you." He held her until her sobs subsided. "Is it true, White Dove? Are you with child?"

Leslie looked into his eyes and reached up to stroke his cheek tenderly. "Yes, my love. I do believe I am. The gift I was born with has never proven wrong. I have no reason to question nor deny a child grows within me now."

They stayed in their matrimonial hut for another five days, enjoying their time alone together. Leslie knew that once they returned to the compound, her life as a sachem's wife would be tremendously different from the life she lived as the daughter of a clan sub-chief. Her responsibilities would be great as well, and Winnokin had taken this special time spent together to inform her of those duties expected the wife of a Sachem. Leslie was confident she could fill the role honorably and wanted nothing more than to make her husband proud of her.

She looked forward especially to the upcoming role of mother, a joyous fulfillment that had been lost to her with the death of her first child. She knew that her life with Winnokin in some ways would be similar but also very different than if he were a trapper or farmer from the settlement. Life certainly had a way of shaking things up, and Leslie anticipated that her future with Winnokin would be filled with many more surprises and new experiences.

She still had much to learn and looked toward their new life together as one filled with adventure and wonderment. On the eve of their last night together, she had most of their belongings packed and ready to go for their departure the following morning.

Running Elk was expected to bring another one of her stallions by mid-morning in order to transport most of their possessions to their new lodge, which Running Elk had supervised during their absence. After the next upcoming holiday known as the Green Corn Festival was over, Little Raven would return with Leslie to gather the skins from the tepee and the few incidentals she would leave behind for the short term. She was happy she would have her sister to keep her company the seven days Winnokin and Running Elk would be gone.

They received a jovial welcome upon their return. Both were the recipients of teasing and playful heckling. The warriors, particularly, enjoyed harrying Leslie when she turned two shades of red each time one of them sent an amusing quip her way and Winnokin could not help but chuckle.

The first crop of corn harvested to the Seneca was a beautiful and spiritual sight, because to them it meant that mother earth was fertile and had not failed them.

The thanksgiving began at high noon on the day of their return. A full day assemblage of young and old alike was summoned by the Faith Keepers, who were male and female dignitaries appointed for their duty by each individual clan.

Little Raven was chosen to represent the Hawk Clan and very proud of her responsibility. The villagers set on either the right or left side of the council lodge, and Leslie was escorted to the left front row to sit opposite her husband.

Strong of Heart began the ceremony, expressing the entire tribe's gratitude to all the spiritual forces: the earth, water, grasses, trees, animals, thunder and rain, wind, sun, moon, and stars, and finally the Great Spirit, for the bounty they had been blessed with.

Leslie was moved by the emotional and spiritual depth of the words her grandfather spoke. She knew the world of the Seneca was full of invisible spirits, and earthly symbols of them appeared everywhere. To the Seneca, the world in which they lived was one where the forces of good and evil were inherent in all things evolved from nature. She never realized how holy and reverent the Indian truly were until she witnessed their first public prayer of thanks when she was adopted and again during her wedding ceremony. Her new people prayed often and thanked the Great Spirit after each war for those who came home safely and those who fought bravely, after each prosperous hunt, and at the end of every season for the bounties bestowed upon them.

Strong of Heart ended his prayer with a chant, and the Faith Keepers responded in kind. When the chant was finished, he announced the forthcoming Feather Dance, which Leslie knew was a very spirited and graceful show. Following the dance, a small feast would begin for all to attend if they so desired.

Because Winnokin was sachem and not expected to move into the lodge of Leslie's family, he opted for their own private dwelling, knowing his new bride would have preferred it that way.

When Leslie learned of them being alone as husband and wife, she was extremely grateful that her standing in the village made it all possible. The intimacies they shared were private and special. She did not feel comfortable with the thought of others being able to hear what went on between her and her husband, no matter how much sharing a home was a part of their culture. Even though platforms could be subdivided into separate petitioned chambers, or protected by lowering private curtains, moments spent with her husband were less than quiet. It would be difficult to follow a more subdued and moderate level of propriety once they were caught up in the heat of passion. It was a facet of her life she wanted not to change.

The long house Winnokin had constructed for them was of the same elm wood framework and measured only seventy-five feet in length as opposed to the usual 100–150 feet. Each end was crested with the Bear Clan seal, and a totem representative of Winnokin's standing in the tribe was raised before the main entrance. It pleased her to know their newly constructed home would be the permanent settlement of their own lineage, beginning with the birth of the child she carried within her.

Leluna and Little Raven were thrilled to learn she was with child. They never questioned how far long she was, nor did they disbelieve the visitation by the lake foretelling her condition. What was even more pleasing, was learning that Little Raven was expecting her firstborn as well shortly after when Leslie would be due.

Winnokin was ecstatic to learn that same evening his dearest friend would become a father as well.

"We can teach our sons together to become great warriors," he replied proudly as he traced her nose with the tip of his finger.

Leslie rolled to her side; her brow raised in question. "And what makes you think it is a son I carry, husband?" She pushed his shoulder playfully.

Winnokin shrugged.

She could not help but smile when she noticed the smirk playing at the corner of his lip.

"A warrior knows when he has sired a son." He pounded his chest.

Leslie leaned up on her elbow. "Well, great warrior, we will see, won't we? I suggest you prepare yourself for the slightest chance there will be another female under this roof," she replied.

Winnokin growled as he pulled her into his arms and lavished sweet kisses up and down the length of her neck.

She purred like a kitten when his attentions turned more amorous, transporting both to that familiar plane where time passed slowly, and they took the greatest pleasures renewing the love that bound them forever.

Chapter Twenty Four

The second day of the festival began at mid-afternoon with another speech of thanksgiving, followed by a dance that was constantly interrupted with more speeches expressing gratitude to the individual spirits by each Faith Keeper on behalf of their clan.

Singing was the major activity on the third day; solo performances were given by the men, who wished to sing their own personal songs of praise to the spirits.

On the last day, a game of chance, which was known as the bowl game, was played by members of the four clans: bear, wolf, turtle, and deer.

Winnokin chose Leslie to represent the bear clan. Once she found out it was simple enough to play, she relaxed and enjoyed the competition. A bowl, which measured about eight inches in diameter and was carved from soft, white pine, was used. It contained six peach pits. One side was charred black and the other left white. The bottom of the bowl was divided into four sections; each quarter had an intricate design representing each of the four clans carved into it.

Each member played an opponent by rapping the bowl sharply against the ground. If five or six pits turned up the same color, the member scored and went again. If not, the opposing member took their turn, and if they scored five or six, the first player got a turn again. If they were not lucky the second time around, they lost, and the second player went on to play another clan member. Whoever won over three opponents claimed victory of the game for their clan.

Leslie proved victorious her first time playing. She could tell her husband was amazed with her beginner's luck, but his enthusiasm was not at the level she had expected.

Toward the beginning of the evening, Winnokin had become quiet and withdrawn. Even their lovemaking hinted at desperation.

During the last two days, he clung to her like a shadow and watched her every move. Whenever their eyes met, she found him watching her intently, as if memorizing every physical trait and expression. She knew he was apprehensive about leaving on the hunt the following morning. Her dismay was just as great, if not more, but she fought hard not to show it. She promised herself that she would do everything in her power to make his departure less stressful. She walked with a happy gait to where he sat watching her. She beamed happily at those she passed who proudly patted her back and shoulder for her victorious wins. She sat down beside him with a light bounce, and her face beamed happily.

"Are you not happy that I was victorious for our Clan?" She asked.

He reached out and touched her cheek softly.

"I am most proud of my wife. The skills you portray each day make me love you more and more." He smiled warmly.

He wrapped his arm about her waist, and she cuddled close to his side. She rested her head upon his shoulder as they watched the festivities together. She knew it was getting late and wanted to spend some quality time alone with him. She caressed the inside of his bare arm and glided her hand slowly up and down and could feel him shudder beneath her touch.

He looked at her out of the corner of his eye, and his lips slowly curled into a smile.

She reached up lightly to kiss and nibble his ear.

Winnokin growled and buried his face in the soft curve of her neck, sending chills to dance up and down her spine as his tongue tantalized the area below her ear.

"I think my wife is trying to tell me she wants to leave." He smiled.

Leslie's eyes glazed with desire. "You know me well, husband," she confirmed.

Winnokin rose and took her by the hand. "Come. We will go and spend our last night together making magic."

Leslie's cheeks turned scarlet, and she looked about demurely to make sure his words were not overheard.

Winnokin chuckled at her embarrassment.

"Should we not say good night?" She tugged at his hand.

Winnokin turned and pulled her chin toward him, drawing her lips to his.

"They do not care, my wife. Our world is much different than the one you came from. When one is tired, they leave. When a husband desires his woman, he leads her home."

Their lovemaking that evening was not filled with a sense of urgency or desperation. Rather, it was a night of pliant teasing, soft strokes, and a rapture that branded their very souls. Their hunger to hold, to taste, to kiss was never ending. They wanted the time they spent in each other's arm to mark a memory they could draw upon later when they were apart. Their heated desire fed their passion's flame, bringing them close to near madness until their bodies had no strength left and yielded to love's sweet release.

Chapter Twenty-Five

Leslie shifted her weight on her sleeping pallet, stretched, and yawned. Her nose was assailed with a sweet scent, and she sniffed the air, detecting a fragrance of flowers. She patted the furs besides her, and her fingers touched upon soft, velvety petals. She opened her eyes and found her husband gone. In his place was a colorful bouquet of flower petals spread out in splendid galore. She smiled and raised her head slightly to look about.

Rubbing the sleep from her eyes, she could see two water pouches were over laden with a massive arrangement each of wildflowers and ferns. Tears misted her eyes as she rolled to her side and drew the enchanting collection of orange tiger lilies to her and sniffed them deeply. It must have taken him some time to find such a variation in size and color. There was a mass of delicate white daisies, green ferns from the forest and bright black-eyed Susan as well.

She sighed deeply, missing him already and reflected on the loving and tender evening they had shared, and smiled to herself. She knew she had seven long days ahead of her but was determined to do her best and muddle through. She rose and dressed quickly and wondered if Little Raven was up and feeling as miserable as she was. She scooped a small ladle of fresh water and nibbled on a slice of corn bread when she heard a light tap coming from the entrance of her lodge.

"White Dove, it is I, Little Raven. May I enter?"

"Ya, Little Raven, come in," Leslie answered happily.

They exchanged glances, and Leslie moved forward to greet her sister and tenderly hugged her.

Little Raven gasped when she noticed the colorful bouquet of flowers spread about the furs on Leslie's sleeping pallet and also filling the water pouches.

"And what is this?" She smiled.

Leslie turned and sighed deeply. "Winnokin's way of saying goodbye. I awoke to their beautiful scent, but sadly, he was already gone."

"Our men are very dramatic. My bouquet was not blossoms but sweet, tender kisses and passionate embraces as we watched the sun rise together."

"We better keep ourselves busy, sister. For sure we will go mad if we constantly dwell on the passion our husbands can arouse in each of us." Leslie chuckled.

Little Raven joined in her laughter as they sat to share a light meal and plan out their day together.

A short while later Leslie bridled three of her stallions. One they used as a pack horse and the others to ride. She wanted to return to their marriage tepee and retrieve the rest of the belongings they had left behind. It was a beautiful fall day. Cones dropped from their massive pines, and needles skirted the forest ground, mixing with foliage from neighboring maples and elm trees.

The blazing red, brilliant gold, and vibrant rust leaves made a colorful carpet for their steeds to tread upon in passing. Often, their conversation centered on their husbands and the babies growing within them. They agreed their lives could not be better. No maiden in the village could be more blessed than they were.

Little Raven spoke of their husbands as young men and how the three of them had always been close, even as children. She admitted loving Running Elk like a brother in the beginning and never looked upon him in a romantic way. It wasn't until puberty when their bodies began to change that a more intimate closeness grew between them, and his soft eyes would melt her heart. The slightest touch of his hand would send shudders coursing through her.

"Winnokin was the one who made us realize how deep our love had blossomed," she told Leslie. "We were so caught up in being close like brother and sister we honestly thought it was wrong to desire each other."

Leslie smiled warmly. "Look at what you would have missed if it was not for my husband?" she remarked as she raised her eyebrows devilishly.

Little Raven chuckled and nodded her head in agreement.

Once they reached their destination, Little Raven walked the horses to the river to drink and offered to tether them nearby, while Leslie went inside to begin gathering up what was left to pack and start dismantling the tepee.

When Little Raven entered the tepee, she halted immediately, puzzled by Leslie's actions.

Leslie was strewing belongings about wildly as she ranted and raved in frustrated English.

"White Dove, what is it? Have you misplaced something?"

Leslie was not only bewildered, but an unsettling feeling came over her. She ran her fingers through her hair and turned in all directions, overturning items she had already flipped over before. Perplexed, she stopped and threw her hands in the air.

"Two days before Winnokin and I left, we roasted some meat. I stored a little away for when you and I returned. I know I left a mat for us to sit upon and two fur pelts in case the weather turned cool. But they are not here!"

Little Raven shrugged and followed Leslie outside. Together they walked around the tepee and checked behind the rocks, bushes, and trees nearby.

Leslie stopped abruptly and listened, her eyes scanning the dense trees with an intensity that made the hairs at the back of Little Raven's neck stand on edge. Leslie was certain they were being watched, and a warm sensation that was all too familiar washed over her.

Little Raven came up behind her and tapped her on the shoulder.

Leslie turned to face her but peered over her shoulder one last time to take another look and scanned the tree line behind her.

"White Dove, perhaps you packed the mat and furs and forgot, or some animals sniffed out the meat?"

Leslie gazed at her sister, and her brows knitted tightly as she shook her head in disagreement.

"I think not."

"White Dove, really! There is no other explanation," Little Raven countered.

Leslie shook her head again and walked back around to the front of the tepee.

Little Raven followed.

"I stored them in one of my pottery bowls and sealed the top with skin and sinew. The container is gone as well," Leslie replied as she drew in a breath and released it slowly.

Little Raven contemplated her words. She saw the expression on Leslie's face and realized what she was thinking. Little Raven shook her head and spoke before Leslie could open her mouth.

"No! No one would dare enter the land of the Seneca. They would never get past our patrols and sentinels, White Dove. Only a few know where they are posted. You had to have misplaced the container or forgot that you packed it. You said you waited until the last moment to leave and rushed to get back in time for the festival, remember?"

Leslie appeared perplexed and raised her hands in question. "Perhaps a raccoon stole the container and worked it open," she said. A wide smile spread across her face when a thought came to mind. "Back home when the weather was warm, I would leave the windows open. There were two such raccoons ... brothers ... I think," she chuckled, "and what a mischievous pair they were too. They liked my pies. Every time I placed them on the windowsill to cool, one would be stolen if I did not keep an eye on them."

Little Raven smiled. "The day is getting warmer," she said. "Let us take down the tepee before it is too hot. Then we can go for a swim and pick some berries later to snack on before we return home."

They took their time and worked well together. In almost an hour the leather ties securing the skins to stakes driven in the ground were undone. The lengths of sewn skins were pulled from the elm pole frame, folded, and ready for packing.

They splattered their faces and arms with cool water beside the river's edge and sat down upon a thick mat of grass to catch their breaths and relax.

Leslie wiped the sweat from her brow and puffed loudly. "Now I know why all the women are so fit and trim." She laughed.

"Ya, my sister. The work is hard. At times I am tempted to lie about and let the sun warm my face. But if my chores fall behind, there is twice to do the next day," Little Raven said. "Then I am mad at myself for being lazy."

Leslie laughed at her sister's logic. "That is why I like to rise early and have mine done by noon," Leslie said. "The rest of the day is mine to swim, sew, collect berries, or love my husband when he is in a playful mood." She laughed.

"If he is anything like Running Elk," Little Raven chided, "it is often."

"Yes, often. And I would not have it any other way," Leslie replied.

They both rose to finish their task. Leslie stopped instantly and clutched her lower back as a sharp pain passed through her and slowly radiated to the front of her abdomen. She doubled over in pain and went down on one knee.

Little Raven moved to her side instantly. "White Dove, what is it?" Her voice trembled with concern.

By the time Leslie lowered herself to the ground the pain dulled and nearly subsided.

Little Raven knelt beside her; worry etched upon her beautiful face.

"Do not worry, Little Raven, I am fine," Leslie responded as she reached out to caress Little Raven's cheek.

Little Raven was not convinced, however. The weak smile Leslie offered did not reach Leslie's eyes.

"Do not lie to me, White Dove. I know you well. Tell me what it is that you feel," she insisted sharply.

Leslie showed her the spot where the pain started and stopped. "A really sharp pain hit me here. It is gone though, now, and just feels more like a throbbing ache. I must have pulled something in my back, that's all."

Little Raven did not want to speculate and hammered out the situation in her mind before speaking. "You will stay here off your feet. I will go for berries."

Leslie opened her mouth to protest, but Little Raven was adamant and waved a finger before her face. "Do not argue with me, sister," she said. "There is nothing strenuous about picking berries, I agree. If you did sprain your back, I would rather you undress and go float in the cool water. It will do your back good. I will return shortly and join you."

Leslie hesitated and noticed the stern look and stubborn stance her sister was taking and nodded her agreement. She began to undo the ties at the shoulder of her tunic.

"I will do as you ask, my sister."

Little Raven nodded her approval and turned to retrieve a swatch of skin to use as a satchel. She looked over her shoulder and smiled at Leslie when she noticed her slowly wading out into the river then turned to enter the woods where Leslie had shown her earlier that berries could be found.

Leslie had to agree that the cool water was comforting as she floated upon her back. It was such a glorious, hot fall day, and she knew that there would not be many more of them left to enjoy before the river got too cold. A sigh escaped her throat as her body began to render itself to the soothing relaxation. She maneuvered close to shore so she could rest her head upon the shoreline, allowing herself to float freely without sinking to the bottom. Her mind voided itself of all unnecessary thought, tuning in on the melodious chirps of the birds overhead, the soft rustle of leaves, chatter of squirrels, and cry of an eagle as it soared in the near distance overhead.

Subconsciously she escaped as pleasant memories filled her mind of lovers kissing in the night, murmurs of delight, and the vision of her last evening in the arms of her husband. Her lips curled absently in a smile as she lost herself to that blissful memory. Several moments passed, and once her mind and body relaxed, she drifted off to sleep, all thoughts of her pain and Little Raven gone.

Leslie was jolted awake, and she banged the back of her head on a rock as her ankles were grabbed and she was dragged out into deeper water. Before she could react, her face was pushed beneath the surface. The weight of someone straddling her stomach to hold her down filled her with a fear beyond none she had ever felt.

She began to thrash about and tried to release the hands from her throat but could not budge them away. She realized that her frantic actions would be for naught and would use up whatever precious air remained in her lungs. One thing was certain ... she was an excellent swimmer and had the ability to hold her breath longer than most. She forced herself to relax her body and stopped combating her attacker.

Once the ripples in the water cleared, she almost gulped a mouthful of water from the shock of seeing Nuchzetse's face above her, a vehement look of hatred etched on her face. Leslie was confident it was the maiden's intent to kill her, and Leslie forced herself to remain calm and stare back at her with a blank look.

She tried desperately to relax and force her arms and legs to naturally become buoyant. It was hard to leave her eyes wide open and not let her lids blink as Nuchzetse stared down at her. She could feel the pressure expand in her lungs, and her throat began to burn, and her eardrums pounded from the pressure building up in her head.

If she does not release me soon, I will die, she cried to herself. The thought of her unborn child gasping for air as well made her stronger. She refused to let her life slip away so easily. *Please, dear Lord, please*, she prayed silently. *Do not let me die, not now, not this way, not after everything I have been through. Help me, Lord. I beg of you. Give me the strength to survive this, to combat this wicked woman.*

Slowly, Nuchzetse's hold began to relax around her throat.

Leslie knew that Nuchzetse was starting to believe she accomplished her terrible feat, and that Leslie was now dead.

Nuchzetse shifted her weight. Once she removed herself, Leslie's body floated to the top and broke the surface.

Leslie was so very thankful that her long, thick hair had fanned out, covering her face, giving her the opportunity to tilt her head slightly, open her lips, and draw fresh air into her lungs. She remained motionless, and the urge to gasp and cough was overwhelming.

Nuchzetse laughed devilishly. "My day of victory, White Dog, has finally arrived," she barked as she grabbed a handful of Leslie's hair viciously and pulled her toward shore.

Leslie willed herself not to respond. Her eyes filled with tears as hair was pulled from her scalp. She peaked through cracks of her wet hair and could tell Nuchzetse's other hand was free. Leslie could not tell if she was concealing a knife. The thought of Little Raven came to mind, and Leslie wondered where she was. She should have taken the warning she felt earlier more seriously. She knew they were being watched, and she ignored it.

What if Nuchzetse attacked Little Raven in the woods and she lay bleeding and in need of care. She knew she had to do something. When she felt the river's bottom roughly scrape along her backside, she growled loudly, reached back, grasped her attacker's wrist, and turned it viciously. She heard Nuchzetse yelp, and Leslie smiled. The element of surprise was on her side.

Nuchzetse fell backwards into the water when Leslie grabbed her legs from behind and tugged with all her might. Leslie did not wait as she drew back her arm and with all her might, she punched Nuchzetse's nose with a tightly clenched fist. She heard the snap of bone and watched as her attacker coughed and gulped for air after she swallowed a mouthful of water. Leslie shook her painful hand as her knuckles swelled from the force of the blow. Blood streamed from Nuchzetse's nose, but Leslie did not hesitate.

She encircled her throat with her hands and began to squeeze with all her might. Tears streamed from her eyes as she sobbed loudly. She shook Nuchzetse's head violently in and out of the water as her mind filled with hatred for the woman who tried to ruin her life and had possibly harmed her sister.

An uncontrollable wrath filled her. She wanted to kill this woman, strangle every breath out of her body. She felt out of control as visions of the past flashed before her eyes: Red Farmer's eyes wild with wanton lust, Shaun's body being stabbed like a pin cushion by warring Huron, and her father's lifeless body in her arms. Her own loud, screeching screams filling her ears brought her back to reality, and she stared at Nuchzetse's pallid, lifeless face.

Leslie finally realized what she was doing and instantly stopped. She did not want to be like this woman and forced to turn into a callous, vindictive murderer like her, insensitive to human life. She slowly released her grasp around Nuchzetse's throat, and her body shuddered uncontrollably as tears continued to flow from her eyes. She moved and grabbed her under the arms and dragged her up onto the bank. She bent low and listened for sounds of breathing and a heartbeat.

Nuchzetse's pulse was shallow, and her breathing had stopped.

 Leslie tilted her head back and blew two, sharp breaths into her mouth and listened for air to escape. There was none. She depressed down hard on Nuchzetse's abdomen to push water from her lungs and swore every curse word she could think of out loud while she continued to get her to respond.

"Come on, you bitch! Breathe! I will be damned to hell before I let you die! Breathe!"

She blew twice more into her mouth and pressed down again on her middle.

 "My satisfaction will be keeping you alive so, you are forced to carry out your punishment. Breathe, Nuchzetse! By the grace of God, breathe!"

She repeated the process two more times and was soon rewarded.

Nuchzetse began to cough up water and gulped air into her lungs.

Leslie moved off her and rolled her to her side.

Nuchzetse threw upriver water and continued to cough violently.

Leslie moved to quickly gather two lengths of vine from a nearby poplar and took advantage of Nuchzetse's weakness and tied the woman's ankles tightly. She pulled her arms behind her back, crisscrossed them at the wrist, and secured them as well.

Nuchzetse slowly came to her senses and realized what had been done to her. She thrashed about and spit out threats that she could not keep. Her weakened state deterred her from breaking the bonds, and soon she gave in and lay very still.

"What have you done to Little Raven?" Leslie screamed as her eyes snapped with both anger and hatred.

Nuchzetse did not reply, and Leslie went to her belongings and pulled out her skinning knife.

"You will tell me, woman, or I will slice your pretty face so no man will look upon you with desire ever again!" Leslie threatened. She knelt beside her and pressed the point of her blade against Nuchzetse's skin and drew blood.

Nuchzetse spat in Leslie's face and swiped at her ankles with her restrained legs, knocking Leslie backwards.

Leslie swore out loud and righted herself. "I have had just about enough of you!" she squealed and threw her knife like the expert she was.

Nuchzetse's eyes went wide with shock, and she screamed in pain as the blade embedded into her upper right thigh.

Leslie moved forward and stomped her foot down hard on her thigh.

Nuchzetse screamed again.

"You have one last chance to give me the answer I want, or I drive this knife into your cold heart."

Leslie pushed on the blade even harder to strengthen her threat.

Nuchzetse gasped and dug her heels into the ground, trying to drag herself backwards and away from Leslie. She gulped, and her eyes reflected fear as Leslie moved closer, still naked, her tanned skin covered with dirt and mud.

Leslie's voice was low and menacing. "If you have escape on your mind, forget it. I suggest you take my threats seriously. One ... last ... time ... where is Little Raven?" she asked through gritted teeth.

Nuchzetse remained silent. In one swift movement Leslie slashed the strap from her shift and ripped it off her shoulder. She pierced the tender skin of Nuchzetse's left breast with the honed point of her blade. Nuchzetse nodded her head frantically in the direction of the woods to the east and scooted backwards until her back collided into the lower trunk of a massive elm tree.

"That way ... behind those trees. I ... I only hit her over the head." Nuchzetse watched as terror turned to wrath on Leslie's face. She shook her head as panic filled her heart when Leslie moved toward her. "No! I did not kill her. She was breathing. I checked. I vow this is so," she screamed.

Leslie ran and grabbed her dress. As she tossed it over her head, she ran toward her supplies, grabbed a length of sinew and rope, and returned to tie Nuchzetse's arms behind her and then secure her body to the tree. In a flash she ran in the direction Nuchzetse gave, crying out Little Raven's name.

It was not long when she heard Little Raven's weak voice and followed the sound. She found her slumped over, concealed behind a patch of blackberry bushes. Her face, legs, and arms were scratched and lacerated from the thorny bushes. Her hair was matted with wet blood from a deep, open gash in the back of her head. Leslie expressed her thanks to God openly and cried as she ran to where Little Raven lay.

Chapter Twenty Six

Leslie exerted every ounce of strength she could muster to half carry Little Raven back to the campsite.

Little Raven could barely stay awake and vomited twice the short distance back to the camp site.

Leslie knew she was suffering from a concussion. How severe it was, was too hard to tell. She sobbed openly as Little Raven's blood seeped all over her shift from the multiple cuts that covered nearly every inch of her exposed skin. She wanted to scream at the top of her lungs and feared that her sister had a good chance of losing her unborn child. She tried desperately to awaken her each time she started to fall into a deep sleep. Her dead weight was unbearable.

Leslie stopped beside the nearest pine trunk and pushed Little Raven upright against it to catch her own breath. The clearing to the camp was only a few more feet away. Leslie took a few deep breaths and then let Little Raven slouch over her shoulders from behind. Slowly, she took one step at a time as she carried her like a sack of flour. Her knees threatened to buckle, and her back seared with pain, but Leslie continued to move forward one small step at a time, gritting her teeth the entire way.

When they finally broke through the tree line, Leslie noticed Nuchzetse had slumped to her side, and a large pool of blood soaked the ground beneath her wound. She instantly sprang into a sitting position when she noticed their approach. The fear on Nuchzetse's face did not bother Leslie. She knew the woman would not be going anywhere, and Leslie couldn't care less whether she bled to death or not.

Her number one concern was tending to Little Raven. Her attention was instantly drawn to Little Raven when she screamed. Leslie huddled over and slowly lowered her to the ground.

Little Raven's eyes were wide with fear as she grasped her middle and drew her legs into a fetal position. She groaned loudly as a spasm of pain coursed through her midsection.

 Leslie chewed on her lower lip and knew she had to move Little Raven closer to the campsite where the supplies and fire pit were, and the river was close by.

 "I must move you, Little Raven, so I can tend you. Can you try to stand?"

Little Raven whimpered as she looked at Leslie. Her face was void of color, and she nodded her head slowly. "I ... will ... try."

Leslie prayed for strength as she bent to help her stand. She took all Little Raven's weight on her hip, half carrying, half dragging her along until she found an area suitable near the riverbank where Little Raven could stretch comfortably upon the ground. She moved into action immediately and folded one long skin from the tepee into the shape of a head rest. She stretched out two more upon the ground and topped them with furs then helped Little Raven slide upon it. She folded a few more skins into squares to elevate Little Raven's feet and hopefully still any bleeding and further cramping.

Little Raven reached out and touched her hand, and Leslie bent low as she whispered weakly into her ear.

Leslie could not believe it when she learned that Nuchzetse had kicked Little Raven in the stomach before she hit her in the head with a thick tree limb. Leslie looked over her shoulder and sent Nuchzetse a look of disdain.

"It will be all right, Little Raven. We will get through this, I promise. Be still now, sister. Close your eyes and try to relax."

Leslie covered her with the remaining fur blanket and went in search for roots she would need to medicate her wounds and hopefully stop the cramping. It was not long before she found the bright yellow patch of a three-foot high wild indigo Winnokin had shown her last week. She drew her knife and dug deeply into the ground until she found the rootstock that she would steep and use as an antiseptic for Little Raven's head wound and scratches. She followed the river a short distance to where it branched off into a stream. She sighed with relief when she saw the flat, long sword-like leaves of sweet grass.

She walked out into the stream and again dug into the murky bed until she located the root. She would clean it then boil it into a mild tonic that should help stop Little Raven's cramping.

Little Raven was in tears when Leslie returned. She had started to spot, and Leslie quickly prepared the roots and administered them right away.

It took her almost an hour to clean all the blood from Little Raven's wounds and steep both of the roots to their proper potency before she could leave and get help.

"Are you sure you want me to do this, Little Raven? We can stay here together as long as it takes to get you up and back on your feet again. I don't feel right about leaving you out here all alone."

Little Raven shook her head. "I do not think I will be better by morning." She grimaced with pain. "It is best you go and bring Strong of Heart here and tell the council what has happened. I will be fine until you return. We are not that far from the village, remember?"

"I do not know, Little Raven. It will take me almost an hour before I get there and another to return."

"White Dove, enough! The tonic is working, and my cramps have subsided. I promise not to move, and Nuchzetse I do not think will be going anywhere." Little Raven's tone grew louder and was filled with hatred. "She knows my aim is deadly, and I will not hesitate to kill her no matter how much pain I am in if she dares to move but an inch," she threatened as she sent Nuchzetse a venomous look.

Leslie stroked Little Raven's forehead softly as tears overflowed from her own eyes.

"I will do as you say, sister. The tonic is here beside you. Promise me you will take a sip now and then until it is all gone."

Little Raven nodded and smiled weakly. "I promise, White Dove." She waved her hand. "Now go and ride like the wind."

Leslie bent forward and kissed both of her cheeks softly. "I love you, Little Raven. I will return soon."

"My love goes with you, White Dove. Do not fear. The wife of Running Elk is strong."

Leslie smiled and then turned around to look at Nuchzetse.

Nuchzetse refused to meet her gaze.

"I know you are a smart woman," Leslie spoke with conviction. "If you know what is good for you, you will not move or utter a sound. Nothing my sister could do to you will equal my wrath if you attempt to escape."

Nuchzetse slowly raised her head, and her eyes were expressionless.

Leslie glared at her. "Do you understand my meaning?"

Nuchzetse nodded her head in agreement and swallowed nervously.

"You are wise," Leslie said as she rose, turned on her heels, and mounted her stallion.

Leslie rode hard and did not allow her horse to slow his pace. The landscape passed quickly before her. She was oblivious to the colorful grandeur of autumn's fall showing. She clung to her beautiful steed's strong neck as it carried her toward home. She could not help but sob openly as visions of Little Raven flashed before her eyes.

Her horse followed a course without her direction, as though some spiritual force guided it back to the village and halted abruptly outside the village stockade. As soon as the gate opened by the warrior on duty, she kicked her stallion into motion and rode with break-neck speed through the village with Strong of Heart's lodge her destination. The villagers stopped from doing their chores, halted their conversations, and turned to gander at the rider who passed them in a hurried whirl of dust and dirt, the look of utter fear reflected upon her face. They knew something terrible was amiss with their sachem's new wife and quickly followed her with concern.

Strong of Heart was sitting outside his lodge, smoking his pipe and conversing with a group of elders when Leslie's horse came to a quick stop and reared slightly. She dismounted in front of the group and fell to her knees sobbing and gasping. Strong of Heart rose instantly and ran to her side, his brows furrowed with concern. He took her in his arms while she continued to gasp and try to catch her breath.

"What is it, my child? What has happened? Where is Little Raven?"

Leslie huffed and puffed between words, relaying the entire story of what had transpired since they left the village that morning.

Strong of Heart called out to four warriors to prepare for their travel. He called for a quick counsel with the elders present to determine Nuchzetse's fate.

Leslie implored that Nuchzetse's parents not be advised of what happened, in order to spare them the additional hurt and shame. She asked the warriors to be sworn to secrecy. Once the elders heard her testimony, she was asked to leave while a quick decision was made. She paced back and forth in front of the lodge, deep in thought and worried about Little Raven alone in the woods in pain and afraid of losing her child. She wished that Winnokin and Running Elk were there with her, and her tears began to stream down her cheeks again. Her lip burned from the skin she'd chewed away earlier.

She started to chew on the skin of her fingers as she prayed the council's decision would be swift. It was only a matter of minutes for them to decide Nuchzetse's fate. Leslie was called into the lodge and told four warriors would accompany Strong of Heart and be sworn to secrecy. Two warriors would escort Nuchzetse back to the village from whence she came with a message delivered on Strong of Heart's behalf. Whatever punishment their brothers the Oneida decided upon would be honored by the Seneca. The two remaining warriors would help aide and escort Strong of Heart in bringing Little Raven safely home, and Nuchzetse's parents would be spared the hurt of their daughter's shame.

Leslie bowed her head reverently to show her respect and quickly said a prayer of thanks.

Strong of Heart entreated she stay behind to inform Red Eagle and Leluna of what had happened, as well as the council's decision. He requested that she prepare specific potions and poultices for immediate administration upon their return. It was not difficult for Strong of Heart to read the disappointment in Leslie's eyes regarding her staying behind.

"You did well, White Dove. The medicines you have already given her have probably given great relief. But it is not necessary for you to return," he stated strongly. "What is left to be done, the warriors will do. I will make sure she—"

"But, Grandfather," Leslie interrupted, "Little Raven is afraid of losing her baby! She needs me to assure her everything will be all right. I must go. You do not know where the camp is!" she pleaded.

Strong of Heart reached out and touched her shoulder tenderly. "I understand your concern. Your place is here to do as I requested ... to prepare for her return. I will give her a potion to calm her right away and make her sleep. I know of the spot where your ceremonial camp is, as I chose it for you. You will stay."

As much as she was tempted to plead one last time, she knew that Strong of Heart would not relent once he made up his mind.

"I will stay, Grandfather, and do as you ask." She bowed her head respectfully. As soon as they left, Leslie hastened to inform her family of the disheartening news.

Chapter Twenty-Seven

Five days had come and gone, and Little Raven was still with child. For nearly two full days the bleeding and cramps persisted heavily. Due to Strong of Heart's wisdom and devout attentions, the severity dwindled substantially with every hour that passed, until the threat of losing the baby altogether was no longer a possibility.

Leslie doted on Little Raven and stayed by her side with a loyalty that touched everyone.

Leluna's daily warnings of Leslie overdoing it and not taking care of herself went ignored. Warnings be damned, Leslie thought. She needed to be sure Little Raven stayed off her feet completely and took the medicines prescribed to her religiously. If anything happened to her baby, Leslie knew she could never forgive herself. She felt terribly responsible for everything that took place. If she had not asked Little Raven to come along with her, she would not be there lying before her, fighting to keep her baby safely growing within her.

If she had not met Winnokin, Nuchzetse would never have felt threatened and banished from her home and people. As stupid as it seemed, Leslie felt sorry for the troubled maiden despite all the pain and trouble she caused. She wondered what other trouble her presence could bring to these beautiful people. If the authorities got word of her living amongst the Seneca, would they automatically assume she was an imprisoned slave and take action against them to rescue her?

Leslie could not help but feel that her living amongst them was proving to be more of a hindrance than a blessing with every passing day. She hated living with the fear of always looking over her shoulder, always feeling as though she was being watched, always worrying that Nuchzetse would escape again and again and make good her threat. What would Nuchzetse do once she learned that Leslie had given Winnokin a child? Would the news of him becoming a father send her even further over the edge? She had a child growing within her as well. Could they have a safe, wonderful life living here amongst the Seneca? Would it be better if she left? Would her own kind be as accepting if she returned to the settlement to have her child?

Leslie's worrisome concerns kept her awake many nights. No matter how much it made sense to leave, she knew it was insane. She was madly in love with Winnokin, and he would never let her go. Even if she attempted to get away, he would find her. They were two ... living and loving as one. They finished each other's sentences, knew each other's thoughts, and sensed each other's feelings.

She knew life without pain and heartache and challenges was not living, that every man and every woman had to confront whatever trials came along the way. If she was to be tested more than most, she knew in her heart she could endure anything if Winnokin was there by her side to give her love, to be supportive, to protect and to guide her.

By the sixth day, Little Raven's cheeks took on a healthy blush. Strong of Heart allowed her to sit up for short periods of time. It was during those intervals that she and Leslie would cut out patterns and work on sewing clothes for their expectant children. They talked endlessly about the return of their husbands and, most importantly, the birth of their children in the spring. They vowed to be present during each other's birthing and stay until their babies were delivered.

Little Raven told Leslie how the Seneca made a soft compress of maize powder to soothe the sting in the newborn's navel once the umbilical cord dried and was removed. The child was also put to the breast right away to induce the mother's breasts to swell with milk, and the child was nourished until two or three. Leslie told her how she nursed her first little boy until his teeth broke through. He was such a ravenous eater, it was impossible to stop him from biting down on her nipples, so she began to feed him fruits and vegetables that she'd steamed and mashed.

It still saddened her greatly to think upon him, the life he would never know and the happiness and joys he would never experience.

Little Raven listened quietly as she spoke. She knew it was important to let Leslie release the pain and grief of such a terrible loss whenever it surfaced, as she knew that Leslie would do the same for her.

Leslie was curious how the Seneca raised their children. She asked Little Raven to tell her of other Seneca customs. She listened intently and was full of questions. She wanted so much to learn and do the right thing so Winnokin would be proud. Because the men were frequently away, she learned the mother was the driving force behind raising the child. She was loving in her treatment but careful not to spoil or soften them. The mother encouraged her son to fight other boys with sham war clubs made of cornstalks. Frequently she told him stories of the bravery of their ancestors. Both boys and girls were taught to eat sparingly, and to be a glutton was a sin.

Leslie chuckled when Little Raven relayed that little ones were told too many corn cakes dipped in maple syrup brought about the bogeyman, Long Nose. The children were toughened with regular baths of cold water to ward off winter colds and sickness. When they were eight, they were made aware of their duties. A girl did light chores in the long house and helped in the fields. A boy was free to wonder in the woods for days on end with his peers, living off berries and tubers and small game they snared or shot with their bows and arrows or blow guns. When the time came that a boy killed his first deer unassisted with a bow and arrow, he was allowed to join the adult hunting parties.

Leslie admitted it would be one of the proudest days in her husband's life to hunt with his own son. Little Raven told Leslie she would have to learn many stories, because it was their way of teaching the children about their ancestors and carrying on tradition from one generation to the next. The one all little Seneca boys loved to hear was about the Four Iroquois Hunters. Leslie begged Little Raven to tell her the story and she finally did.

Once, not long ago, four hunters spent the winter together trapping in the North. They had much luck and brought their furs to the trading post. They were given much to buy all the things needed for their families, including one new rifle. They had a problem, however. Although they hunted and trapped as brothers, for they all belonged to the Bear Clan, they did not live together. One hunter was from the People of the Great Hill, the Seneca. Another was from the People of the Mucky Land, the Cayuga. The other was from the People on the Hills, the Onondaga. And the last was from the People of the Flint, the Mohawks. It was easy to divide provisions among four people, but how could they divide one rifle? It was decided, the man who told the tallest story about hunting would take the gun home.

The Mohawk hunter spoke first.

"A man was walking along after hunting all day. His mind was not on hunting, and he used up all his bullets for his old muzzle. As he walked, he ate cherries that he had picked earlier and spit the pits into his hand. Then he saw a big, big deer in front of him, but he had no bullets left to use. He thought quickly, poured powder into his gun, took the cherry pits, loaded them, and fired. The deer fell, got right back up, and ran away. Years later he went hunting in the same place with no luck. At the end of the day, he saw at the edge of a clearing a tall tree covered with ripe cherries. "Ah," he thought, "at least I can eat! He put down his gun and began to climb. When he reached lower branches, the tree began to shake back and forth, and the hunter had to hold on with both hands. Then the tree lifted straight into the air and he was thrown out. As he looked up from the ground, he saw the tree was growing between the antlers of a huge deer, which shook its head one more time before running into the forest. And that," he said, "is my story."

The Onondaga warrior began his story.

"One time my uncle was hunting. He had only one shot left in his gun and wanted to make it count. He came to a stream where he saw a duck. In front of the duck there was a large trout leaping from the water to catch flies. On the other side of the stream, he could see a deer sniffing the wind. Back on a small hill was a bear on its hind legs, scratching its paws on a tree. My uncle got down on his belly. He crawled to the stream, took careful aim, and waited. When everything was just right and the trout jumped again, he pulled the trigger. The bullet went through the trout and killed the duck. It ricocheted off the water, struck the deer, went through the deer, and killed the bear. The amazing thing you will find hard to believe is when he went to skin the bear, he turned it over to find a fox it had fallen upon, and the fox had a fat rabbit in its mouth."

The Cayuga hunter took a very deep breath.

"Many seasons ago my grandfather was out hunting and saw a deer. He could not get close enough for a good shot but ran so fast he went right past the deer. When the deer saw my grandfather go by him, it got scared. The deer turned around, jumped as hard as it could, and sailed right over a stream Grandfather jumped too, but when he got halfway over the stream, he saw he could not make it to the other side. He turned in mid-air and jumped back. The deer hid behind a hill so my grandfather could not see it anymore. Now, my grandfather was angry. He did not want the deer to get away. He put his gun between little maple trees and bent the barrel. Then he aimed and shot. The bullet curved right around the hill and struck the deer.

When he saw the fallen deer, he got excited. It was as if it was the first deer he had ever shot. He started to skin the deer, but it was not dead. And just when he reached the horns and was about to pull the skin off, the deer jumped up and began to run around. My grandfather tried to grab the deer, but it was too slippery. He chased it around and around. Then the skin got caught on the bark of a hickory tree. The deer backed off and pulled hard. The skin came right off over its horns, and the deer ran away, leaving grandfather with only its skin. If you do not believe me, go to grandfather's lodge. The skin is still hanging there."

Now, only the great Seneca hunter was left. He looked around at the other three warriors, laughed out loud, and shook his head.

"Wah-ah," he said. "(I am sorry.) The mighty Seneca never tell tall stories about hunting."

The other three hunters looked at each other and knew they had been duped. Without another word, they handed the Seneca warrior the brand-new rifle.

Leslie rubbed her belly thoughtfully and hoped the life within her was a boy. It was a good story to remember and one she would enjoy sharing with a son. When she gazed at Little Raven, she knew her sister shared her thoughts as well. Their eyes filled with happy tears, and they could not help but laugh and leaned forward to hug each other.

It had been a long afternoon full of exciting chatter. Little Raven yawned openly. It did not take much coaxing from Leslie to get her to settle down for a nap. Once she made Little Raven comfortable and gave her, her medication, she went outside in the afternoon sun to work awhile on the cradleboard she had begun. The sun was warm upon her skin and shone brilliantly amongst a cloudless, azure sky.

She sighed deeply and felt so very content and happy about the way things had finally turned out. She wondered what had happened to Nuchzetse, since they never heard anything regarding her fate. Despite all the pain and misery, she caused, Leslie knew she would feel bad if she learned she was dealt with harshly because of what she had done. She shook her head and felt a sense of sadness despite it all.

Nuchzetse was such a young, vibrant, and beautiful woman. To let jealousy consume her had been the cause of her own self-destruction. She could have found true love if she had given herself the opportunity and the chance to open her heart, to start anew with the Oneida.

Leslie realized there would always be people like Red Farmer and Nuchzetse in the world causing pain and suffering to others. With Winnokin in her life, however, they would be able to rise above the sorrow and strife in the world and make best with what they had—what they shared and created together as man and wife.

She started to rub the soft, white pine board positioned between her thighs. She worked the special oil into the grain to further soften the wood so she could carve the designs she had sketched earlier on paper Winnokin had given her. She looked at the pattern and smiled and was pleased with her artwork. It was an intricate design of brightly colored butterflies resting upon a soft, delicate rose open in full bloom.

Mindlessly, she rubbed in a circular motion as she thought of Winnokin and how much she was missing him. The last six days had gone by quickly as she occupied her time caring for Little Raven and doing both of their chores. The villagers were told Little Raven's horse had been startled by a rattler, taking her by surprise and dismounting her into a thicket of thorns and knocking her unconscious.

The warriors who had aided Strong of Heart in returning Nuchzetse to the camp of the Oneida were further instructed to meet up with Winnokin's party and inform him of what transpired during his absence and requesting that the hunt be discontinued and to return home immediately.

Leslie could feel her heart beating rapidly in her chest, knowing that at any hour, her husband would be returning home. She could not wait for that moment to arrive. She decided to stop what she was doing and placed the cradleboard quietly inside her family's lodge. She looked around for Leluna and found her next door visiting with some of the women. She asked her mother to look in on Little Raven while she went for a long, relaxing swim.

Leslie retrieved a change of clothing and headed toward the river. She stripped quickly and hesitated at the water's edge when her toes encountered the shocking cold water. She knew the swim would be invigorating once her body became accustomed to the temperature. She stood and pondered for a moment, looking at the calm surface before her and then the reflection of the beautiful colorful foliage along the surrounding bank.

"All right, Leslie," she spoke out loud to herself, "just go ... on the count of three." She stepped back and counted, "One ... two ... three!"

But she did not move. She stomped her foot with annoyance. "Coward!" she remarked and took a deep breath.

She shook her hands rapidly at her sides and ran in place to stimulate her nerves.

"Okay. You're a Seneca now. You can do this. On the count of three ... no ... five." She poised herself to make a mad dash. "One ... two ... three ... "

On the count of four, strong arms encircled her waist and masculine hands cupped her breasts from behind. Long, tapered fingers began to knead her soft nipples, stimulating them to hardened points.

"Umm. I have missed you, my wife," Winnokin moaned softly in her right ear as he slowly kissed her neck.

Leslie gasped and turned in his arms.

Winnokin dug his fingers through her golden tresses and brought her lips to meet his in a demanding kiss.

She moaned in response as he lifted her into his arms and carried her swiftly to the protection of a cove sheltered nearby, by thick brush. She tore at his loin cloth and shirt and clung to him desperately. Their need was great, and there was no time for words as their lips devoured each other and their breaths came in short, excited gasps.

Leslie's fingers encircled the cause of her husband's desire. Slowly she caressed and massaged him until he could not stand her splendid torture any further.

He shifted her quickly and placed her atop him as he slowly lowered them to the ground. Her long, beautiful hair tickled his chest, and she maneuvered over his wonderful fullness and sighed with splendid joy when she took him deeply within her. She missed the joy and pleasure that coupling with him brought.

"Welcome home, my love," she cooed as she began to move. "I have missed you terribly." She sighed as she rotated her hips seductively, and he matched her rhythm.

She bent over him to drink of his lips, kissing him ardently, their tongues intermingling, playing, and arousing. She savored the feel of him, not wanting to rush the intimacy she had craved, longed, and hungered for the past five days.

His hands moved over the velvety softness of her skin, kneading the roundness of her bottom, gliding over the curve of her waist, and capturing her breasts once more in his hands.

She moaned as she fought to control the arousing urgency growing within her and threatened to explode. She leaned forward and kissed her husband's eyes, nose, each well-defined cheek, and the sensual cleft of his square jaw.

Winnokin reciprocated and ran his tongue along the fullness of her lower lip and nipped her chin playfully, moving slowly downward and back up again. He stopped at her ear and spoke sweet, endearing words of love.

"I love you, White Dove and missed you more than Mother Earth would miss the sun and rain. I could not run fast enough when I heard what happened to you. Seeing you as you were beside the water's edge your belly slightly swollen with our child sent fire coursing through my veins. You are my life ... my reason for being."

With one easy sweep, he lifted and rolled her beneath him. Leslie clung to him as their bodies melded.

All she could do was sigh as her hands slowly ran over the hard roundness of his backside and down to the top of his muscled thighs.

"I have missed you too, my husband. But no more talk. Love me ... just love me."

Her husband was happy to oblige. He would save the rest of his sweet words for later and love her like no man had ever loved a woman before.

THE END

Nuchzetse and Leslie's story doesn't end here. Find out more how their journey continues and how Nuchzetse is challenged to grow and the love she finds for herself. Here's a taste of what's in store

CHAPTER ONE

Nuchzetse (New-zet-see) threw the large pile of soiled buckskins she was carrying upon the ground. She vented her frustration as she kicked at the pile wildly and scattered them in all directions. She shrieked like a mountain lion and glared at them with a hatred that should have evaporated them into thin air.

I am the daughter of a Clan Leader, she huffed; and will not be forced to serve like a slave and do such menial tasks. She stomped her foot repeatedly as though following a musical tune playing silently in her mind.

"I am not a wash maid! No man tells me what to do. I will not do this!" she ranted as she punched the air with clenched fists, startling the wildlife within ear shot as she continued to create a dust storm about her.

A brusque male voice resounded loudly from behind.

"I would bridle your temper cast away or, your stay in my village will be short lived."

The intrusion enraged her, and she spun about ready to lash out at the person who dared to chastise her actions. She jumped with a start when she recognized the handsome Oneida Bear Clean leader, Lone Star, standing nearly three feet away. The scowl upon his face clearly indicated his anger. He stood tall and proud and wore the traditional breech clout, his sculpted muscles mirroring the obvious harm he could flay upon her if he so dared.

His powerful arms were crossed at his chest as he moved forward to stand before her. The intensity of his fixed stare was unwavering, and it made her gulp with nervous apprehension. It was only the third time she had seen him since arriving to his village less than two weeks ago. His glare was no worse than the first time he laid eyes upon her when she was forced to stand in judgment before the entire council of elders to receive her punishment and instructions of duty.

Her heart began to constrict with a tightness that made it difficult for her to breathe as her eyes devoured his powerful presence. The breech clout he wore barely covered what she really wanted to gaze upon, and she was sorely tempted to reach out and glide her hands along the smooth copper skin of his chest. It took every ounce of control she could muster to keep her arms straight by her side. When it came to men, practicing restraint was not one of her strong points, she admitted quietly. Her brow lifted slightly as the thought of what she would like to do to the handsome warrior standing before her played out in her mind.

Can you read my thoughts warrior, she wondered?

She watched the furrows deepen across his forehead transforming his rugged good looks to a menacing frown. She lifted her chin with a defiance that made him grimace even more. She stood her ground, mimicked him and crossed her arms at her breasts forcing them to rise above the low cut of her neckline. She knew the vision she presented and the power her beauty had over men. It was exhilarating.

Despite her attraction for the handsome leader, she hated being embarrassed and reprimanded especially by him. She despised the division of rank between men and women and the boundaries placed on her because of them. She balked authority at every opportunity, despised being dictated to and did the reverse of what was expected while living in a world controlled by men.

How dare he?

She lifted her head proudly and pulled her torso taller to show him that his grimace did not scare her.

"I am not your squaw. Save your preaching for her!"

It took only a matter of seconds for Lone Star to close the distance between them and she flinched slightly. She wondered if he found her captivating as her own pulse thundered like a herd of wild stallions through her veins. She watched as his eyes directed to the rise and fall her breasts beneath the tightly fitted doeskin shift, she wore. Despite her petite frame she refused to shirk at his towering presence or show any sign of fear. She knew that her insolence and lack of respect for authority was unacceptable but refused to back down.

The sweet scent of lavender that drifted up to his nose as she stood parallel to his chin caught Lone Star by surprise. He wanted nothing more than to run his fingers through the maiden's long raven tresses, grab her by the back of the neck, and draw her lips to his in a ravenous kiss that would brand her his woman forever.

It was hard to ignore the passion she inflamed within him, and he could not help but wonder of the delight the woman standing before him could bring to a man's pallet and he wanted badly to be that man. Taking her right there and now would be more than worth the risk, he admitted quietly, and the corner of his lip curved slightly as he envisioned it in his mind.

She would be like no other woman he had ever been with. The thrill of being the one to tame her wild side was a challenge he would gladly accept. The desire to ravage her nearly overpowered him and it took every ounce of warrior strength and training to restrain from pulling her into his arms. Her enticing beauty and the seductive curves of her body were enough to drive any man over the edge. He could not forget, however, the reason why she was sent to his village. Her dishonor could not be ignored, despite the physical attraction he felt for her.

For one fleeting moment Nuchzetse recognized the desire he tried to mask in his eyes, but the wrath in his voice, bespoke of an entirely different emotion.

"You are no guest here, Woman, but merely a means to favor the chief you chose to dishonor," he recoiled.

Nuchzetse's insides quaked from the hatred that emanated in his light brown eyes. She stood her ground, however, and refused to show how his venomous words affected her and tried with all her might to stall the tears which threatened to moisten her eyes. She wanted this man's favor, not his disgust and the idea of it rattled her resolve. She was not used to doing a man's bidding. Her father had spoiled her since birth and gave her the freedom to do as she pleased. She never once succumbed to the desires of anyone.

She never once bowed to the will of any man except her father respectfully. There was something different about the man now standing before her. The intense, virile power that radiated from him she found to be unsettling yet intoxicating. Only one man ever manipulated her senses so easily and rattled her nerves to the depths of her soul and the Oneida clan leader before her won her favor without her granting it willingly. She did not like losing such control.

There was something about this man that intrigued her and left her spellbound. There was something that made her question the type of woman she had become. She wondered if given time she could have him bending to her will just like all the others that had come and gone in her life.

Perhaps it will not be so dismal here after all, she thought.

"As Bear Clan leader, the well-being of my village, is my concern. It will suit you well, Maiden, to learn your rightful place amongst us. Your evil ways and outbursts will not be tolerated here. Heed my warning for you will not hear it again," he threatened.

His retreat was as immediate as his entry and did not avail Nuchzetse the opportunity to lash out a response as she watched him disappear into the cover of the forest.

She could not believe the emotion that engulfed her and how his words made her feel. Her eyes overflowed with tears, and she opened her mouth to scream out a retort at his retreating back but decided it would work better in her favor to hold her silence. She wiped the tears staining her cheeks away with the palms of her hands as she watched him fade from her view. The last thing she wanted was for him to take away her freedom to move about the village.

She sniffed repeatedly and ran her forearm beneath her nose and forced herself to gain composure over her feelings. It bothered her that he made her feel so emotional, and it was a weakness she found extremely discomforting. She could not ignore the sadness which began to embrace her like a heavy cloak. She could not understand why his words and actions tore at the very pit of her being and left her disturbed, tense and sensitive.

Why should I care what he thinks of me? He is just a man and no better than the rest! And like them all, she sniffled, he will do my bidding.

She nodded with a determination to emphasize her point. Nuchzetse made the rules and did what she pleased. Every man she took into her arms melted like the harsh snows of winter when embraced by the warm breath of spring. Ever since she could remember, she did what she pleased whether it met with anyone's approval or not. She was opinionated and quick-tempered. And even though they were not her greatest strengths, her physical attributes made up for her obvious short comings. Despite her fathers' numerous warnings over the past year, she had yet to learn how to bridle her tempestuous behavior.

Still, Lone Star's biting words and hated gaze cut deep like a knife, and she felt it all the way to the very core of her soul. She knew being banished from her Seneca home would follow her like an ominous storm cloud. In all her twenty-three winters, no man had ever looked at her in such a way and it was a look that would haunt her a very long time.

Why does his opinion bother me so? She wondered. Why do I care what he thinks and how he looks at me?

As quickly as she asked herself those questions, she knew the answer. The moment she had arrived at the Oneida village, she heard much talk about the great warrior Lone Star. She remembered the image she had created of him in her mind's eye, and it was pleasing to learn firsthand her vision proved true right down to the simplest of details. He was a proud specimen of man and handsome in every way imaginable from his regal stature to his striking honed features. The masculinity he exuded was not only hypnotizing but it left her breathless. His people held him in the highest regard not only for his many heroic feats, but also his compassionate heart, accomplishments as a hunter, fierce warrior, and strong, noble leader of his clan.

Since their head sachem, Rain Dancer, had three daughters and no male heir, it was expected by all that Lone Star would be proclaimed the next in line for the honorable title of Sachem once, Rain Dancer succumbed to the land of the Great Father. Nuchzetse understood why Lone Star would be chosen. He was the epitome of power, stood for the highest degree of honor, and a valiant leadership quality, which would serve to protect his people well.

Even though she felt a strong attraction towards him, she knew she could never be one with his people. At least ... not right now. They regarded her as a servant, looked upon her with contempt and excluded her from all social activities. She was a prisoner amongst her own kind and there was no way she was going to stand for it. She had made up her mind. Once she had that old fool Gray Owl convinced, she could be trusted and had finally accepted her sentencing to be his ward, she would make good her escape.

She knew it would take her some time to ration away some supplies to some secret hiding place, if that was the route she decided to take. Nuchzetse knew she would have to be careful and patient. Lone Star would be watching her closely now that he marked her as untrustworthy. She was accomplished at tricking people into believing whatever she wanted them to, and a seductress with the talent to bewitch as well. She was confident she would succeed but also knew that right now, time was her enemy.

She smiled to herself. She knew Lone Star found her attractive. She caught the look of desire in his eyes before he skillfully masked it. Nuchzetse would take great pleasure in tormenting him and create a hunger so desirous; he would find it worse than the most bothersome of toothaches. She sighed deeply and chuckled with a gaiety that made her feel like a pampered child.

Yes, she thought. He will be a worthy opponent for that I am certain, she nodded.

The questions she still needed to ask herself; however, were would she be successful casting a spell over him? And would she still want to leave the Oneida village if she did? The thought of sharing both his home and pallet were more than enticing, she sighed. Was it even possible she could live a happy and fulfilling life with the Oneida if she played the game well? Could she commit herself to only one man? Did she really want to? The more she thought about it, the more she realized that no one told her she could never return home to her people.

Being cast out was only a short-term punishment and not a permanent banishment. Would she want to return, she wondered? Was there truly anything left for her there? She knew she had made a lot of enemies amongst the other Seneca maidens. They were probably thrilled she was no longer there and would never want to see her return. Then too, she did not care. She could not help it, if all the warriors thought she was beautiful and desired her for their own. Why would she ever want to return?

The face of her mother appeared before her, and an extreme sadness engulfed her. She loved her parents immensely and felt bad that her actions caused them an incredible pain and embarrassment. The last thing she wanted to do was dishonor her family. Still, there was truly nothing to draw her back home. The man she loved all her life and consumed her every waking moment for as long as she could remember had given his heart away to another ... a white woman. Being spurned by him was the greatest humiliation ever inflicted upon her. Her heart still tightened within her breast when she thought about it. She remembered how as children they played together.

They flirted throughout the innocence of adolescence and shared long talks of what their hopes and dreams for the future would be together. Their entire village had expected they would wed someday. Nuchzetse sniffled as the pain she felt nearly suffocated her. It all began once her beloved Winnokin participated in his first vision quest and their relationship changed dramatically.

Kindness for her remained in his heart, yet his actions took on that of a brother rather than the admirer she had adored and loved. It was then she realized that his destiny would be interlinked with a woman not of his culture and from that day forward he waited for fate to cross their paths. It was from that day he forgot all about Nuchzetse and the dreams they had once shared.

Nuchzetse could not halt the hatred that began to build and churn deep within her again as the vision of Winnokin's new bride flashed before her eyes. The white woman, Leslie now known as White Dove to the Seneca, had taken her place in Winnokin's heart and in his life as his bride.

 The feelings she still harbored for the woman were dangerous and had gotten her into the terrible situation she now found herself in. She had lost face with her people, dishonored her family, and tarnished her reputation when she tried to kill White Dove. She knew it would be a renewed death wish if she allowed those old feelings to resurface and fester inside of her now. But the hate she felt for White Dove was so deeply rooted, it flowed through her veins like a venomous poison.

She knew she needed another challenge ... a new diversion. Nothing would be more challenging than trying to win Lone Star's favor, she smiled devilishly. She would weigh all her options carefully before putting them into motion. Until the right time afforded itself, she would continue to play the role of a dutiful maiden and perform all the chores expected of her while a prisoner in Gray Owl's lodge.

Nuchzetse wrinkled her nose with disgust as she looked at his clothes strewn about before her. Catering to the elder's needs was not her idea of fun. It would have been more sporting to cater to the needs of a virile widowed warrior instead she rationalized. Still as pleasing as the thought was, she quickly dismissed it. Nothing was more important than the new conquest she set for herself, and that was turning Lone Star's chastises into whispers of desire.

She had to be careful. If she did not watch herself, she could easily be cast out of the tribe without a thought to her survival. She shuttered at the idea for it held no appeal. To be free of bondage was paramount, she nodded. Thwarting her chances of attracting the mighty Bear Clan leader was just as important as making good her escape if her attempts proved unsuccessful.

Nuchzetse was hopeful; however, for she was confident her seductive talents could win the handsome warrior's affections. She knew it wasn't going to be easy chipping away the apparent disapproval he harbored for her presently. But the difficult task was exhilarating and worth the risk and reward in the end.

If the odds worked against her, Nuchzetse knew she would have no other choice than find another means of escaping the village when the first opportunity availed itself. It would take some time to find an adequate hideaway, steal cooking utensils, weapons, clothing, a horse, and food to survive on her own. Patience was not one of her virtues. She would learn, she sighed softly. She would learn.

She turned and gazed at the encampment in the distance.

Like her Seneca village, the Oneida community was protected behind a tall stockade wall, surrounded on all sides by a double row of wood palisades. A deep trench had also been dug that encompassed the entire outside. It was much wider than her own village and the entire length of its bottom was embedded with sharp stakes and tips shaved bluntly to impale human flesh with deadly force.

There were always sentries posted outside the entrance throughout the day and evening. Two warriors guarded each angle of the stockade walls considering recent enemy attacks and the ever-increasing encroachment of whites and British soldiers to the area.

She knew Lone Star's warriors were well instructed to watch her. They skulked like wolves on the prowl, keeping constant visual over everything she did, watching wherever she ventured. It seemed the entire village made it their business to know her every move. She would not put it past the Bear Clan Leader to demand daily reports as to her whereabouts and activities.

She scrunched her nose and frowned at the clothing still scattered about on the ground. Still venting her anger helped to alleviate all the frustration and annoying, irritating squabbles with the other maidens and stupid tasks she had to carry out daily. It did not even bother her that Lone Star had witnessed her temper tantrum and she chuckled for it did her a world of good, and that was all that mattered.

Slowly she bent down and gathered the buckskins into her arms one piece at a time and moved toward the water's edge to finish her menial task.

As she knelt upon her knees and began soaking Gray Owl's shirt and leggings the vision of Lone Star came into her mind.

"If he thinks the tirade witnessed a few moments ago was something," she giggled, "he hasn't seen anything yet!" she vowed as she leaned forward and began to scrub a tunic beneath the water.

Deep in thought as to how she could master Lone Star's heart, Nuchzetse was unaware that someone was watching her from the cover of trees just a short distance away.

Monsumi squatted low behind the massive chestnut tree in front of her as she continued to gaze upon the beautiful maiden with confused intensity. She wondered what was going through her mind just now after witnessing the exchange with her uncle.

She had not meant to eavesdrop when she happened along while collecting medicinal herbs for their Shaman, Gray Owl.

A bothersome mosquito buzzed about her tiny ear, and she mindlessly swatted it away. She could not explain why, but she felt great sadness for the Seneca maiden. After noting her reaction to her uncle's stern forewarning. She knew Nuchzetse did not possess an evil heart like most of the adults in her village believed. She was not quite certain how she knew, but Monsumi felt the maiden's heart was heavy because of something else. She saw the pain upon her face after her uncle stormed away. She felt as though the maiden was lost and Monsumi wanted to help Nuchzetse find her way.

She was a curious and normal ten-year-old. Monsumi wondered what caused such hate for someone so beautiful.

Why was she sent to our village? What did her uncle mean when he spoke about Nuchzetse's evil ways? She wondered.

Monsumi shook her head. It was most difficult; she thought to try and understand adults. She was not too young to realize, however, that living amongst strangers, separated from the love and protection of family and friends, away from familiar surroundings and personal belongings must be terribly difficult for anyone. She felt the maiden's pain.

Monsumi loved her uncle. She could tell he was attracted to Nuchzetse from the way he did not make his presence known at first. She watched as he studied the maiden from afar with a smile on his face. She even had to contain herself from giggling out loud when she watched the maiden's display of temper earlier.

Yes, she nodded absently. Adults were certainly difficult to understand at times. Why they pretend to feel one way, when they act another was the biggest mystery of all. Being a grownup was not going to be easy, she contemplated as she shook her head and quietly rose and retreated in the direction of her village. Now was not the time to become acquainted with the beautiful maiden, she thought. But she would do so soon, that she was certain of. She had to learn more about the woman who clearly had stolen her uncle's heart, even if he did not know it yet himself.

CHAPTER TWO

Nuchzetse rose quietly from a fitful sleep and exited the house she shared with Gray Owl with a basket dangling from her arm containing an assortment of colorful beads, quills, feathers and sewing utensils.

The morning sun was just beginning to rise, and she noted how its golden rays cast an incandescent glow over the still waters of Lake Owasco.

Gazing across the calm water, a wave of extreme loneliness overwhelmed her. And even though she could not see clear to the other side, she knew her family and people were there, soon to rise and begin another new day without her. She missed the familiarity of her surroundings, her mother's daily routines and her sweet words of welcome each morning when Nuchzetse would rise.

She could not blame her banishment on anyone, but herself. Her attempts to scare, then nearly kill, her chief's newfound love was no one's fault but her own. Without a doubt, her punishment could have proved more severe if not for the merciful pleas of her parents and the empathy expressed by the very woman she tried to harm.

Nuchzetse could not help but dwell on how lucky she was despite it all. She could have been whipped to death, dismembered, or banished high in the mountains without food, water, and a means to protect herself, if Winnokin had his own way. But the Council was compassionate and fair on her behalf.

Her eyes filled instantly with tears.

"I would have died for you, Winnokin," she whispered softly into the wind.

If it had not been for his fateful encounter with the white woman, she was certain she would be his bride right now despite what his damnable vision had foretold. But it was not to be.

She paid dearly for her foolhardy mistakes. Her wanton desire to be his soul mate and partner for life consumed her and ruined her fine standing amongst her people. For this she was sincerely sorry.

Somehow, she would find a way to make it up to them. One thing was certain, she nodded absently, and she still refused to change for anyone. Yes, her temper was far from passive. Opinionated, strong-willed and stubborn certainly characterized her personality.

"I am who I am," she sighed deeply.

For nearly three weeks she found herself tormented by the same haunting nightmare. She wondered if the Great Spirit, Hawenneyu, was punishing her for the many bad decisions she had made in her life.

Nuchzetse trembled slightly as she replayed bits and pieces of the dream over in her mind as she started to walk toward the lake.

Panic and fear consume her as the mare she rides bare-back races through an eerily dark and cold forest. Low-lying branches whip and tear at her bare flesh and clothing as she clings to the beast's massive neck. They are being chased by an unseen demon. She can hear the loud raspy snorts of its own stead as it follows dangerously close behind them, while the gruesome bellows of its rider cuts through the silence like the haunting shrills of displaced spirits in the night.

Since dreams were considered sacred amongst the entire

League of Iroquois, which included the Seneca, Oneida, Cayuga, Mohawk, and Onondaga tribes, she feared the meaning behind her own. It frightened her terribly because if anyone was to know of hers, then she would be required by law to hers interpreted by the tribe during a traditional spiritual ritual. Some form of satisfaction, or fulfillment had to be met toward defining what they meant, as it possibly could be detrimental to the tribe she now lived with, or even her family.

For a moment she wondered what would happen if she did not confess the dreams which held possession of her mind. Did Gray Owl already know she wrestled with such haunting dreams, she wondered? Perhaps she cried out in the still of the night or thrashed about upon her sleeping robes without realizing. Was he waiting for her to come forward and acknowledge them to him?

Absently she chewed at her bottom lip and flinched when she pulled a small patch of skin away and tasted her blood in her mouth.

Maybe I should design a Dream Catcher like the one mama created when I was little and hang it outside our quarters. She thought.

It was such a beautiful circular design made from a willow branch and entwined with corn husks, she remembered. She had helped her mother soak corn husks in a special liquid to keep them soft and pliant. They suspended them from the circle on strings of colored beading and young turkey plumes that were dyed a light blue to match the color of the sky.

The Dream Catcher was a sacred token to all Iroquois and used to protect the occupants residing in a lodge from having nightmares.

Her people believed a Dream Catcher guided good dreams

through the special webbing, allowing them to pass through the center hole so they gently drifted off the feathers into the life of the dream, to be experienced each night thereafter. She remembered when she was little how her mother told her that bad dreams did not know the magical way around the webbing and would become tangled and perish at the rising of the morning sun.

Nuchzetse looked down at the basket she was carrying and silently prayed her beads and feathers would contain the same strong medicine as it did when she was little. She vowed to treat the Dream Catcher she would make with honor and respect, so it would cast away the nightmares that had haunted her since she first came to the Oneida village.

In a few short months all Iroquois would be celebrating the sacred Midwinter Festival, a six-day event that would focus mainly on sharing and interpreting dreams. Everyone, young and old, participated in the process. Even though she was not Oneida, she was still Iroquois and would be expected to openly share her dreams, good or bad.

She knew Gray Owl would make her come forth to have her nightmares interpreted and the thought of doing so scared her to death and left her feeling vulnerable. She knew that the Oneida would look upon her as a weak individual and possibly even a bad seed or omen.

The thought of strangers guessing, even trying to analyze her dreams petrified her terribly.

Dream guessing, or what their people called the Ceremony of the Great Riddle gave each member the opportunity to tell their dreams to the tribe. Certain experts in interpretation would be consulted to give hints regarding its meaning.

In addition, the whole tribe would offer suggestions and

respond by sharing their feelings of what it meant as well. Even if she felt their interpretations could be helpful, Nuchzetse feared acknowledging her deepest thoughts and fears to people who really did not know anything about her except for what they were told or heard through gossip.

The ceremony was extremely intense. Although often serious, it held strong spiritual significance and the rituals motivated tribal members to challenge each other.

That's all I would need, she dreaded.

"The last thing I want to do is draw more attention to myself!" she admitted aloud.

She knew dreamers would be expected to sing, shout, dance, and demand that their own vision be "guessed". Some tribes even challenged and competed to see who could guess right the first time, while others might walk from house to house, hinting at what their dream might be and goading occupants to guess it.

Her heart began to race rapidly in her chest. Somehow, she had to regain control of herself, change the negative aura surrounding her and create a more positive force in her life. She knew she had to try and enrich the way she lived and perhaps make amends for some of the terrible things she had done without feeling trapped and smothered. She certainly was not about to pantomime her dream in front of a group of strangers. She continued to walk along the shoreline until she came upon a willow tree with branches, she could use to assemble her Dream Catcher. She stood up on her tip toes and snapped a small branch away from a low limb. She then walked to the water's edge and soaked the branch for a couple of moments. Once it softened, she knelt and began to shed away its leaves and shape the long thin branch into a circular ring.

She gazed upon her reflection in the clear, mirrored surface of the lake. Her heart-shaped face was framed with thick raven tresses that hung way below her waist and gleamed in the morning sun. She was surprised that the constant turmoil which raged within her did not show in the beautiful reflection looking back at her.

Her large, round green eyes were uncommon for her race. Her full sumptuous lips sorely tempted the willpower of any man, and she enjoyed the spell she could cast over them.

She became acutely aware of her beauty very early in life but was also taught conceit was evil and would breed hatred, pain and disappointment.

Why is this happening to me? She questioned silently. Why have I ignored everything I have been taught, everything my people believe in?

"Oh, mother!" she cried, "How I wish you were here with me now," she whimpered.

She could see her mother's face in her mind's eye. It had always been her mother's ritual to ask Nuchzetse each morning since she was a child if she had dreamed, for each one was supposed to be cultivated and attended to.

To the Iroquois many times dreams indicated whether an individual would have a special ability in warfare, hunting, medicine, and the like. They foretold not only the causes of an illness and an individual's power to cure, but also the means of maintaining good fortune in various aspects of life.

"Good fortune!" she huffed as she stood and kicked up dirt with her foot. "My life has been riddled with nothing but failure!" she cried out in frustration. "No wonder my dreams are nothing but nightmares!"

"The dream is the spirit of the Great Father within us all," Gray Owl interrupted.

The willow circle she was forming flew from her grasp as Nuchzetse screeched, tripped on a log behind her and fell with a thud to the ground onto her backside.

Gray Owl circled in front of her, and his brow furrowed deeply with concern.

His full head of white hair lay long and straight upon his broad shoulders. Surprisingly he was in fabulous shape for a man of sixty-three winters. His teeth were still a vibrant white, straight, and full of set. Most elders lost the lustrous sheen of their eyes but, his soft brown ones were still bright and clear.

"Light will not shine from within, when the soul is shrouded by doubt, self-pity, and remorse, my child." he continued.

Nuchzetse moved backward a few inches on her haunches and lowered her eyes. She was afraid of him and thought beyond a doubt some mystical power kept him young. She feared his powers were so great he could penetrate the deepest recesses of her mind.

"You cannot hide what I have already seen in your eyes. You do not have the power or the knowledge to fight those forces which hold your dreams prisoner," he continued.

Nuchzetse's head snapped up and she gasped with surprise.

Gray Owl nodded slowly.

"Ya. Yes. This old man knows your torment."

He pointed to the willow circle lying on the ground beside

her.

"A Dream Catcher is powerful medicine, but first we must speak about what has stripped away your honor."

"Ya Niu. It is so, Wise One," she whispered and bowed her head reverently.

Gray Owl lowered himself to the ground and crisscrossed his legs in front of him. He rested his palms atop his thighs and gazed intently upon her.

"This torment will haunt you like a cat on the prowl, or chase you like demons in the night, Nuchzetse if you do not speak openly of your fear. Tell Gray Owl what makes you cry out in the night. I will decide if we must speak of it during the time of the Great Riddle Ceremony."

Nuchzetse kept her head downcast. She was afraid to look into his eyes. She feared his power but most importantly, the possibility that she may have to share her weakness openly and expose to the world the person she had become.

His ability to see all and know the truth before it was spoken before it was acted out was a mystery to all. She could not lie to Gray Owl for he was a visionary and would know the minute the words passed from her lips whether she was speaking with truth from her heart.

At that exact moment she realized being honest with Gray Owl was crucial to her well-being, to her acceptance, to even possibly winning Lone Star's respect and that of his people. Absently, she shook her head and shrugged from the hopelessness she felt.

What was she thinking? Why should she even care what the two of them thought of her? She felt confused, uncertain what to say, what she wanted, how much she should share with the wise man sitting before her. Her hand lifted and rubbed at her right temple which began to throb painfully.

Gray Owl reached forward and took a hold of her hand and held it between his palms.

"There is much goodness in your heart, Nuchzetse. Do not fight to keep it deep inside for this is the cause of the evil, which separates you from your people."

Nuchzetse's jaw dropped, and her eyes grew wide with surprise. How did he do that? She swallowed the huge lump that formed in her throat and threatened to cut the air from her lungs. Slowly she lifted her head to gaze into his eyes.

An intense heat radiated from his hands. The warmth coursed up her arm, across her shoulder and down through her chest. She felt so calm and at peace with herself while in his magnificent presence. All a sudden she no longer feared him, but yearned to share, to pour out her heart and soul and all her secrets and inhibitions to him.

A sense of inner peace, a calming spiritual strength embraced her at that moment. All a sudden it did not matter what she needed to confess, for she knew in her heart Gray Owl would not judge her in a negative light.

"I feel so humble in your presence, Wise One," she whispered.

Gray Owl patted her hand and clucked.

"I am but a man, my child, guided by the Great Manitou who knows and sees all. I cannot help if you do not relay what truly plagues your dreams and rules your heart."

Nuchzetse slid her hand free from his grasp and tugged at a blade of grass. She twirled it about her finger as she pondered for a moment what she might tell him, how much she could entrust to this stranger who now sat beside her. Even though he was considered a most holy man, Gray Owl was not a leader like Strong of Heart, the Seneca's Medicine Man, whom she had known all her life and had the greatest respect for despite the conflicts which had grown between them over the last few years.

In a way she wished it was Strong of Heart sitting before her. She would like nothing more than to wipe away all the bad feelings she created because of her stupidity and selfishness.

It bothered her terribly to be cast out of the village she was born into and loved. The sentiments shared by her own people were cultivated by the white woman, who came into their lives, stolen the heart of the man she dreamed since birth to join one day as his wife. If it had not been for White Dove, Nuchzetse knew in her heart she would not have turned into a spiteful, vindictive person and had done everything in her power to get rid of her.

Gray Wolf leaned forward and lifted Nuchzetse's chin with his finger, forcing her to look into his eyes.

"Then I will tell you. Hatred has distorted the beauty of your face, Nuchzetse. It is reflected there now because of the negative thoughts you keep in your mind. It is this evil which holds your heart captive. To be free of it, you must let it go, look beyond it and open your soul to new beginnings. Love and happiness will not find you when your heart is black with hatred and deceit," he said.

Nuchzetse shook her head slowly, amazed by his words.

"We are strangers, yet you know me so well, Gray Wolf. How can that be?"

Gray Wolf leaned back and smiled warmly.

"It takes no special power to see the sadness which burdens your heart, the hatred which cloaks your eyes, or the vengeance, which consumes your spirit. Sadness can be replaced with joy, but hatred and vengeance will be the cause of your destruction, young one. Those are my concerns and should also be yours.

Your heart does not like what your mind controls. Hatred and vengeance are monsters. They will overpower and consume your soul, not only during waking hours, but your dream state as well. Do you not wish more for yourself?" he asked.

Nuchzetse nodded in reply.

"Ya. Yes." She answered softly.

"Know my child; these two evils are the monsters which haunt your dreams. You cannot change what the Great Manitou has destined for you, even if it is not what you desire. If you do not rid these evils from your life, your spirit will never soar, and my people will not see you for the person you truly are. You will never experience joy in your life until you first reconcile the mistakes you have made.

I am certain we need not share your dreams during the time of ceremony. It is only you who will be affected by whatever path you chose to venture. You are the only one, who can change the course of your life and make your nightmares disappear.

Look deep inside yourself, child. The answers are here."

He leaned forward and gently touched her heart with his palm.

"They are here also," he touched the side of her head and then raised himself up to kneel before her.

"They are woven by the love of your mother and father, nurtured by the culture of your proud people and heritage."
Gray Wolf placed his hands upon her shoulders and shook her slightly as he continued.

"You have lost your way ... led astray by demons which taunt each of us ... but <u>you</u> <u>are</u> <u>Seneca</u>, <u>you</u> <u>are</u> <u>strong</u>, and <u>you</u> <u>will</u> find your spirit once again. This I know to be true ... you must believe in yourself before it can be so. Know that I do not view you as an outcast, but as a guest in my home. What is mine is yours." he vowed as he cupped her face between his warm palms.

Nuchzetse felt as though a whirlwind of emotion and feelings erupted deep inside her belly. It was as if all her sins and past transgressions were erased ... wiped clean. She could not believe Gray Wolf had such faith in her ability to change.

She knew in her heart she was not a bad person. At times she did not know why she did the things she did. She could not stop the tears which began to fill her eyes and run down her cheeks.

Gray Wolf's smile was genuine and warm. With much affection he brought her to him and enfolded her into the strength of his arms and petted the back of her head tenderly.

"Believe, my child," he whispered against her ear and then kissed each cheek softly before he rose and left her to dwell on the words he had spoken.

CHAPTER THREE

Nuchzetse's spirit was restless even though she and Gray Owl had made peace with each other. There seemed to be a more common bond between them. Despite the fact he knew so much of the torment which plagued her; he was the only one who did not ostracize himself from her. She still felt very much like a stranger in his village.

She wondered if it would be worth the effort. It would take nearly a miracle to win acceptance by his people. She was certain the Oneida knew in part of the wrongs she had committed. It would take a long time to convince them she was not an evil person, but rather a female misguided by love.

Nuchzetse was certain returning to her Seneca village was out of the question for quite some time. As much as she surrendered to the marriage between Winnokin and White Dove, she knew it would err greatly to witness their love daily until she could come to terms with it in her heart.

Living amongst the Oneida was the only option she had. Making the best of her present situation was up to her and no one else. She knew that it would not be easy and there would be days where bridling her temper would be most difficult. Knowing that she had Gray Owl in her corner was the very strength she needed to get through each new day that approached and knowing she could talk to him any time kept her fear of failing at bay.

She would give herself until the end of summer to make this village her home, perhaps develop friendships and hopefully sway Lone Star's opinion of her to a cordial favorable alliance. If nothing changed, she would leave and slip away under the cover of night.

When she learned from Gray Owl a special council had been held the previous evening regarding the ever-impressing stress placed on the Oneidas by the colonists, she craved to be with her family even more. Her conversation with Gray Owl that very evening about the event lasted well into the night.

They talked relentlessly about the difficulties which lie ahead and what their concerns and personal fears had been. She knew the same apprehension and alarm was being felt by the Seneca, since the entire League sent a representative to attend the discussions.

The air was oppressive with tension when she exited the lodge, she shared with Gray Owl the following morning after they shared the morning meal. As she looked about the faces of the villagers, she knew it also dwelled heavily on many of their minds. The Old One's clustered in small groups, the burden of despair weighing heavily on their limp, bent shoulders. Moving further through the village she heard mothers trying to quell their children's fears of going to war, losing their homes and perhaps their brothers, uncles, and fathers.

The devastating war with the League's enemy, the Huron, nearly three years prior had left many lodges without the care and protection of a warrior. From the sixty long houses in the Oneida village alone, thirteen families depended on the generosity of Lone Star and his Bear Clan warriors to provide for their households.

She was grateful she could fend for herself if the need arose. She knew how to throw and use a knife, could string a bow, and shoot a straight arrow and ride as well as any warrior. Personally, she thought it was unjust that maidens were not taught at an early age how to do just that in case the male head of a lodge was killed in battle or injured severely. No Seneca shunned her skills but her outspoken ideals were always thwarted by the same argument that it was the responsibility of the warrior clan to protect and provide for those members of the tribe who were without the protection of a male provider. Maidens were meant to attend to domestics, give voice in council and nothing more.

Nuchzetse still could not quell the logic behind how they could possibly protect themselves should another massive attack befall them unexpectedly.

Her pace quickened through the village and was driven by an extreme desire to escape the heavy melancholy already weighing heavily over the village at the start of a new day.

Since Gray Owl had told her she had access to all which was his, she steered towards the exit to the stockade, determined to seek out his small herd of horses and lose herself in a long ride through the countryside, if perhaps, even a small game hunt of her own. She had promised him, she would not escape, and she would hold true on that promise. As she adjusted the bow and quiver of arrows hanging from her shoulder, she tested the sturdiness of the belt around her waist, which held the sheath containing her hunting knife.

Her worried thoughts were interrupted by a small group of maidens who had instantly appeared and stepped forward to block her way. One female was squat and rotund of frame. Her dull black hair was haphazard about her face, pulling free from the single strip of otter fur, which held the unruly mess together behind her shoulders.

Nuchzetse knew her as Plum Blossom, but felt Plump Turkey was more befitting of a name as her eyes grazed over her from head to toe. Protectively her hand glided to the sheath of her knife as she glared at the short, ugly woman.

"Step aside, woman. I am in no mood to deal with your feeble, little mind today," Nuchzetse warned.

Plum Blossom looked about quickly. Satisfied no one was close to hear her other than the two supporters standing directly behind her, she took one step closer, turned her back and openly passed gas before Nuchzetse.

Nuchzetse's eyes grew large with rage at the insult and the disgusting smell which wafted up toward her nostrils. She wanted to pummel Plum Blossom with her fists until the woman's skin turned black from her fury.

The women behind Plum Blossom jeered and goaded Nuchzetse, trying to push her to a limit of acting without honor. But Nuchzetse was much wiser, than to fall victim to their scheme. Even though their social standing within the community was of little importance, Nuchzetse was smart enough not to risk further defaming her reputation for their mere pleasure and entertainment.

Nuchzetse inched her toes closer, touching those of Plum Blossoms. She pulled her knife from its sheath and pressed it against the fat underside of the woman's stomach. Her towering height over the obese woman was gratifying as she spit out her rebuttal in a vehement tone.

"Remove your fat, rotting paunch from my path woman, or I will gut your belly where you stand!"

Nuchzetse relished the joy of watching the color drain from Plum Blossom's face. The woman gasped sharply when Nuchzetse increased the pressure of her knife. The sharp point broke through the woman's shift which was heavily stained with dirt and grime and pierced her skin. A cold, nervous sweat dotted the woman's brow and the area above her thin lips.

Plum Blossom quickly backed away, bumping into her two cohorts. They shrieked lightly with fear when Nuchzetse glared in their direction. Without thought, the three simultaneously turned about in the same direction, departing as quickly as their legs could carry them.

Nuchzetse instantly placed her knife back in its sheath and looked about slowly to see if anyone stood watching. Thankfully all were busy with their daily chores and had not witnessed the foray which just took place. Camp dogs were barking at children while they ran about and played, woman was either cooking outside their lodge fires, or working on the skins of deer that were felled the day before.

She sucked a long deep breath of air into her lungs and released it slowly to relax the quivering tremors dancing deep within her gut.

It was the fourth negative encounter she experienced with the same group of women since her arrival one month earlier. She wondered what she had done to invoke such reactions from them. What did they know about why she was there? Or were they simply just jealous and unhappy with her intrusion into their community?

What else would transpire between them, Nuchzetse wondered silently? She prayed she scared them enough into leaving her alone. But she also knew one's strength and courage were increased ten-fold when backed by supporters. Time would tell, she thought. Now more than ever she would have to be on the alert.

Exiting the high palisade walls of the stockade she caught sight of the mighty herd of stallions, mares, colts, and geldings belonging to all the Oneida families grazing upon the crest of the hill to her East. Nuchzetse sighed deeply as she walked towards the base of the rise.

Since it was the responsibility of the adolescent males to tend the herds daily, it would be a relief not to have to explain what she was doing or where she was going. Even Lone Star and his warriors knew enough not to question Gray Owl's open proclamation that she was now a guest in his home and had free access to his personal herd. A heated encounter with any one of them right now would not fare well, particularly in her present state of mind.

She knew Lone Star's braves found her incredibly attractive. She caught their looks of praise many times while she worked or walked through the compound. There were also times when their body language reflected the very turmoil churning inside of them and it gave her a supreme sense of control.

She was not about to change in that regard she vowed silently, even if it meant not winning their total favor and appreciation quite yet.

She thought about her father at that moment and smiled softly. Like any man, he had hoped for a son but, it never dawned on him to treat her any differently. Ever since she was a toddler, she displayed an instinct to learn the skills of a warrior and her father saw no harm in teaching them to her. The bond that grew between them was much like one of a father and son because of the respect between them throughout her years of learning.

Nuchzetse adapted instantly. Her arrows shot straight and always hit their mark. She could track, ride, skillfully handle a knife and down a deer as well as any brave. She knew that the Oneida women did not appreciate the fact she carried a bow and quiver of arrows with her often. Still, she could not change that part of her, and she secretly hoped that one particular warrior would find honor in her abilities should he ever find out.

If anyone could bridle her wildness, and accept her unique qualities, Lone Star would be such a man. She had to believe that. And it would be an interesting challenge to put him to such a test; she chuckled lightly as she walked up to the young brave who was helping tend the herd.

The look of utter shock that registered on his face when he noticed the bow and quiver of arrows strung over her shoulder made Nuchzetse laugh at loud.

"Close your mouth, young brave," she teased, "or you will surely swallow flies."

The young lad's jaw shut tight as he turned to look over his shoulder and see if his comrades noted who was standing there before him.

Nuchzetse followed his gaze and noticed the other boys had stopped as well and were gaping openly in her direction. She sighed deeply, shook her head, and directed her attention at Gray Owl's herd. A slow smile graced her lips when her eyes fell upon a beautifully spotted Cremello mare. She walked forward while reaching her hand into the small pouch she carried at her waist to retrieve a crisp honey cake as an offering of friendship.

The attentive mare lifted her tall neck and shook her proud mane as in greeting and snorted as her nostrils flared catching the scent of the sweet Nuchzetse was bringing towards her and lifted in her direction. A soft neigh of welcome escaped the mare's throat and she trotted forward slowly with grace and elegance.

Nuchzetse placed the sweet cake in her palm and lifted it before the mare when it stopped directly in front of her. The stunning animal delicately took it into her mouth and then let Nuchzetse caress her muzzle softly with the palm of her hand.

"Oh, you are a striking beauty," Nuchzetse spoke delicately as she ran her hands up and down along her neck. "We are going to become the greatest of friends."

As if in understanding, the mare nestled her head upon Nuchzetse's shoulder and whinnied invoking a chuckle from her newfound female friend.

Nuchzetse placed a tender kiss on the side of her nose and offered the mare another treat before she grabbed a handful of its mane and lifted herself upon its back. She looked over her shoulder at the young braves and noticed they were still standing where she last saw them with a look of utter amazement registered on each of their faces. She could not contain her glee and laughed happily as she waved in their direction, squeezed her thighs tightly to the mare's barrel and kicked lightly to engage the mare forward.

"Let's go my beauty and ride like the wind together," she yelled happily.

Her heart pounded in her chest from not only the exhilarating joy her freedom offered, but also because of the wind blowing wildly through her hair and the lithe power of the steed beneath her ferociously pounding the earth at break-neck speed.

Her mind wondered aimlessly, first in reflection, then contemplation as she passed the dense forest rich in pine, ash, oak and elm. Her eyes fell upon an abundance of game large and small and streams she knew would be bountiful with trout.

Would her people really lose all this, she wondered? Since the beginning of time, they lived in peace and harmony with nature and the abundance that Mother Earth provided them to survive. They had always only one enemy to contend with, the Huron. They had the strength of their combined brethren within the League to sustain their livelihood, but she could not help wondering if it would be enough, if it would all be lost to them as the whites grew larger in numbers and continued to invade their lands.

For many years, the foreigners were very few, and kept a comfortable distance from their lands, generally settling along the banks of the mighty rivers. The focus of their interest and greed for the beaver pelts and animal furs they could trade.

But now, the European people were too numerous to count bordering and spilling over into the homelands of the Iroquois League. Their land was becoming the most sought-after form of wealth. It seemed all non-Indians wanted a piece of what their people owned for as long as they could remember.

Once the military and trading post of Oswego was built, the roughest sort of trappers and traders encroached upon their land and intensified with the building of Fort Stanwix by the red coats known to all as the British.

She knew the Oneida shared the Seneca's views on the increasing invasion. In the beginning, their leaders' response was practical, creative, and peaceful. They adopted many aspects of foreign life, which was necessary for their survival and useful for preserving the sovereignty of the League and its core traditions. They adapted to what was new to keep alive their heritage, culture, and the practices of their ancestors.

Nuchzetse slowed her mount to a slow canter as she remembered Gray Owl sharing his vision, a vision that war was imminent and there would be a great revolution amongst the non-Indians in gaining ownership of the land they were colonizing. He feared the League would be drawn into their battle, forced to take sides to survive as a nation onto themselves.

Nuchzetse knew her Shaman, Strong of Heart also felt fighting for the cause of American liberty and independence would force an alliance with either the colonists or British and send many of their warriors into the battleground. The price they would pay would be beyond thought or, comprehension.

Yet, it was a consequence that was way beyond her control. She silently prayed her people would rise above the adversity and remain a strong, thriving nation. It was her greatest hope of all.

After a few hours of riding and circling back into the direction she came from, her cramped backside cried for relief. Nothing would prove more comforting she thought than an exhilarating swim. She focused her attention on finding a secluded spot since she knew she was not far from the lake.

Shortly she came upon a small cove and scanned the area quickly to be sure her privacy would not be invaded and then disrobed with lightning speed.

The cooling, spring-fed water caressed her sore muscles like a lover's soothing massage. She sighed with resplendent joy as she floated upon her back, letting the afternoon sun warm her body with the heat of its rays.

She cherished quiet moments such as these for they held a promise all was right with the world. Being one with nature opened her to become more attuned with all her splendorous surroundings: a vivid blue sky, the crisp heavy scent of pine in the air, melodious sounds of birds, squirrels and insects filtering through the woods, the precision flight of an eagle overhead and a mother beaver splattering warning signs to her cubs upon the water's surface with her flat oar-like tail.

Nuchzetse flipped to her belly and expertly dove beneath the surface. She directed herself back to the shoreline, holding her breath for a matter of minutes until she thought she would burst from the pressure building in her lungs.

As she crashed through the surface with her arms reaching high above her head, she sucked the air deeply into her lungs and felt exhilarated. She moaned loudly and a long sigh of contentment escaped from her lips.

This is what I needed, she rationalized, as she began to slowly wade toward the shoreline and stretched out upon a soft bed of grass. Her spirit felt alive as her breaths came in deep, quick gasps. Slowly her heartbeat calmed to a nice steady rhythm.

Lone Star nearly lost his footing as he knelt hidden behind an enormous berry patch and gazed openly upon Nuchzetse's loveliness. Returning from his visit with her people, the Seneca, he recognized her silhouette from afar as she galloped wild and carefree on the open plain. He had followed her to ensure her intention was not to escape despite what Gray Owl had told him.

Blood boiled through his veins with a feverish, wanton hunger as his eyes transfixed upon her full, firm breasts and watched as they rose and fell with every breath she took. His loins ached to join with her and drive them both to and beyond the brink of ecstasy as she lay before him as naked as the day she was born.

She sat up and gathered a mass of her wet hair into her hands and began to squeeze as much of the remaining moisture that she could from the tresses.

Lone Star could not still the craving desire to dry the droplets cascading in slow rivulets along her sleek, silken perfection with his tongue. The more he watched her, the more he realized no woman had ever driven him so near the brink of madness than Nuchzetse. He could not argue that her radiant beauty was hypnotizing. He also argued her willful pride, short temper and sharp tongue were nuisances he needed to tame but not stifle completely.

Winnokin was a powerful, handsome warrior and Sachem of the Seneca. Lone Star could understand why Nuchzetse would have been attracted to his close friend. But he also knew that Winnokin's heartbeat only for his new bride White Dove. Indeed, she was a beguiling female for a white woman, and he respected his friend's choice for a wife, but Nuchzetse was a beauty he craved for himself.

As he watched her roll to her side facing him, he was further enraptured by the curvaceous contours of her long, sleek body. Seeing her in such an alluring manner held him spellbound as she played with blades of grass and softly hummed an old Iroquois love song.

He had reservations as to whether Nuchzetse could change. He was rather disheartened to learn firsthand the turmoil she had caused between White Dove and Winnokin during his visit to her Seneca encampment. To think she attempted to kill White Dove not once but, twice, bothered him greatly.

Nuchzetse should have respected her chief's choice once she realized the love between him and the white woman was strong and forever bonded. To have questioned, to have even tried to alter what was destined and revealed during his vision quests and recognized by the elder council and her people as a fateful event blessed by the Great Father, was surely unforgivable.

Lone Star believed love's driving force could tempt the

sanest man to shear madness as he felt his own tumultuous heart beating within his chest. He had to be strong, he realized. He could not be drawn in by her beauty and the deep attraction he felt towards her. Most certainly, she could not know of his feelings, or she would most assuredly use her beguiling, tempting ways as an advantage to lure or deceive him into getting what she wanted.

He decided he would be patient and reserved and watch her closely. Gray Owl confided he believed there was goodness in her heart and that she had lost her spirit and way. He held his shaman in the highest regard, but his skepticism still strongly guided his path.

He continued to look on as Nuchzetse moved to the water's edge to watch a school of trout feeding at the base of a hardy lily patch growing close to the shoreline.

Quietly she reached backward for her satchel of arrows and drew one out. She then tied a considerable length of string to the arrow and the other end to her wrist.

He sat mesmerized watching as she notched her arrow and took aim. Pride filled his heart, noting the extreme strength it took as the muscles corded with strain in her arms, shoulder and back to control bending the bow as she pulled back on her arrow. Once she released it, it whisked through the shallow pool with precision and speed, striking not one, but two speckled lake trout.

Lone Star's smile was wide and vibrant, and he chuckled quietly when the force of her thrashing catch pulled her forward onto her belly.

"Yahee!" she cheered with delight.

Quickly she twined the string about her hand to ease the

trout's floundering, but the pair fought aimlessly to free themselves. She moved to the water's edge and slowly pulled them to shore, removed them from her arrow and threaded a vine through their gills to keep them together.

Triumphantly she stood with her fists on her hips as she gazed upon her catch.

"I wonder if I can do that again?" she questioned with glee.

Lone Star's heart warmed affectionately as he witnessed a side to her personality he did not think ever existed. She was like a playful child, comfortable with her nakedness, confident and joyful with her task. Her features radiated a tempting sweet innocence which made him want to leap from his cover and join in the simplicity of the moment with her.

He continued to watch as she gazed at the water intensely until the ripples calmed and the surface finally mirrored clear beneath the shallows that the school of trout had not been frightened away. He held true to his belief she would remain to repeat her volley for most of the afternoon and decided to leave her to her pleasure alone.

As his gaze fell upon the trout flapping wildly upon the ground at her feet, his curiosity was peeked.

What did she plan to do with her bounty, he wondered? Would she throw those she did not need back into the lake, take them to Gray Owl's lodge for only them, or would she share her bounty with the needy of his village?

Her decision would be yet another test of her character, he thought.

His heart silently hoped it would be the right one.

****

Please take a moment and share your thoughts and experience reading Wind Warrior. It will prove most helpful toward obtaining future sales and getting me recognized as an author in this genre. I hope your read was enjoyable and thank you so much for spending time in my world. Here is the link https://www.amazon.com/gp/product/B01997CZMU/

Captive Heart, Book 2 of this series is also available on Kindle Unlimited and accessible at the link above as well.

My Collection of Books

Historical Romance ~ Iroquois Series

Wind Warrior ~ Book 1

Captive Heart ~ Book 2

Captive Warrior ~ Book 3

Contemporary Romance

This Too Shall Pass

Love Song Standards Series – The greatest love songs of all times were the American Standard Classics with lyrics that told a story. I've had such a wonderful time creating such stories about relatable, flawed characters … sometimes wounded … sometimes broken who eventually find that soulful kind of love we all dream of attaining in our lifetime.

Unchained Melody

Strangers In The Night

Chances Are

At Last

For Once in My Life

Can't Help Falling In Life

4 New titles coming soon ~ All the Way – It's Impossible – Unforgettable – Sincerely

Suspense Thriller

Keeper's Watch

A Pawn for Malice

Made in the USA
Middletown, DE
29 January 2025